Stephanie had barely lain down, heavy-lidded, on the bed, when something made her eyes suddenly open, though she could recall hearing no sound.

She saw him standing in the doorway. Had he knocked and she not heard? She came to her feet and took a few hurried steps toward him. He came inside and closed the door and took a few steps toward her—after setting down a valise.

"Oh," she said. "This is your room, is it not? I am so terribly sorry. The maid brought me here. Perhaps she did not realize—"

She felt the fingers of both of his hands against her wrists and then moving up her arms until his hands came to rest on her shoulders. She was not conscious of either moving or being moved, but she could feel suddenly the tips of her breasts brushing against his coat. Then his lips touched hers.

She was in the wrong room, she knew now. What he must think of her must have been wrong as well. And what he clearly intended to do was as wrong as wrong could be.

Why, then, did it feel so right . . . ?

The Plumed Bonnet

Mary Balogh

A SIGNET BOOK

SIGNET
Published by the Penguin Group
Penguin Books USA Inc., 375 Hudson Street,
New York, New York 10014, U.S.A.
Penguin Books Ltd, 27 Wrights Lane,
London W8 5TZ, England
Penguin Books Australia Ltd, Ringwood,
Victoria, Australia
Penguin Books Canada Ltd, 10 Alcorn Avenue,
Toronto, Ontario, Canada M4V 3B2
Penguin Books (N.Z.) Ltd, 182-190 Wairau Road,
Auckland 10, New Zealand

Penguin Books Ltd, Registered Offices:
Harmondsworth, Middlesex, England

First published by Signet, an imprint of Dutton Signet,
a division of Penguin Books USA Inc.

First printing, September, 1996
10 9 8 7 6 5 4 3 2 1

Chapter 1

She was trudging along the edge of a narrow roadway somewhere north of London—a long way north of London, though she was not at all sure exactly where, the fuchsia color of her cloak and her pink bonnet with its deeper pink, fuchsia, and purple plumes making her look like some flamboyant and exotic yet bedraggled bird that had landed on the dusty road. Anyone passing by—though so *few* vehicles seemed to pass by, and those that did were invariably traveling in the opposite direction—would surely just keep on passing when they saw her. Her half boots were the only colorless part of her apparel, being as gray as the road, though they were actually black beneath the dust, an old and shabby black. She clutched a creased and worn reticule, which contained her pathetically small and much depleted store of coins—frighteningly small, frighteningly depleted. It was no longer even plural, in fact. There was one coin left.

Anyone seeing her now—and anyone within five unobstructed miles could not fail to see her and even be blinded by the sight of her, she thought with a grimace—would never guess that she was an eminently respectable young woman and, in addition, a very wealthy one. She chuckled with a humor that only succeeded in frightening her more when she heard the sound of it. By her reckoning, it was going to take her days, perhaps even weeks to walk to Hampshire—she could not be more precise than that. But by her far more precise reckoning, she had enough money left in her reticule to buy one loaf of bread—one small loaf.

Could one loaf of bread sustain her through many days of walking? What would happen if it could not? She pushed the thought firmly aside and quickened her pace. It would simply have to do, that was all. When there was no food left, she would have to go on without it. Water would sustain her. There was always plenty of that to be had. She just hoped that the weather would stay fine and would not turn too cold at night. It was early May after all. But she shuddered anew at the thought of having to face yet another night out of doors. Last night, even before she had had cause to do so, she had felt distinct unease. She had huddled on the field-ward side of a hedge. She had had no idea that a night could be so dark or so filled with unidentifiable noises—every one of them starkly terrifying. Later, of course, there had been real terror, from which she had been saved in the nick of time.

She could not believe this, she thought, stopping briefly to look back along the road. She just could not believe it. It could not be happening. Not to her. She had lived the most dull, the most drab, the most blameless of lives. Nothing even remotely resembling an adventure had ever come within hailing distance of her. Now she despised herself for ever longing for one. Beware of making wishes, someone had said—she could not remember who—for they might come true. The trouble with dream adventures was that they were always happy and jolly affairs. This one was anything but those things. Indeed, she would be fortunate to survive it.

The thought was so horrifying and yet so very realistic that she chuckled again. She had always accused the children of being melodramatic. She had always advised them not to exaggerate in the stories they told of their escapades.

Did nothing ever travel along this road? It was a main thoroughfare between north and south, was it not? But all she had seen all day—and it must be noon already—was a farmer's cart laden with manure. It had been traveling hardly any faster than she, and it had stunk terribly, but nevertheless she had begged for a ride. Strange how easily one could take to begging when the need arose. She wondered if she would beg for bread when her one remaining coin was spent. It was a ghastly thought. But the farmer, black teeth interspersed with gaps, had gawped at her as if she were some strange bird indeed, and had muttered something totally unintelligible before driving on a few yards and then turning into a field.

And of course both a stage and a mail coach had gone by. They did not count. One could hardly beg a ride on a public vehicle. Of course there had been whistles and catcalls from drivers and male passengers alike, all dreadfully mortifying for a woman who was accustomed to being invisible.

She turned to walk determinedly on again. Perhaps it was as well that her valise had been stolen and did not therefore have to be carried, she thought briefly, until she remembered that if it had not been stolen, she would be on a stagecoach right now, considerably closer to her destination than she was. She could still hardly believe how stupid she had been to keep her traveling money and her tickets in her valise and to entrust that valise to the care of a friendly, stout, seemingly respectable country woman who had traveled the first leg of the journey with her, talking to her in most amiable fashion all the way. All she had wanted to do was go inside the inn before the stage drew up in order to use the necessary. She had been gone for five minutes at the outside. When she had returned, the stout woman had gone. And so had her valise, and her money, and her tickets.

The stagecoach driver had refused to take her. The innkeeper had refused to call a constable and had looked at her as if she were a worm—a gray worm. She had still been wearing her own gray cloak and bonnet at that time.

Something was coming at last—something a little larger than a cart. It must be another stagecoach or post chaise, she thought with a sigh. But she stopped walking. She moved right off the road to press herself against the hedgerow. She did not want to be bowled over by a coachman who believed he owned the road.

It was a private vehicle—a plain coach drawn by four rather splendidly matched horses. The coachman and a footman were seated up on the box, both dressed in blue uniform. Obviously someone grand was riding inside, someone who would not only look at her as if she were a worm, but also tread her underfoot or under wheel without sparing her a thought—especially considering her present appearance.

Nevertheless, as the carriage drew closer, she held up one hand, at first tentatively, and then more boldly, reaching out her arm into the road. Panic welled into her throat and her nostrils. She did not think she had ever felt lonelier in her life—and she was an expert on loneliness.

The carriage swept past without slowing. The two servants did not even deign to turn their heads to glance at her, though the eyes of both swiveled in her direction, and they were nudging each other with their elbows and grinning before they passed from her sight. She bit her lower lip. But suddenly, a little ahead of her, the carriage not only slowed, but actually stopped. The coachman turned, somewhat startled, and looked back at her with a face that had lost its grin. She hurried forward.

Oh, please. Please God. Dear, dear God.

A passenger was pulling down the window on the side closest to her. A hand, expensively gloved in cream leather, rested on top of it. Someone leaned forward to look at her as she approached. A man. He had a haughty, bored, handsome face topped by thick, carefully disheveled brown hair. His voice, when he spoke, matched his expression.

"A bird of bright plumage painting the landscape gay," he said. "Whatever is it that you want?"

Had she not been feeling so weary and so hungry, not to mention footsore and dusty and frightened—and embarrassed, she might have answered tartly. What on earth did he *think* she wanted, out here in the middle of a roadway, miles from anywhere?

"Please, sir," she said, lowering her eyes to her reticule,

which she clutched with both hands as if to make sure that that too would not be snatched away from her, "would you allow me to ride up with your servants for a few miles?" She did not fancy riding up between those nudging, grinning two, but doing so was certainly preferable to the alternative.

"Where are you going?" She was aware of his gloved fingers drumming on the top of the glass. She could tell from his voice that he was frowning.

"Begging your pardon . . ." the coachman said with a respectful clearing of the throat.

"For coughing in my hearing?" the gentleman said, sounding even more bored than before. "Certainly, Bates. Where are you going, woman?"

"To Hampshire, sir," she said.

"To Hampshire?" She could hear the surprise in his voice, though she did not look up. "That is rather a distant destination for an afternoon's stroll, is it not?"

"Please." She raised her eyes to his. As she had suspected, he was frowning. His fingers were still drumming on the top of the window. He looked toplofty, arrogant. This looked like an impossibility. "Just for a few miles. Just to the next town or village."

The coachman cleared his throat again.

"We really must get you to an apothecary, Bates," the gentleman said impatiently.

And with that he opened the door and jumped down to the road without first putting down the steps. She took an involuntary step back, aware suddenly of the emptiness of the road to left and right and of the fact that there were only three strange men confronting her. He was a large gentleman, not so much in girth as in height. He was a whole head taller than she, and she was no midget. She was horribly reminded of last night.

"Well," the gentleman said, turning and bending to let down the steps himself, though the footman had vaulted hastily from his perch, "to the next village or town it is, Miss . . . ?" He turned back to look at her, his eyebrows raised.

"Gray," she said.

One eyebrow stayed up when the other came down. "Miss Gray," he repeated, reaching out a hand for hers. She had the impression that he was mentally naming off all the bright colors of her attire and considering the incongruity of her name. Belatedly, she wondered why she had not thought of pulling the plumes from her bonnet this morning and tossing them into the nearest hedgerow.

He expected her to ride *inside* the carriage with him? Did he not know how very improper . . . ? But clinging to propriety seemed absurd under the circumstances. And the prospect of being inside any structure, even if only a carriage, was dizzying.

"I did not expect to ride inside, sir," she said.

"Did you not?" He made an impatient gesture with his hand. "Come, come, Miss Gray. I shall try to curb my appetite for dining on tropical birds until after we have reached the next village."

She set her hand in his and immediately noticed the hole worn in the thumb of her glove, twisted around and perfectly visible. "Thank you," she said, feeling horribly mortified. And then as she settled herself on one of the seats, her back to the horses, and felt the warmth and softness of the blue velvet, she had to swallow several times to save herself from a despicable show of self-pity. She twisted the thumb of her glove inward in the hope that he had not noticed its shabbiness.

The gentleman closed the door again and seated himself opposite her, and the carriage lurched into well-sprung motion. She smiled at him a little uncertainly and tried not to blush. She could not remember another time when she had been quite alone with a gentleman.

Alistair Munro, Duke of Bridgwater, was on his way to London to take in the Season. His mother was already there, as was his sister-in-law, Lady George Munro. George was there too, of course, but his presence was without threat. And both of his sisters were there with their respective husbands. Bridgwater knew perfectly well what the presence of his female relatives in town during the Season was going to mean for him. He was going to be paraded to every ball, concert, soirée, and whatever other entertainment the *ton* could invent for its collective amusement, the ostensible reason being that they could not function without his escort—though presumably they had done very well for themselves during the first part of the Season, and all of them had husbands to be dragged about with them except his mother, who needed no escort at all. The real reason, of course, would be to expose him to the view of all the young beauties who were fresh on the market this year and of their mamas. His mother and his sisters—and his sister-in-law too—were determined to marry him off. He was, after all, four-and-thirty years old—alarmingly old for a duke with no heir of his own line.

The trouble was, he had been thinking gloomily before his thoughts had been happily diverted by the sight of a brightly flamboyant ladybird standing beside the road, one arm outstretched—the trouble was that he was beginning to lose his resistance. He was very much afraid that he might allow himself to be married off soon. For no other reason than that he was filled to the brim with a huge ennui, a massive boredom with life. Why not get married if his mother was so set on his doing so? It was something that must be done sooner or later, he supposed. There was that dratted matter of a nursery to be set up.

He was horribly bored—and restless—and depressed by the knowledge that life and love were passing him by. He had used to be a romantic. He had dreamed of finding that one woman who had been created for him from the beginning of the world. He had not found her all through his hopeful twenties. And then he had become nervous. Some of his closest friends had been tricked or forced into marriages not of their choosing, and he had panicked. What if the same thing should happen to him? There was Gabriel, Earl of Thornhill, for example, who had become involved in a reckless scheme of revenge and had ended up snaring an unwanted bride for himself. There was his closest friend, Hartley, Marquess of Carew, reclusive and unsure of himself, who had married for love one of the loveliest ladies in the land and had then discovered that she had married him under false pretenses. And there was Francis Kneller, who had kindly taken the gauche and alarmingly reckless Miss Cora Downes under his wing despite her being a merchant's daughter, and had ended up having to marry her after he had inadvertently compromised her. That last disaster had happened six years ago. Bridgwater had avoided any possible romantic entanglement since then.

And so he was bored and restless and none too happy. He had taken to staying away from home at Wightwick Hall in Gloucestershire, which could only remind him of the domestic bliss he had once dreamed of and never found, and instead wandered about the country, going from one house party to another, from one pleasure spa to another, in search of that elusive something that would spark his interest again.

He was coming now from Yorkshire, from an extended Easter visit with Carew and his lady at Highmoor Abbey. He had also seen a great deal of the Earl of Thornhill, whose estate adjoined Carew's. And as fate would have it, Lord Francis Kneller had been staying there for a visit, though he and his family had returned home a few weeks ago. Three couples, three marriages, all of which had frightened the duke out of his dreams of love and romance and happily ever afters. Three couples who were ironically proceeding to do what he had once dreamed of doing himself. Three happy and prolific couples. The two estates had seemed to teem with noisy, unruly, exuberant, strangely lovable children— Thornhill's three, Carew's two, and Kneller's four.

Bridgwater had never felt more alone than he had for the last several weeks. He had been a valued friend of everyone, a spouse and a lover of no one. He had been a favored uncle to nine children, a father to none.

He was desperate for diversion. So desperate, in fact, that he rapped on the front panel almost without hesitation as a signal for his carriage to stop when he spotted the little ladybird who was standing out in the middle of nowhere begging a ride when no respectable woman had any business doing either. Of course she was no respectable woman. She looked ludicrously out of place in her surroundings. She looked as if she might have just stepped out of a particularly lurid bawdy house—or out of a second- or third-rate theater.

Well, he thought, if love and romance had passed him by, there were other pleasures that assuredly had not—though he preferred to draw his mistresses and even his casual amours from the ranks of the rather more respectable.

She was disconcertingly dusty and shabby and wrinkled despite the splendor and gaudiness of the garments she wore. She was unconvincingly meek and mild, clutching at her shabby reticule with both hands as she stood beside his carriage and directing her eyes downward at it as if she expected him to wrest the wretched item from her grasp and give Bates the order to spring the horses. He was sorry in his heart that he had stopped. He was really not in the mood for the kind of gallantry that her type called for. And one never quite knew how dangerous it was to dally with total strangers. He felt irritable. But he had stopped. It would be cruel to drive on again and leave her standing there just because he was bored and not really in the mood, after all. Someone else had obviously kicked her out of another carriage and abandoned her, creating a rather nasty situation for her.

He just wished she would not play the part of demure maiden. It was rather like an exotic parrot masquerading as a gray squirrel.

But then she raised her eyes and looked full at him, and he saw that they were fine eyes—hazel with golden lights. They were large and clear and intelligent. They coolly assessed him. He sighed and hopped out to hand her in. He could not, after all, allow her to squeeze in between Bates and Hollander and distract them from the serious business of conveying him a certain number of miles before nightfall without overturning him into a ditch. Perhaps it would relieve his boredom somewhat to discover between here and the next village why she was in the process of walking all the way to Hampshire with only a small and shabby reticule for company.

Miss Gray. Miss *Gray*. It was too laughably inappropriate to be real. Miss Whatever-Her-Name-Was was also traveling incognito, he thought. Well, let her keep her real name to herself if she so chose. It mattered not one iota to him.

In addition to the fine eyes, he noticed, studying her at his leisure after his carriage was in motion again, she had a pretty face, which he was surprised to see was free of paint. Her auburn hair, just visible beneath the appallingly vulgar bonnet, clashed unfortunately with everything she wore—except for the gray dress he could glimpse beneath the cloak. She was younger than he had at first thought. She was not above five-and-twenty at a guess.

Her eyes, which had been directed at her lap, now lifted and focused on his. Oh, yes indeed, very fine eyes, and she was experienced at using them to maximum effect. He resisted the impulse to press his shoulders back against the cushions in order to put more distance between them and his own. He raised his eyebrows instead.

"Well, Miss *Gray*," he said, putting a slight emphasis on her name to show her that he did not for one moment believe that it was real, "might one be permitted to know why you are going to Hampshire?"

It was an impertinent question. But then she was no lady, and he had a right to expect some diversion as payment for conveying her a few miles along her way.

"I am going to take up my inheritance there," she said. "And I am going to make an advantageous marriage."

He folded his arms across his chest and felt eternally grateful to the fates that had arranged for him to spot her beside the road as his carriage sped past her, though he had been dozing a mere five minutes before. He was not to be disappointed in her. She was going to regale him with a wonderfully diverting and extremely tall story. As tall as Jack's beanstalk, perhaps? She also, he noticed, spoke with a refined accent. Someone had invested in elocution lessons for her.

"Indeed?" he said encouragingly. "Your inheritance?" Having made such a bold and vivid start, surely she would need only a very little prodding to continue. He would explore the inheritance story first. When they had exhausted that, he would prompt her on the advantageous match story. If she was very inventive, he might even agree to take her on to the next village but one.

"My grandfather recently died," she said, "and left his home and his fortune to me. It is rather large, I believe. The house, I mean. Though the fortune is too for that matter, or so I have been informed. It was a great surprise. I never knew him, you see. He was my mother's father, but he turned her off when she married my father and never saw her again."

He would wager half his fortune that the father would be a country vicar when she got around to describing him. It was the old cliché story—the great heiress marrying the poor country curate for love and living happily and poorly ever after. Bridgwater had hoped she would be more original. But perhaps she would improve once she had warmed to her story.

"Your father?" he asked.

"My father was a clergyman," she said. "He was neither wealthy nor wanted to be. But he and my mother loved each other and were happy together."

They would both be deceased, of course. Now what would Miss Gray have done when they died? She would have taken employment, of course, rather than go begging to her mother's wealthy father. Of course. Nobility and pride would have conquered greed. Employment as what, though? Something suitably genteel. Not a chambermaid. Never a whore. A lady's companion? A governess? The latter at a guess. Yes, he would wager she would decide on the governess's fate. But no, that would be impossible. She would not be able to choose the governess's role convincingly when she was dressed as she was. He wondered if she would think of that in time.

"They are both deceased?" He made his voice quiet and sympathetic.

"Yes."

He was pleased to see that she did not draw a handkerchief out of the reticule to dab at her eyes. She would have lost him as an audience if she had done so. Abjectness, even as an act, merely irritated him. More important, she would have doomed herself to getting down at the very next village. He wondered who had booted her out of his carriage a few miles back and why. His eyes moved down her body. The cloak was rather voluminous, but he guessed that it hid a figure that was perhaps less voluptuous than he had first thought.

"I took a position as a governess when Papa died," she said. "In the north of England." She gestured vaguely in his direction.

A very strange and eccentric governess she would have made. He amused himself with images of her in a schoolroom. He would wager that she would hold the fascinated attention of children far more easily than the gray, mouselike creatures who normally fulfilled the role. The mistress of the house might have an apoplexy at the sight of her, of course. The master of the house, on the other hand . . .

"And then," he said, "just when you thought you were doomed forever to that life of lonely drudgery, you received word of the demise of your grandfather and his unexpected bequest."

"It *was* unexpected," she said, looking at him with an admirable imitation of candor. "He did not even reply to Papa's letter telling him of Mama's passing, you see. Besides, my mother had a brother. I suppose he must have died without issue. And so my grandfather left everything to me."

"Your grandfather lived in Hampshire?" he asked.

She nodded. She looked at him with eager innocence. With a butter-would-not-melt-in-my-mouth look. He wondered where she had slept last night. Her cloak looked distinctly as if it might have been slept in. The dreadful plumes in her bonnet looked rather sorry for themselves. And he wondered too how much money her reticule held. Certainly not enough to buy her a stage ticket to wherever it was she was going. Unless, of course, she disdained to spend money so senselessly when she could cajole bored travelers like himself into giving her carriage room in exchange for stories—and perhaps, if not probably, in exchange for something else. Perhaps if he asked her given name, she would call herself Scheherazade. Scheherazade Gray. Yes, it would suit her. Was she hungry?

But he did not want to feel pity for her. He wanted to be amused. And so far she was marvelously diverting. He had cheered up considerably.

"And so," he said, "having discovered what a great heiress you had become, you were so filled with excitement and the desire to exchange one sort of life for the other that you rushed from your employer's home in the north of England, carrying only the clothes on your back and a reticule, in order to walk to your new home in Hampshire. You are an impetuous young lady. But then, who on hearing of such a reversal in fortune would not be?"

She flushed and leaned back in her seat. "It was not quite as you imagine," she said. "But close enough to be embarrassing." She smiled at him to reveal a dimple in her left cheek—not to mention white and even teeth. Her eyes sparkled with merriment and with mischief. Yes, definitely. And he would wager that she knew the effect of that smile on her male victims. On his guard as he was, he felt his stomach attempt a creditable imitation of a headstand. Yes, indeed—an accomplished ladybird.

"They were to send a carriage for me," she said, "and servants. I was very tempted to wait for them and to tell my employers of my good fortune. They had not been kind to me, you see, though the children were dears most of the time. They made pretensions of being grander than they were and treated me as if I had been born of a lesser breed. I know that they would have turned instantly and despicably obsequious if they had found out. They would have fawned on me. I would suddenly have become their dearest friend in all the world, one whom they had always loved as if I were truly a member of their family. It was tempting. But it was also sickening. I did not wish to see it. So I did not wait for the carriage to arrive. I left very early one morning without giving notice—though that did not matter since I had not been paid for the last quarter anyway."

He pursed his lips. He had to admit it was an amusing story. He could almost picture her mythical governess self striding down the driveway of the home of her erstwhile employers, not looking back, her plumes nodding gaily in the breeze.

"And so," he said, "you left without even enough money in your reticule to get you to Hampshire—unless you either walked or begged rides."

She flushed again, more deeply than before, and he felt almost sorry for his unmannerly words.

"Oh, I had enough," she said. "Just. I bought my tickets for the stage and still had enough with which to buy refreshments on the way and even a night or two of lodging if necessary. Unfortunately, I put both the money and the tickets in my valise for safekeeping."

And the valise had been stolen. It was priceless. Actually, the predictability of her story was proving more amusing after all than originality might have been.

"My valise was stolen," she said, "while I was changing stages. I left it for no longer than five minutes in the care of a woman with whom I had been traveling. She seemed so very kind and respectable."

"I suppose," he said, "no thief worth his salt would advertise his profession by appearing unkind and unrespectable and expect naive travelers to entrust property to his care."

"No, I suppose not," she said, looking up at him again. She smiled fleetingly. "I was very foolish. It is too embarrassing to talk about."

And yet she had talked about it to a complete stranger.

"And so," he said, "you have been reduced to walking."

"Yes." She laughed softly, though she was clever enough to make the laughter sound rueful rather than amused.

"And do you," he asked, "have enough money in your reticule to feed yourself as you walk?"

"Oh yes." Her eyes widened and the flush returned. "Yes, indeed. Of course I do."

A nice little display of confusion and pride. But really, how much money *was* in her reticule?

He had not noticed the approach of the village—a strange fact since it was the approach of villages and towns and inns with which he had attempted to relieve his boredom during his journey. The carriage was slowing and then turning into an inn yard. It was a posting inn, he guessed. Time to change the horses and have something substantial to eat.

"Oh." His companion turned her head to look out the window. She too seemed surprised—and a little disappointed. "Oh, here we are. I do thank you, sir. It was kind of you to take me up and save me a few miles of walking."

But he had not yet heard about the advantageous marriage. Besides, perhaps she was hungry. No, *probably* she was hungry. And besides again, only the very smallest of dents had yet been made in his massive boredom.

"Miss Gray," he said, "will you give me the pleasure of your company at dinner?"

"Oh." Her eyes grew larger, and he read unmistakable hunger in their depths. For a moment she was forgetting to act a part. "Oh, there is no need, sir. I can buy my own dinner. Though at the moment I am not hungry. I will walk to the next village before stopping, I believe. But thank you."

"Miss Gray," he said, "I will take you on to the next village. But first I must dine. I am hungry, you see. And if you are to sit and watch me eat, I shall be self-conscious. Do force yourself to take a bite with me."

"Oh." He knew suddenly for a certainty that she had not eaten that day and perhaps not yesterday either. It must have been yesterday, not today, that she had been tossed out of that other carriage. "You will take me one village farther?

How kind of you. Very well, then. Perhaps I can eat just a little." She laughed. "Though I did have rather a large breakfast."

He raised his eyebrows as he vaulted from the carriage and handed her down the steps. He escorted her toward the private dining room that Hollander had already bespoken for his use. A gentleman and his ladybird. He read that interpretation in the eyes of the ostlers in the yard and in the eyes of the innkeeper when they went in and in those of the barmaid they passed inside.

Well, let them think what they would. Even gentlemen had to be amused at times. And even ladybirds suffered from hunger when they had been abandoned by their protectors and had not eaten for a day or longer.

Chapter 2

S he was sorry she had accepted the invitation to dine with him. She was sorry she had been tempted by his offer to take her just one town farther along her way. Her legs were shaking so badly by the time she stepped inside the private dining room he had bespoken—he must be *very* wealthy—that she wondered they still held her upright. Her hands shook so badly that she would not for the moment try raising them in order to untie the ribbons of her bonnet.

She was so very accustomed to being invisible. Well, almost so anyway. It was true that the male guests Mr. Burnaby had brought to the house far too frequently for Mrs. Burnaby's liking—he was a gentleman who enjoyed shooting and hunting and used them as an excuse for having company and carousing for days and nights on end—it was true that those guests sometimes noticed her. It was true too that she had sometimes had difficulty in shaking off their attentions. But on the whole she had crept about the house in her gray garments and been invisible to both the servants, of whom she had not been quite one, and the master and mistress of the house. Mrs. Burnaby had even insisted that she wear a cap in order to douse the one splash of color she might have carried about with her—her hair.

She was certainly not accustomed to being looked upon as if she were an actress—ironical that, really—or a wh—. But even in her mind she could not fully verbalize the word. Her hands developed pins and needles as well as the shakes.

And yet that was exactly how everyone outside and inside the inn had just looked at her.

"Miss Gray," the gentleman said from behind her in his characteristic voice of hauteur—and yet it was a light and pleasant voice, she thought—"do please take a seat and make yourself at home."

"Thank you." She collapsed in a rather inelegant heap onto the nearest chair and reached for her bonnet ribbons. But no, it just could not be done. The offending monstrosity must remain where it was for a while longer.

And then she realized another cause of her distress, which had been drowned out so far by the looks she had been given as she entered the inn. There were strong smells of cooking food in the air. Her stomach clenched involuntarily, and she swallowed convulsively. She drew her gloves off one at a time, holding her hands in her lap so that she could control their shaking. And then her stomach protested with a loud and deep and prolonged growl.

"The horses will be changed here," the gentleman said, not waiting for the room to grow silent again. "I wish to press on as far as possible until nightfall. I find travel somewhat tedious. Would you not agree, Miss Gray?"

He was making an attempt to save her from embarrassment. She wondered if he knew she had lied about the large breakfast. She liked him. It was true that he was handsome and elegant and looked more than a little haughty and even bored, but he had been kind to her. It seemed such an age, an eternity, since anyone had been kind—or courteous. He had shown her courtesy despite her appearance and circumstances. She had almost forgotten what her own voice sounded like, except as she used it with the children during their lessons. But he had listened to her story and prompted her with questions and had seemed genuinely interested in her answers.

And now he was going to buy her dinner and take her a little farther on her way.

"Yes, I do, sir," she said in answer to his question, and she smiled at him.

His eyes dropped a fraction from hers. She had the feeling that he was looking at her dimple. Her dimple always embarrassed her. It seemed somehow childish. And Mrs. Burnaby had once told her she must bring it under control or else cease to smile at all. She had ceased to smile.

He sat down on the chair opposite hers, the table between them. The door opened again at the same moment, and the innkeeper himself came in carrying a tray from which rose steam and a smell that set her stomach to clenching again. The innkeeper set a bowl of oxtail soup before each of them, and a basket of fresh rolls on the table between them.

She swallowed and tested her hands in her lap, squeezing each in turn. Yes, the shaking had gone. She would be able to pick up her spoon and eat. She tried not to rush and waited for the gentleman to pick up his first.

"Miss Gray," he said as he did so, "do you have another name to go with the surname?"

She stared at him for a moment, desperate though she was to eat. No one had used her name, her given name, for so long that she no longer thought of it as public property. It was her own, private to herself, as certain parts of her body were. But there was no impertinent familiarity in his manner. He was looking at her in polite inquiry. His gray eyes, she thought irrelevantly, were so light that they might almost be described as silver. They were keen and rather lovely eyes. She wondered briefly if he was married. How fortunate his wife was to have such a handsome and such a gentlemanly husband.

"Stephanie," she said.

For a moment his eyes appeared to smile. She had noticed a similar expression a few times in the carriage as she talked.

"Alistair Munro at your service, Miss Stephanie Gray," he said and lifted his spoon to his mouth.

She did likewise and immediately thought that the idea of swooning with ecstasy was not quite as silly a one as she had always thought it.

"Ah," he said. "A cook of indifferent skills. A pity."

She looked at him in surprise. Food had never tasted even half as good as this soup did—and as the rolls did when she tried one, though it was true that it was a trifle doughy in the center.

"It is obvious, Mr. Munro," she said in the sort of voice she had sometimes used on the children, "that you have never had to go hungry."

His spoon paused halfway between his mouth and his bowl, and his face became coldly haughty. Then he half smiled at her.

"You are quite right," he said. "For a moment, Miss Gray, you sounded far more like a governess than a, ah, an heiress."

She laughed. "I have not become at all accustomed to the knowledge that I am wealthy," she said. She really had not. The reality of it still amazed her. She still expected to be able to pinch herself and wake up. "But I hope I will never cease to be grateful for my good fortune. I hope I will never squander my wealth or horde it all selfishly to myself."

"Or complain about food that is indifferently prepared," he said.

She felt herself flushing. She had scolded him even though he was showing her incredible generosity.

"One has a right to an opinion," she said. "You are paying for my meal, sir. Perhaps that gives you a right to complain about your own."

The innkeeper returned with two plates piled with hefty portions of steak and kidney pie and with potatoes and vegetables. He removed their empty soup bowls and bowed himself out of the room. If she could only eat every mouthful of the dinner, Stephanie thought, it would surely fortify her for the rest of today and even tomorrow.

"And what *do* you plan to do with your riches, Miss Gray?" Mr. Munro asked. "Perform philanthropic good deeds for the rest of your life?"

She had a thought suddenly. She flashed him a smile of bright amusement and noticed that his eyes stayed on her face even though he had already taken up his knife and fork.

"What I should do," she said, leaning slightly toward him, "is offer you a large sum to take me all the way to Hampshire. To be paid after I have been safely delivered, of course, since I am unable to pay in advance."

She was instantly sorry that she had spoken. It had been meant as a joke, of course. But he looked at her so intently and so haughtily, his eyes roaming her face and moving upward so that she was reminded of the ridiculous bonnet, which she never had taken off—she almost squirmed. She had been a mouse for so long a time. Was it possible that she had actually suggested something so very brazen and improper even as a joke?

"And *are* you offering, Miss Gray?" he asked.

He was undoubtedly a wealthy man. He must be hugely offended.

"No." She laughed again. "It was a joke, sir. No, of course not."

"Of course not," he repeated quietly, and then unexpectedly his eyes had that half-amused expression again. "But you have not told me of the advantageous match."

She wished she had not mentioned it to him in the carriage. He had been wonderfully polite and kind, listening to her story when it could be of no interest whatsoever to him. And yet she had never been much of a talker, even when she had lived at home with her parents. Certainly she had never talked on and on about herself. She had always been too conscious of the fact that she must be of no particular interest to anyone except herself. And marriage she knew was a subject that fascinated women far more than it did men. Mr. Munro could not really wish to hear about hers. He was just being polite again.

"You would not really wish to hear about it, sir," she said. "I must have bored you dreadfully in the carriage with the other details of my story."

"On the contrary, Miss Gray." When he raised his eyebrows, he looked downright arrogant, she thought. "You have saved me from a few hours of dreadful tedium. I will feel cheated if I do not hear about the advantageous match."

She chewed on a mouthful of pie. He was the complete gentleman, it seemed. He knew how to listen and appeared genuinely interested. She liked him a great deal despite his general air of lofty grandeur. Had she seen him from afar in other circumstances, at Mr. Burnaby's, for example—though she could not quite imagine him as a participant in any of Mr. Burnaby's rowdy gatherings—she would have disliked him on sight, seeing him as cold and arrogant and insufferably high in the instep. How looks could deceive!

"I am to be married," she said, "within four months. Actually, it was six months. That was what my grandfather stated in his will. But it took them two months to find me."

Mr. Munro pursed his lips. "Let me guess," he said. "You inherit from your grandfather only on condition that you marry within six months of his death. Otherwise the inheritance will pass to someone else."

How had he guessed? She nodded.

"To a distant relative?" he asked, his voice quietly sympathetic. "There always seems to be a distant relative waiting in the wings to seize one's property at the first glimmering of an opportunity—usually a *wicked* distant relative."

"I do not know him," she said. "I know none of Mama's family. But I doubt he is wicked. Very few people are in reality, you know. Only in fairy tales or Gothic stories. Most of us are a bewildering mixture of near-goodness and near-badness."

"But usually one of the two predominates," he said, smiling and revealing himself as a man who was purely handsome with the layers of aloof pride stripped away. "And who is the fortunate bridegroom?"

"Actually," she said, "my grandfather's will did not state who he must be. After all, I might have been married already, might I not? I am six-and-twenty, you see. All he did state was that I must be married within six months, and that if I was not already married before his death, my choice must be approved by both his solicitor and his nephew on my grandmother's side. The nephew apparently has a nephew of his own who is prepared to marry me. He is a man of substance and impeccable reputation and has not yet passed his fortieth birthday. I suppose I will have him. I will not have a great deal of time to find someone of my own choosing, will I?"

She smiled. In truth, she was somewhat elated at the prospect of marrying, even though she had not yet met the man and knew about him only what her grandfather's solicitor had written. All she had ever really dreamed of achieving in life was marriage and a home and a family. She had ached for all three since her father died when she was twenty. For six years she had lived a life of loneliness and invisibility as a governess. She had long ago given up the dream and adjusted her expectations. She was to be a spinster for life. All she could hope for was a post someday that would give her more satisfaction and that would bolster her self-esteem better than the first.

Yet, now suddenly she was wealthy and independent, and would remain so provided she married soon. It was no difficult condition. Indeed, the prospect of being married lifted her spirits even more than the wealth and the independence did—both would pass into her husband's hands once she was married anyway. It was true, perhaps, that she would have liked to choose her own husband. It was true that deep within that original dream had been the hope that she would marry for love as her parents had. But this was the real world. In reality many people—*most* people—married for reasons other than love. And most marriages were to a greater or lesser degree arranged.

Mr. Munro had finished his dinner—he had eaten everything on his plate. He set his napkin on the table and leaned back in his chair. "You would cheerfully enter into an arranged marriage?" he asked. "When for twenty-six years you have preserved your independence?"

Ah, he had a man's blindness to some of the more bitter realities of life for a woman.

"I believe that marriage, sir, even an arranged marriage, is preferable to a life of independence as a governess," she said.

His eyes gazed deeply into hers. "Of course," he said, his voice sympathetic. His eyes looked above her head to the gaudy plumes of her bonnet. "But do you not dream of a love match, Miss Gray?"

"Dreams have no part to play in the waking world, sir," she said. "Besides, love can grow where there is respect to begin with. Or if not love, then at least companionship and affection."

"A life without dreams," he said so quietly that it seemed he was talking to himself more than to her. "Ah, yes, it is a lesson one learns with the experience of years, is it not? Have all your dreams been destroyed, Miss Gray?"

"If they have," she said, "I have not allowed their destruction also to destroy me, sir. There is always some satisfaction to be drawn from life. And there is always the future and always hope, even if there are not dreams."

"And yet," he said, looking fully into her eyes again, the half smile back in his, "some of your dreams—or perhaps they seemed too impossible even to be dreams—must have come true for you recently."

"Yes, indeed," she said. "My point is proved, you see."

"If you have finished," he said, "we should be on our way. I hope to be considerably closer to London before nightfall forces me to stop."

She had been unable to finish everything on her plate, much to her regret. She knew that even before the day was out she would look back with longing on the abandoned food, but she could hardly ask the innkeeper if he would wrap it up for her so that she might take it with her. She got to her feet.

"Yes, of course," she said. "It is kind of you to be willing to take me on to the next village."

"It is my pleasure, Miss Gray," he said. "We will while away the time in conversation. You must tell me about your life as a governess. Did you have just one charge or several? Were they eager to learn? What did you teach? Did you have influence over the formation of their characters as well as their minds? I shall be interested in hearing what you have to say."

He looked interested—almost amused. She could not imagine why he would be interested except that he was kind despite appearances, and he was a gentleman. And of course it would be very embarrassing to occupy the confined space of a carriage together if they had nothing to say to each other. She would talk to him then. She was finding it strangely exhilarating to tell someone about her life and her good fortune. The telling was helping her forget the ill fortune of the day before—and of the night. And somehow it helped her to regain the identity she had submerged six years before in order to make her fate as a governess bearable.

She smiled and preceded Mr. Munro through the door. But the smile quickly faded. She had to walk the gauntlet of insolently staring guests and servants again in order to reach the haven of the waiting carriage.

She regretted the loss of her gray cloak and bonnet perhaps more than that of her valise. And she marveled at the respect Mr. Munro showed her. He was the only one.

He could not quite make up his mind about her. What was she, exactly? An actress? She was certainly able to play a part. Sometimes she spoke so earnestly about her prospects and about her past life that he was almost convinced. But then she would flash him that smile, and his insides would turn over before he could catch himself. She must never lack for male admirers and protectors. It was difficult not to be drawn by the practiced mixture of innocence and artlessness on the one hand and the bright invitation of her eyes and her smile—and her dimple—on the other. And there was her beauty, of course. She was extremely pretty, despite the bright clothes, which if she only knew it, detracted from rather than enhanced her beauty. He would love to see her hair without the bonnet and without the pins.

Or was she merely an adventuress, setting out for the

south, where she expected life to be more lively and more lucrative? Had she dressed this way on the mistaken assumption that she would look more fashionable? Or had she come north with a protector who had abandoned her? That was the interpretation he rather favored. But why would any man abandon her in the middle of nowhere? What had she done to displease?

She was clearly in search of another protector; there was no doubt about that. Her invitation to him to take her all the way to Hampshire and be paid after she was safely delivered there had been artfully done, but she had used every weapon in her considerable arsenal before withdrawing and pretending that it had all been a joke.

He was half inclined to take her up on her offer. She sat now on the seat opposite him, her head turned so that she could gaze through the window, though she was occasionally dozing. She had stopped talking, and he had stopped asking questions just for the amusement of discovering how inventive she could be. They had passed through several villages since they had stopped for a meal. At the first she had looked inquiringly at him and sat forward in her seat. Since then she had almost visibly held her breath every time a cluster of buildings appeared through the carriage windows.

Soon he must stop for the night. The landscape was growing gray with dusk. He could not quite decide what to do about her, Miss Stephanie Gray. She must have regretted the very dull surname she had given herself and had made up for it with the Christian name. Should he let her down and forget about her? Give her some money, maybe, so that if she was serious about going to Hampshire, she could take herself there on a stagecoach? Or should he keep her with him?

He was surprised and somewhat alarmed at the tightening in the groin he felt at the latter thought. He always chose his bedfellows with meticulous care—never as the result of a simple flaring of lust. But it had been a long time. And she was both pretty and attractive—and willing. Doubtless she would be delighted to provide him with a couple of nights of pleasure in exchange for a ride to wherever she was going and food along the way. And a bed in which to sleep even if she must work first in order to earn that sleep. Not that he would make the work unpleasant for her. He liked to pleasure the women who pleasured him.

But she was a stranger with vulgar appearance and refined tongue. And she was the most accomplished liar it had ever been his privilege to encounter. Some other man had recently abandoned her for offenses unknown.

It would be better to set her down and give her money—and sleep alone.

And then her head jerked forward with such force that it brought her whole body with it. He had to lunge with both hands in order to save her from falling right off the seat.

"Oh." She looked up at him with blank eyes from a pale face. He kept his hands on her upper arms until awareness came back into her eyes and she sat up and leaned back again. "I am so sorry. I must have fallen asleep."

Deeply asleep. He did not believe it had been an act this time, a plea perhaps to give her a bed for the night.

"How much sleep did you have last night?" he asked her.

"Not a great deal." She bit her lower lip. "It was the only night I have ever spent out of doors. I did not sleep a great deal. I am sure I will sleep better tonight. I am more tired."

She smiled at him rather wanly. It was a masterful expression. He would have had to be a monster not to respond to it. Especially as he believed this one part of her story. She had spent last night alone out of doors and she had been terrified.

"I will be stopping at the next inn and taking a room for the night," he said, his mind made up at last—but what choice did he have, really? "You will stay there too, Miss Gray. And perhaps I will take you a little farther tomorrow. I still have not heard about your life at the parsonage."

He was alarmed and even a little embarrassed to see her bite hard on her upper lip while tears sprang to her eyes. Her face even crumpled for a moment before she brought herself under control.

"Oh," she whispered. "Thank you. You are the kindest

person I have ever met. How will I ever repay you? Money will not do it, I know. You must tell me how I can show you my gratitude."

Shortly, Miss Stephanie Gray, he told her silently with his eyes. *But I doubt I will have to tell you how.* He was glad suddenly that her genuine distress and her ability to turn that distress to her own advantage had made his decision so easy to make.

He wanted her.

"Ah," he said, looking up as the carriage made a sudden turn to the left. "It appears that we have arrived."

Chapter 3

A servant showed her to her room while Mr. Munro went back outside on some errand. The maid was obsequious while he was still in sight, and almost insolently abrupt once they were at the top of the stairs. She tossed her head before going back down and looked Stephanie over as if she were a sideshow at a summer fair.

Stephanie was too tired to care a great deal—and too relieved. She still felt on the verge of tears. The terrifying prospect of having to spend another night out of doors had been hammering at her brain for the last several hours. She stepped inside the inn room and stood against the door, her hands clasping the handle behind her back. Her own room. Four walls and a floor and a ceiling and privacy. She closed her eyes and allowed herself to feel the luxury of safety.

It was a large room with sofas and chairs and a table as well as a large bed and the usual furnishings of a bedchamber. He need not have been so generous. A tiny attic would have sufficed. She felt a rush of gratitude. How would she ever repay him?

He had not said anything about another meal tonight, though it was hours since they had eaten. But she was not really hungry. Only a little thirsty. It did not matter. Surely there would be breakfast in the morning before they left. That would fortify her for the day. How far would he take her tomorrow? She thought of the blessed miles they must have covered today. It would have taken her a few days to walk as far.

She crossed the room to set her reticule down on the dressing table and caught sight of herself in the looking glass. She felt a shock of horror. The bonnet looked even more gaudy and vulgar on her head than it had looked in her hands. Perhaps the way its colors clashed with her hair had something to do with it. And the cloak looked garish, to say the least. Was it any wonder that everyone who had seen her today had looked at her askance? The horrified face in the mirror changed expression and registered amusement despite herself.

Oh, she looked quite, quite dreadful. Though of course *he* had not looked askance at her. He had been unfailingly courteous and kind.

She undid the ribbons with some haste and pulled off the offending bonnet. She plucked at the plumes, twisted them, pulled them. But whoever had put them there had intended that they stay there. With a sigh she set the bonnet down on one end of the dressing table. She unbuttoned the cloak and draped it over a chair. There, she thought, looking back at her image. Now she looked like herself again. Except that her hair was hopelessly flattened and tangled.

She drew out the pins. Ah, it felt so good to shake her hair free and to feel it loose and light against her back. It looked wild and curly, of course—its natural state, alas. It would take her all of five or ten minutes to tease a comb through it. She was just too tired. She took the few steps to the bed, sat on the edge of it, kicked off her half boots, spread her hands on the bed slightly behind her, and leaned back, bracing herself on her arms. She tipped back her head and shook her hair from side to side, her eyes closed. She sighed with contentment.

Something made her open her eyes and lift her head again, though she had not been conscious of any particular sound.

He was standing in the doorway, holding the door open, watching her. Had he knocked and she had not heard? She came to her feet and took a few hurried steps toward him. He came inside and closed the door and took a few steps toward her after setting down a valise.

"I am sorry," she said. "I did not hear—"

"It is beautiful," he said. His voice sounded husky, as if perhaps he had caught a chill. He was looking at her hair. "But I guessed that it would be."

She felt horribly mortified. She felt almost naked. No one ever saw her with her hair down.

"I am sorry," she said again. "I did not know—"

But he had taken several more steps toward her, and he had lifted one hand and was running the backs of his fingers lightly down her hair.

Gentlemen were very easily tempted, Mama had always said. It was a lady's responsibility to make sure that she never *ever* teased.

"Your beauty does not need to be enhanced with bright clothes," he said. "It speaks for itself. The gray dress, now, is a very clever touch."

"Oh, well," she said, horribly embarrassed. She wanted to take a step back, but it seemed unmannerly. "That cloak and that bonnet, you know . . ." And then with the corner of her eye she saw his valise again. And the ghastliest of ghastly certainties struck her.

"What is it?" he asked. His eyes, which had been on her mouth, lifted to hers. They really were quite silver, she thought irrelevantly, but they were saved from fading into insignificance by the dark outer lines—almost as if someone had taken a stick of very dark charcoal and outlined the irises.

"Oh," she said, closing her eyes tightly. "This is *your* room, is it not?" How could she have believed even for a moment that such opulence was intended for her? Doubtless her room really was an attic. That malicious servant girl!

"Yes," he said softly. "This is my room."

"Oh, I am so *sorry*," she said. "The maid brought me here. Perhaps she did not realize . . . Though I am sure she did."

She felt the fingers of both his hands against her wrists

and then moving up her arms until his hands came to rest on her shoulders. She was not conscious of either moving or being moved, but she could feel suddenly the tips of her breasts brushing against his coat.

"She was insolent?" he said. "Well. We will forget about her, Miss Stephanie Gray. She is of no significance."

His lips touched hers.

Her eyes snapped open, and her head jerked back. She had come to the wrong room, and she had let down her hair, and now look what had happened. Gentleman though he was, he was losing control. Mama had been right. Gentlemen—even the best of them—were weak creatures.

And then another thought struck her—ten times worse than the last. Perhaps he thought she had come *deliberately*. Perhaps he thought that when she had spoken in the carriage about repayment for his generosity, she had meant . . .

"No," she said. The word came out as a thin, wavering whisper of sound. It did not sound at all convincing even to her own ears.

"No?" His haughty, rather cold look was back.

One of his arms, she realized, was about her waist, and her waist and her abdomen were pressed to him. He seemed alarmingly muscular and masculine. And yet she was not frightened—not of him—only distressed by the misunderstanding that she had caused, or that the chambermaid had caused.

"No," she said more firmly.

She was not surprised when his arms fell away from her, and he took a step back. He was quite different, after all, from those other men with whom she had occasionally scuffled at Mr. Burnaby's. She had known that all day, and she knew it now too. She felt no fear, only embarrassment and regret that she had inadvertently tempted him. He was looking at her, eyebrows raised, waiting for an explanation.

"I *am* grateful," she said, forcing herself to look into his eyes. She clasped her hands at her bosom. "Believe me, I am, sir. More than I could possibly put into words. One day I will repay you."

"One day," he said very softly, and that gleam almost of amusement was back in his eyes.

"I think," she said, "I should like to go to my own room now, Mr. Munro. Can you direct me, or shall I ask the maid to do so?"

"Ah," he said, clasping his hands behind his back, "but I believe it is agreed that the chambermaid is unreliable, Miss Gray, if not downright malicious. It will be better if you stay here and I take the room that was intended for you."

"Oh, no," she protested as he turned toward the door and bent to take up his valise. "Oh, no, please. I could not allow—"

"Miss Gray," he said, and he spoke in a voice that she guessed his servants were accustomed to hearing and obeying, though he did not raise it at all, "I must insist. You will give me the honor of your company for breakfast—at eight?"

"Oh, please," she said, "I feel dreadful. This is *your* room. It is so very splendid."

He looked around him and then at her. "Indifferently pleasant," he said. "I assure you that the one intended for your use is in no way inferior to this."

He spoke to make her feel better. She did not believe him for a moment. But there was no point in arguing further. He was determined to be the gentleman.

"Thank you," she said. "You are so very kind."

And then, before turning and leaving the room and closing the door behind him, he did what no one had ever done to her before. He took her right hand in his, raised it to his lips, and kissed the backs of her fingers.

"Good night, Miss Gray," he said. "Have pleasant dreams."

She closed her eyes and set her fingertips to her lips, prayer fashion, after he had gone. Oh, how dreadfully embarrassing. How would she ever face him tomorrow morning? She had come to his room and taken the pins from her hair. She had been on the bed when he arrived. And naturally he had thought . . . And yet, as soon as she had said no, he

had let her go. Not only that, he had left her in possession of
his room and asked for the *honor* of her company at breakfast tomorrow.

If she had lost faith in the male species during the past six
years—and sometimes it had been difficult to believe that
there were other men like Papa in the world—then that faith
had been restored today. Oh, how *fortunate* his wife was, if
he had a wife.

But perhaps not either. Stephanie was not naive enough to
believe that he had intended only kisses a few minutes ago.
He had intended— Well, he had intended to do *that* to her.
Not that she could really blame him. It must have appeared
as if she were offering a quite blatant invitation, and being a
man—as Mama would have said—it had not occurred to
him to resist it. But surely he *would* have resisted if he had
a wife. Surely he would. He must be a single man.

She was glad he was a gentleman. She shivered when she
remembered the very real danger she had just been in. She
had been alone in a bedchamber with him. She had inadvertently inflamed his passions. And she had felt two things
during the brief moments when he had held her against him.
She had felt his strength, against which she would have been
powerless had he chosen to exert it. And she had felt something else. She swallowed and would not verbalize in her
mind what that something else was.

She felt grubby and stale, she thought, turning her mind
determinedly from the disturbing images. She needed to
wash. She was going to take all her clothes off and wash all
over. She was going to wash out some of her undergarments
and trust that they would dry by the morning. And she was
tired. So tired that both her mind and her limbs felt sluggish.
She was going to lie down once she was clean, and sleep and
sleep and sleep.

But half an hour later, before she had had a chance to lie
down, a knock on the door heralded the arrival of a servant—not the chambermaid who had misdirected her—
bearing a tray laden with food and a steaming teapot.

She bit her lip and wondered if this was perhaps Mr. Munro's dinner. But no.

"With the compliments of the gentleman, ma'am," the servant said with considerably more respect than anyone else had shown her today—except for Mr. Munro himself, of course.

He was lying on a narrow, lumpy bed in a little box of an attic room, his hands linked behind his head, staring up at a water-stained ceiling. Surprisingly, he was feeling amusement.

The landlord had been deeply apologetic that there was no other room available. He had even offered to turn some lesser mortal out of another room so that His Grace might pass the night in more pleasant surroundings. Bridgwater had declined the offer. He was only thankful that he was not doomed to spend the night on a wooden settle in the taproom.

Of course, the servants were all probably making delighted sport of the fact that he had been kicked out of the best room at the inn by the brazen whore he had brought there with him. Well, let them enjoy their amusement. The duke had never cared a great deal what servants thought or said of him. There were more important things in life on which to fix his thoughts and emotions.

He chuckled. She really was quite priceless. It was a long time since he had been so vastly entertained. He should be feeling both angry and sexually frustrated, of course. She had outmaneuvered him. She had teased him dangerously— but then he supposed she would not have been *very* upset if he had insisted on taking what she had been so artfully offering when he had opened the door to the room.

He felt an unwelcome tightening of the groin again when he remembered how she had looked on that bed, her slender body arched back against her supporting arms, her gorgeous mane of hair swaying from side to side behind her, her face lifted to the ceiling, as if in sexual ecstasy. He wondered how many hours she had spent before a looking glass before she had perfected the posture. And then she had affected surprise and confusion to find that he was standing in the doorway, watching her.

He chuckled again.

The gray dress really was a masterpiece. It complemented the glorious auburn of her hair to perfection, and its simplicity somehow enhanced her long-limbed, slender beauty. She did not have a voluptuous figure, but he had no doubt at all that she knew exactly how to make the most of what she had. Certainly she had succeeded in bringing him to painful arousal even before he had touched her.

He was not sorry she had said no. Well, perhaps that was not strictly true. He still felt uncomfortably warm as his mind touched on the imagined picture of that wavy, tangled hair spread on a pillow beneath him and of those long slim legs twined about his as he worked his pleasure on her. No, he could not pretend that he had not really wanted her. He had and he did.

But he was not sorry even so. One did not know with whom she had been last or with how many she had recently been. The mistake he had made, of course—but perhaps after all it was a fortunate one—was in offering her lodging for the night and in taking the room and sending her to it before agreeing to terms. He had been given the impression that she had enjoyed enormously evicting him while pretending to wish to evict herself. He wondered again if she really was an actress. She seemed almost too good. For there had been nothing melodramatic in her performance. It had been neither understated nor overstated. It had been almost convincing.

He smiled again. She was wonderful, he thought. A woman who lived by her wits and who knew how to use them to her own best advantage. What intelligent woman, after all, would willingly give herself an hour or so's strenuous work in bed when the bed might be had without the work? She had maneuvered him into offering the one without first extracting an agreement about the other. Very wise of her. Undoubtedly she was very tired. She needed to sleep tonight, not to work.

He wondered if she was sleeping peacefully. He would wager she was. And he wondered too if tomorrow night he would plan more carefully and make his conditions clearer. But he doubted it. It amused him to allow her to play out her hand.

Tomorrow night? Was he planning to have her with him again tomorrow night, then? Was it not time to set her down somewhere along the way? With the wherewithal to continue her journey in comfort, of course.

No, he knew he would not set her down. Neither would he go directly to London, he realized. He would take her to Hampshire, if that indeed was her destination. He would take her to the exact place she was going, if she did have an exact place in mind. He was curious to know where it was and why she was going there. And he looked forward to seeing her try to worm her way out of allowing him to travel the whole distance. She would not want to have all her lies exposed, after all.

So they would have a battle of wits. But this was one he intended to win. A night of sexual frustration notwithstanding, he had had more enjoyment out of today, and he had a brighter anticipation of the morrow than he had felt for a long, long time. It was a thought that made him feel a twinge of guilt when he remembered how eagerly and kindly Carew and his wife had entertained him for the past few weeks.

Miss Stephanie Gray—or whatever her name was—had succeeded where they had failed.

It was raining heavily when she got up the following morning. She looked out the window of her luxurious inn room and imagined the misery, as well as the terror, she would have lived through last night if it had not been for the generosity of Mr. Munro.

The rain eased up by midmorning, but it drizzled all day long, and the treetops were tossed about in a fitful and gusty wind. Even inside the carriage, which traveled more slowly than it had the day before because of the state of the roads, the air felt chill and slightly damp.

Through most of the morning she sat tensely in her seat. The tension was caused partly by embarrassment, although he was gentleman enough to make no mention of last evening's misunderstandings. She could not help remembering, though, that she had let her hair down and that he had touched it and called it beautiful—and that he had touched *her* and even kissed her. She could not help remembering that the bed had been behind her and that he had thought she was inviting him to take her there and— Well, she did not need to let her thoughts stray further.

But mostly she was tense because at every village and town she expected him to announce that he had brought her far enough. The long, comfortable journey with him had made her a dreadful coward. The prospect of being alone and destitute again was a terror she could not face, even in her mind. She thought of begging when he finally made his announcement and knew that perhaps she really would.

But so far it had been unnecessary. He had said nothing all morning or into the afternoon, when they had stopped for a meal and a change of horses. And he had handed her back into the carriage afterward, as if he had not even considered leaving her behind. Perhaps he no longer liked to suggest that she leave. Perhaps he expected her to broach the subject. But she would not do so, unmannerly as it might seem.

Please God, let him take her farther. Just a little farther.

He kept her talking all day. She told him about her childhood and her girlhood, about her mother and father. And in the telling, she found herself remembering details and events she had not thought of in years. She found herself becoming more animated, more relaxed, more prone to smiles and even laughter. And then she would remember where she was and glance at him anxiously and suggest that she was boring him. But he always urged her to continue.

She discussed plays with him—those of Mr. Shakespeare and Mr. Sheridan and Mr. Goldsmith. But when he asked her about her experiences with the theater, she had to confess to him that she had never seen a play performed on stage, though she had dreamed of doing so in London, where plays were surely performed at their best. Her only contact with the theater and actors had been a very recent one, but he had not asked about that, and it was something she tried not to remember, though they had been kind to her, of course.

He smiled when she told him she had only read plays, not seen them performed. He would think her impossibly rustic, of course. And he would be right. She *was* rustic. She would not pretend otherwise just in order to appear sophisticated in his eyes. He seemed to like her well enough as she was anyway. He did very little of the talking himself. Yet he appeared interested in everything she said. His eyes smiled frequently.

He had told her nothing of himself, she realized.

"Well, Miss Gray," he said finally when she was trying not to notice that afternoon had long ago turned to evening and evening was threatening to turn to night. "Another night is upon us."

"Yes, sir." She looked at him and kept her eyes on his. She knew that she was gazing pleadingly at him, but she could not muster up enough pride to look at him any other way.

"My coachman will stop at the next inn," he said.

"Yes, sir." She closed her eyes tightly suddenly and lost the final shreds of her dignity. "Please. Oh, please let me stay with you. I . . . It is raining and it is going to be very dark. There will be no moon. I . . . Oh, please."

"Miss Gray," he said, his voice sounding surprised, "I thought it would have been obvious to you by—"

"Please." She would beg and grovel if necessary. "I will do anything. I will repay you in any way you choose." She knew the implication of her words even as she spoke them, though she had not realized it in advance. But she did not care. She would not recall the words or qualify them in any way. She would do anything not to have to face the terrors of the darkness again.

There was a lengthy silence, during which she kept her eyes closed and held her breath.

"No," he said finally. "I think not, Miss Gray, though it is magnanimous of you to offer. Your pleas and your offers are unnecessary anyway." The bottom fell out of her stomach, but fortunately he continued. "I thought it would have been obvious to you by now that I am taking you to your grandfather's home, now yours, in Hampshire. I believe we will reach it tomorrow if the roads do not prove to be quite impassable and if you can tell me exactly what house I am looking for."

He was going to— "You are going to take me all the way?" She opened her eyes and stared at him uncomprehendingly. "All the way there?"

He smiled. "I am afraid so, Miss Gray," he said.

She was glad she was sitting down. Her legs would not have supported her. Her hands shook in her lap. Even so, she had to raise them quickly to cover her face before she lost control of every muscle in it. She swallowed repeatedly, intent on not bawling like a baby.

"Yes," he said. She did not even notice the thread of humor in his voice. "I thought you might be affected by the announcement, Miss Gray."

"Thank you," she whispered. "Thank you. Oh, thank you."

Chapter 4

Sindon Park—he had heard of it. It was said to be one of the grander manors in the south of England. The park, with its rhododendron groves and rose arbors and formal parterres, was said to draw visitors throughout the summer months.

At least, he thought, she was willing to practice deception on a grand scale. He wondered what she would do when she realized that there would be no getting rid of him, when she knew that he intended to escort her right to the main doors of Sindon and even within the doors—if she was allowed within them herself. But she would be—she was with him.

He wondered if she would turn her marvelous inventive skills on the poor unsuspecting inhabitants of the house. Would she claim to be a long-lost relative? He sincerely hoped so. He hoped she would not crumble at the grand scale awkwardness of it all. He would be disappointed in her.

He watched her with appreciation throughout the day. They did not do much talking. She watched the scenery through the window with eager—and with slightly anxious?—eyes. And he watched her.

He was a fool, he thought. He could have had her last night. She had offered herself. Had he accepted, there was no way she could have wormed out of the commitment as she had done the night before. And he had wanted her. He still wanted her. But he had decided not to take on such an entanglement. Or perhaps it had seemed distasteful to him to accept an offer that had been made out of some desperation. He had no doubt that she really had been alarmed at the prospect of having to spend the night out of doors. Somehow he liked to sleep with women who wanted to sleep with him.

Perhaps, he thought, he would take her back to London with him once this charade played itself out to a suitable denouement. Perhaps he would set her up somewhere and keep her for a while, until she found her feet and could make her own way in the metropolis. He had no doubt that that would not take her long at all. Perhaps he would buy her new clothes, ones that were more . . . seemly for a mistress of his. Though he could appreciate the humorous contrast between the flamboyant cloak and bonnet on the one hand and the demure simplicity of the gray dress on the other.

He wondered for how long she would amuse him. Would she succeed in pushing back the massive boredom from his life? She had succeeded admirably for longer than two days. But could she continue to do so? He felt such a deep longing suddenly that he almost sighed aloud.

He waited for her to speak. He knew that she would do so quite soon now. They must, after all, be within ten miles of Sindon. She could not wait much longer.

She was blushing when she looked at him—and biting at her lower lip. Yes, she was setting up the situation very well. He could almost hear already the words that would follow. He was not disappointed.

"Are we close, sir?" she asked him. "Is Sindon Park far off? Do you know?"

"Less than ten miles at a guess," he said, containing his amusement. "Just relax, Miss Gray. I am not about to abandon you now. We will be there in time for tea, I daresay."

Her eyes dropped from his again for a moment, and she played with the shabby glove of one hand, twisting the hole out of sight. "I have been thinking," she said.

He did not doubt it. The workings of her mind had been almost visible to his amused eye throughout the day.

She looked back up into his eyes. She was good with her eyes. They looked purely guileless—and purely beautiful, of course.

"I cannot arrive with you," she said.

He raised his eyebrows and resisted the urge to grin.

"You have been so very kind," she said earnestly. "And it seems so very ungrateful of me. But don't you see? I have no chaperone or even a maid. They will want to know how far you have brought me. I have been alone with you in this carriage for almost three days. I have stayed with you—in separate rooms, of course." She paused to sit back in the seat and to blush with maidenly modesty. "I have stayed with you for two nights. It will be impossible to explain and to make it appear as innocent as it has been." She flushed an even deeper shade.

He would not help her out. He was enjoying this too much. He kept his eyes on her and waited for her to continue.

"And I cannot lie about it," she said. "I am not good at lying."

He felt his lips twitch, but he would not spoil things. "What would you suggest?" he asked.

"I did think at first," she said, "that you might set me down at the gates of Sindon and I would walk the rest of the way. Though it would seem horridly inhospitable of me when you have come so far out of your way and the house is mine, after all. But that whole idea would not do. They would want to know where I came from, and perhaps there would have been no stage or mail coach anywhere near the time I would arrive. I would have to tell the truth after all, and if I were going to do that anyway, then you might as well take me all the way."

"I can see," he said, "that you might be no better off with that solution, Miss Gray."

"And so," she said, "I think it would be best, sir, if you set me down in the next town. I can take the stage from there and arrive properly just as if I had traveled by stage all the way." She blushed deeply again. "Though I will have to beg money to pay the fare. I daresay it will not be much. I will insist on sending it back to you if you will give me your direction in London."

He watched her closely. He was enjoying himself vastly. "I have developed a deep concern for your safety and well-being during the past few days, Miss Gray," he said. "I do not believe that in all conscience I can abandon you now. I would worry too much that after all something had gone awry, and you had not arrived safely to claim your inheritance."

She tipped her head slightly to one side. "How kind you are," she said. "But really—"

"You must remember, Miss Gray"—he gazed benignly at her—"you must remember that you are no longer either a clergyman's daughter or a governess. You are a great heiress. You have a certain degree of power. If you arrive at Sindon timid and cringing and expecting censure for the manner of your arrival, you will find that there will always be men—and women—willing to rule you and control your life. You and I have done nothing improper, apart from indulging in one small kiss, for which I am deeply sorry. *You* have done nothing improper. It would be far better for you to arrive in my carriage with my escort and prove to whoever is waiting to receive you that you are a woman of independent mind as well as means."

"Oh, but—" she said. She stopped to bite her lip once more. "Are you sure it will not appear very improper, sir? I have not really thought a great deal until now about the impropriety of having traveled alone with you because I have been in such desperate circumstances and have been so grateful for your help. But will it not appear improper to others? Will not my reputation be damaged? And perhaps yours too, sir? I should regret that of all things."

"I think not, Miss Gray," he said. "Sit back and relax. I insist on taking you to the door of Sindon Park and delivering you personally into the hands of your grandfather's solicitor and of your grandmother's cousin. I shall not abandon you. I shall see you inside the house, where you will be safe at last. And home at last." He finally allowed himself a reassuring smile.

She said no more, though he could see unease in her face and in her posture. He could almost see her mind racing over the possibilities of last-minute escape.

Think all you like, Stephanie Gray, he told her silently. *And squirm all you like. I have earned this pleasure.* The social events of the Season were going to seem tame indeed when he finally got to town. But then perhaps he would have a new mistress to brighten life for a few weeks or months. Eventually, he would surely tire of her ever fertile imagination. But perhaps not for a while.

She squirmed in good earnest when the carriage finally turned between two stone gateposts and proceeded along an elegant driveway lined with lime trees. He heard her draw a deep breath, which she let out raggedly through her mouth.

"Oh dear," she said, "my heart is pounding and my palms are clammy—and shaking." She held up both hands to prove her point. He had no doubt that she was not acting. "What will they think of me, dressed like this? And arriving with you instead of in the carriage that they have probably sent by now? Will they believe it is me, do you suppose? And what if it is all a hoax after all? What if none of it is real? What if they look at me as if they had never heard of me or anybody of my name?"

Ah, she had been using her time well. She had been thinking of a way out of her dilemma. She was paving the way.

"Relax," he told her soothingly.

"Oh," she said, "that is all very well for you to say. Ohh!"

The last exclamation came out on a note of agony. The house had come into view. It was a house of gray stone and indeterminate architectural design. There were turrets and gables and pillars, all somehow combining to create a surprisingly pleasing effect. The house was larger than he had expected, and the parterre gardens before it were magnificently kept. When he glanced at Stephanie Gray, he saw stark terror in her eyes.

He almost relented. He almost suggested rapping on the

front panel and giving his coachman the order to turn around. He would get her to tell him her real destination. And then he would make his proposition to her. They could consummate their agreement tonight before returning to London. There was something distinctly exhilarating in the thought.

But no. He must see this to an end. And, indeed, it was too late to turn back without incident. The double doors at the top of the horseshoe steps had opened, and three people had stepped out to watch the approach of the carriage—two men and one woman, all of middle years and of thoroughly respectable appearance.

"Oh dear," Stephanie Gray said. Her voice was all breath. "What shall I do? What shall I say?"

"I am sure," he said, his mouth quirking again, "that you will think of just the right words."

"Do you think so?" she asked doubtfully. "You are so kind. But I am not good with words."

And she had just claimed to be a poor liar?

The carriage drew to a halt.

She had not expected to feel such terror. After all, there was no reason for it. She was not coming as a supplicant or as an employee. She had not come to make a favorable impression on anyone. She had come because all this was now hers.

But the thought brought only a renewed wave of fright.

It was *enormous*. And it was *magnificent*. She had somehow pictured Sindon Park as a larger version of some of the prettier, more prosperous country cottages she had seen. She had pictured the park itself as a large country garden. She had expected to feel very grand as the owner of such opulence.

But this . . .

Well, this would dwarf Mr. Burnaby's estate. His house and garden would fit into a corner of this property and not even be noticed. This was a house and a park fit for a king.

She had known that her grandfather was wealthy. But she

had no real conception of wealth. To her, the Burnabys had appeared enormously wealthy. Was she now wealthier than they?

The thought that she owned all this seemed absurd to her, and she was quite serious when she suggested to Mr. Munro that perhaps everything had been a hoax. Surely, it could not be real. She felt at a terrible disadvantage. How could she arrive like this, a woman without baggage, without servants, without even her own clothes, except for her dress? There were *holes* in her gloves. And how could she arrive in Mr. Munro's carriage with Mr. Munro for escort?

It was an impossibility. She was on the verge of leaning forward and begging him—as she had begged him for a different reason last night—to direct his coachman to turn back, to take her somewhere else. Anywhere else.

But of course there was nowhere else to go.

Besides, it was too late. They had been seen. There were people coming out of the house. She could only go forward. And why should she not? She remembered Mr. Munro's words. She was no longer just a vicar's daughter or just a governess—not that there was anything demeaning in either identity. She was an heiress, a wealthy woman, the owner of Sindon Park, the granddaughter of the previous owner.

If she was cringing and timid, he had said, there would always be people willing and eager to rule her. She had had to be timid—and even a little cringing sometimes—for too long. She would be neither ever again. She squared her shoulders and lifted her chin. Mr. Munro had jumped out of the carriage and set down the steps himself. He turned now to hand her down and smiled encouragingly at her. There seemed to be almost mischief in his smile as if he were telling her that this was a new adventure and he looked forward to seeing how well she would acquit herself.

Well, she would not disappoint him.

The three people who had emerged from the house had come to the bottom of the horseshoe steps by the time she had descended from the carriage. She lifted her head to look at them and saw their smiles of welcome fade in perfect unison with one another. Oh dear, her wretched bonnet. The plumes had stubbornly refused to be detached from it, though she had tried again last night. But she kept her chin high and took a step forward, lest she give in to the temptation to hide behind Mr. Munro. This had nothing to do with him. This was her concern entirely.

She curtsied and smiled at them one at a time. "Good afternoon," she said. "I am Stephanie Gray."

They all succeeded in looking simultaneously aghast. Their eyes all swiveled to Mr. Munro. But clearly they got no encouragement from that direction. They all looked back at her.

"Mr. Watkins?" she said, looking from one of the men to the other.

One of them half raised a hand, seemed to think twice about acknowledging his identity, and scratched the side of his nose with it. Stephanie smiled at him.

"After I had your letter, sir," she said, "I decided not to wait for the carriage you offered to send for me. It was foolish of me as matters turned out." But no, she would not be abjectly apologetic. "I took the stage, but at the first change from one to the other, I succeeded in having my valise and my tickets and almost all of my money stolen. I had to spend a whole night in a hedgerow beside the road, and during that night I was robbed of almost everything I had left. Fortunately, those assailants were frightened off by the approach of a carriage. They left me with my reticule and my d-dress, but they took my cloak and bonnet and parasol. The occupants of the carriage were very kind. There were actually two carriages. They were a troupe of traveling actors and offered to take me with them. But they were going in the wrong direction. They did give me a cloak and bonnet, though, from the trunk that contained their stage costumes."

The eyes of all three rose at the same moment to gaze at the plumes of her bonnet.

"It *is* a monstrosity, is it not?" she said and smiled. "But the cloak has kept me warm and wearing this bonnet has been marginally less shocking than going bareheaded. May we go inside?"

Mr. Watkins cleared his throat, and the other man exchanged glances with the woman.

"Oh," Stephanie said. She had omitted something, of course. "Mr. Munro very kindly took me up in his carriage when he saw me trudging along the side of the road. And he has very generously brought me the whole way." She looked them all very directly in the eye. She would omit none of it. Let them make of it what they would. "That was three days ago. Without his help it would have taken me a few weeks to walk here, I am sure, and I might well have perished on the way. I have enough money in my reticule to buy only one small loaf of bread, you see."

"Mr. Munro?" Mr. Watkins said, looking sharply at that gentleman and frowning. *"Munro?"*

"Yes," Mr. Munro said. It was all he said.

"He insisted on bringing me all the way here," Stephanie said, "even though I have brought him out of his way. I owe him a deep debt of gratitude. *May* we go inside?"

"Horace—" The woman spoke for the first time, laying her hand on the arm of the man who had not yet spoken.

Horace cleared his throat. "How do we know you are who you say you are?" he asked. "If you will forgive me for saying so, Miss . . ."

"Gray," she said. "Stephanie Gray. I suppose I do look like a-an actress. Is this proof enough?" She opened her reticule and took out the letter Mr. Watkins had sent her. She handed it to him.

Mr. Watkins took it and opened it and appeared to be reading it, just as if he had not seen its contents before.

"But how do we know," the woman said, "that you did not find this somewhere? How do we know that you and this . . . this *gentleman* were not the ones to attack Miss Gray and rob her?"

Mr. Watkins cleared his throat. "I believe I can vouch for . . . er . . . Mr. Munro, Mrs. Cavendish," he said.

"And I can vouch for Miss Gray, ma'am," Mr. Munro

said, stepping forward and offering Stephanie his arm. She smiled at him gratefully, even though his voice had sounded very much as if there were ice dripping from it. "Shall we step inside, Miss Gray? It occurs to me that you do not have to stand here waiting for permission to do so."

"Thank you, sir." She took his arm.

The other three came up the steps behind them. But she had little time to think about them or the awkwardness of her arrival. Soon they were stepping through the doorway into a marble, pillared hall that quite robbed her of breath. She had expected the whole house to be smaller than just the hall was proving to be.

"Oh," she said and glanced up at Mr. Munro. His face looked strangely like the marble by which he was surrounded. The hall must have taken his breath too, she thought.

But there was another man standing in the hall, obviously a gentleman rather than a servant. He was younger than the other three, of medium height, almost bald, bespectacled. Stephanie smiled at him.

"Peter," Mrs. Cavendish said, "this is her. Miss Gray."

"Yes," Peter said, his voice and whole manner stiff and disapproving. "I heard everything, Aunt Bertha. You came with this . . . gentleman, Miss Gray? Alone with a stranger?"

"For three days," Bertha Cavendish added.

Stephanie could feel the certainty growing in her. Horace was her grandmother's nephew. Bertha Cavendish was probably his wife. Peter was their nephew—her intended bridegroom. Her spirits, already hovering on the lower end of cheerful, took a steep dive. It was unjust to judge on such brief acquaintance that it was almost no acquaintance at all, but in her estimation Mr. Peter Whoever was a man without even a glimmering of humor. He frowned now.

"I do not believe—" he began.

"Sir." Mr. Munro cut into whatever it was Peter did not believe, his voice quite decisive enough to command everyone's attention. And there was no doubt about it now—there was pure ice there. He had turned to Mr. Watkins. "Perhaps

Mrs. Cavendish would be good enough to present herself and these other two gentlemen to Miss Gray. And perhaps she would then escort Miss Gray to the drawing room or a salon for tea. Miss Gray has been traveling for many days. I have been her companion for three of those days. I believe it would be appropriate if I had a private word with you."

Mr. Watkins bowed.

"Well—" Mrs. Cavendish began, her bosom swelling. But Mr. Munro wheeled on her and raised to his eye a quizzing glass that Stephanie had never noticed on his person until now. She remembered the early impression she had had of an arrogant and toplofty gentleman. It was all back, that impression, and clearly Mrs. Cavendish was cowed by it.

"Well," she said with considerably more civility, "if *you* are satisfied, Mr. Watkins, I daresay we must be too. But how foolish of you, my dear Miss Gray, to leave your employer's home without the proper escort. And how rash of you to accept a ride with a gentleman when you did not know him and had no maid with you."

"It seemed preferable, ma'am," Stephanie said, allowing herself to be led toward a magnificently curved staircase, "to dying of exposure and starvation."

Mr. Munro had disappeared with Mr. Watkins. She had not had a chance to speak with him first and to invite him to come to the drawing room afterward or wherever it was that they were to take tea. She must have a chance to thank him properly before he left. And she must offer him dinner and lodging for the night. It would be quite proper to do so when there were obviously other gentlemen staying at the house in addition to Mrs. Cavendish.

It was all very bewildering. But she had arrived at last. The worst was over.

And it was hers. This was all *hers*—if she was married within the next four months, of course. That might be tricky. She was not going to marry Peter Whoever-He-Was. She had made up her mind on that already. He had been about to say that he was not willing to take on a woman who had just spent three days in company with another man and had doubtless been behaving in quite unseemly fashion with that man.

How dare he.

The very idea!

She would rather go back to being a governess than marry such a man.

Though she hoped—oh, how she hoped—it would not come to that.

Chapter 5

He was feeling almost amused. He realized that it was a feeling that would not last—that it was only shock that enabled him to see the humor of a situation that was not in any way humorous for him. But feeling amusement was preferable to feeling stark horror, he supposed.

He followed Mr. Watkins, the solicitor, into a private room leading off the hall—it appeared to be a combination office and library—and waited for the man to close the door behind them.

He had rushed with wide open eyes into a trap of his own making. That had been obvious to him soon after he had helped her down from the carriage. At first he had felt blinding anger against Miss Stephanie Gray. If only she had thought of telling before now the story of the stolen bonnet and cloak and the one about the actors. It seemed to him that she had told him almost every detail of her life history except that one. And it was the one detail that made all the difference.

But perhaps not. Perhaps he would have taken it as one more brazen and clever invention. And he could hardly blame her for not telling him. She was not a prattler. She had talked to him, yes. She had done most of the talking during their days of travel. But everything she had told him had been spoken in answer to his questions. He had not thought to ask her what had happened during that one night she had spent out of doors.

He should have thought of asking. It *did* make all the difference. Without the cloak and bonnet, he realized now when it was too late, she looked to be exactly what she had said she was—a governess living on the edge of poverty. *Why* had he not set more store by her gloves, which actually had holes worn in them, and on her plain gray dress and shabby reticule?

He had built his whole fanciful image of her around such flimsy evidence as a fuchsia cloak and a pink bonnet with its multicolored plumes.

Oh, yes, he had set the trap for her with careful deliberation, and then he had proceeded to walk smiling into it himself. Yes, it really was funny. Hilarious.

Mr. Watkins cleared his throat. "Mr., er, Munro?" he said. "Are you not the head of that family, er, sir? I have seen you in town once or twice, I believe. Are you not the Duke of Bridgwater?"

"I am," His Grace said, turning before the fireplace and setting his hands behind his back.

Mr. Watkins made him a hasty and rather ridiculous bow. "This is an honor, Your Grace," he said. "And an honor for Miss Gray, too. I cannot imagine why—"

"I will, of course," Bridgwater said, bringing one arm forward in order to toy with the handle of his quizzing glass, though he did not lift it to his eye, "be marrying the lady."

He knew even as he spoke, even before he saw the surprise on the solicitor's face, that it was a quite unnecessary gesture. His rank would have protected him. She would have suffered embarrassment and even a measure of disgrace, unless the four people who had greeted her all agreed to say nothing about her manner of arrival at Sindon Park. He would wager that the morally outraged Peter would agree to no such thing—unless he was bound and determined to marry her at all costs. But nobody would censure the Duke of Bridgwater for walking away from the woman. Nobody would expect him to do anything as drastic as offering for her.

But he had known as soon as the truth dawned on him that

he had no choice. There was the annoying matter of his honor.

"You wish to *marry* Miss Gray?" Mr. Watkins said, his eyes starting from his head.

"But of course," His Grace said haughtily, taking his glass more firmly in his hand and lifting it, though not all the way to his eye. "Do you believe I would so thoroughly have compromised her, sir, unless I intended to make her my wife?"

He was thinking about the law of averages. His best friend and those other two friends of his had all been forced into unwanted marriages—though that was not quite true of Carew, who had married for love only to discover that his bride had married for another reason altogether. All three of those marriages had turned out well. Indeed he might almost use that dreadful cliché of them and say that the three couples were in the process of living happily ever after. He knew—he had just spent a few weeks in their company. Three out of three success stories. Now there were going to be four such marriages. It was too much to hope that there would be four out of four successes. The law of averages was against him.

"I believe," he said, "that according to her grandfather's will Miss Gray must be married within the next four months if she is not to forfeit her inheritance?"

"That is correct, Your Grace," the solicitor said. "But Sir Peter Griffin—"

His Grace set his glass to his eye, and Mr. Watkins fell silent.

"I think not," the duke said quietly. "I feel a certain aversion to the idea of allowing another man to marry my chosen bride. Miss Gray is my chosen bride."

Sir Peter Griffin could go hang, he thought. He was probably dangling after her fortune and this impressive property, but he would never let her forget the impropriety of her arrival at Sindon, dressed like a prize ladybird and with a male companion in tow. The man had looked severely displeased at his very first sight of her and had done nothing to hide his irritation.

Though why he should press his point when there was such an easy solution to his dilemma, the Duke of Bridgwater did not quite know. Miss Gray could marry the baronet, he could be on his way to town and his family and the Season, and they would all live happily ever after. No, she would not live happily. He could predict that with some certainty. And he would not have done the right thing.

He wished suddenly that he had not been brought up always to do the right thing, or that he had rebelled against his boyhood education as he had rebelled during his childhood. Good Lord, he had just spent six years being very careful indeed that nothing of the like would ever happen to him.

But he had walked into just such a situation like a lamb to the slaughter.

Mr. Watkins cleared his throat again, perhaps disconcerted by the silence that had stretched a little too long for comfort.

"We will discuss the marriage contract," the duke said. "I wish it to stipulate quite clearly that Miss Gray retain ownership of this property and of whatever fortune she has been left besides. I gather, sir, that her choice of husband must be approved by you and by a relative. That would be Mr. Horace . . . Cavendish, I presume? He is the lady's husband?"

"Yes, Your Grace," the solicitor said.

"We will have him down here, then," Bridgwater said briskly, "and have his approval. Then we will proceed to business. I am expected in London and have no wish to delay. I take it I have your approval, sir?" He raised his eyebrows and favored the poor solicitor with a look that had been part of his early education and had stayed with him ever since, a look that brooked no denial and no insubordination. He did not even use his quizzing glass.

"Oh, y-yes, i-indeed," the solicitor said, visibly flustered. "It is a g-great honor, Y-your Grace. For Miss Gray, I mean. And indeed f-for—"

"Mr. Watkins," His Grace said, "Mr. Cavendish?"

The solicitor scurried to the door in order to summon a servant.

Lord, the duke thought. Amusement was fading fast. Indeed, it had faded to nothing long ago, he realized. Lord, he was about to marry a governess. A governess-turned-heiress. A stranger. Someone for whom he felt nothing. Nothing at all except a certain lust. And that now seemed embarrassingly inappropriate. Good Lord, she was undoubtedly a virgin—a twenty-six-year old virgin. A virtuous woman whom he had been planning to take back to London with him as his mistress.

Good Lord! He dropped the handle of his quizzing glass lest he inadvertently snap it in two.

Her cloak and her bonnet had been whisked away—she fervently hoped that she need never see them again, though she felt woefully her lack of belongings. She had been taken by Mrs. Cavendish, who had requested rather stiffly that she be called Cousin Bertha, upstairs to her room. Actually, it was a whole suite of rooms, quite overwhelming to someone who had made her home in a small attic room for the past six years. She had been given time only to wash her hands and pat her hair into better shape after the removal of her bonnet. Then she had been taken down to the drawing room for tea.

Mrs. Cavendish, Cousin Bertha, presented her properly to Mr. Cavendish, who explained that he was her grandmother's nephew, son of Grandmama's sister, and that she must call him Cousin Horace. And she was presented to Sir Peter Griffin, who bowed stiffly and frowned darkly and explained that he had the honor of being Cousin Bertha's nephew and that he also had the honor of being at her service in the ticklish matter of her grandfather's will.

It was, Stephanie supposed, his way of offering her marriage. She tried not to be awed by his title. He was the only titled gentleman she had ever met. But apart from the title itself, there was nothing impressive, nothing awe-inspiring about the man. She could overlook his lack of good looks.

Though she would prefer a handsome husband if she had the choice, she had to admit, she had been taught from childhood on that a person must not be judged on looks alone. But she could not and would not overlook bad temper. And if Sir Peter Griffin was frowning at her the very first time they met, then one could hardly expect him to smile his way through the rest of the lifetime they might spend together.

Her experience of life might be limited, Stephanie thought, but even she knew that marriage was no easy business, that even the happiest of brides and grooms eventually had to work at achieving contentment and compatibility. Her parents had succeeded, though she could remember arguments and tight-lipped disagreements; Mr. and Mrs. Burnaby had not.

Her companions at tea were at least polite, she found. They appeared to have accepted her story and to have overcome their suspicions that she was an impostor. Cousin Horace was called away after a while, and she was left to converse with the other two. Cousin Bertha made an effort. Sir Peter concentrated on being silently morose. Perhaps he thought to impress her with a show of masculine power. She was not impressed.

She thought about Mr. Munro. She hoped he would not leave before she had had a chance to see him again. It would have been far better if he had done what she had suggested and allowed her to come by stage from the nearest town. Her arrival had been horribly embarrassing, and she was sure that he must have felt the embarrassment too. But all seemed to have ended well.

The thought of not seeing him ever again saddened her in a strange way. He had been kind. He had been a gentleman, even if he had felt temptation when it had presented itself and had shown signs of being willing to give in to temptation. But after he had understood the misunderstanding, he had been the perfect gentleman. She hated to think of such a man going out of her life forever. She had met with so little kindness in the last several years. Perhaps things would change, of course. She was an heiress now—except that she had to marry within four months, and she had already made up her mind not to accept the suitor who was there and ready to oblige her.

The opening of the door heralded the return of Cousin Horace with Mr. Watkins. Stephanie looked eagerly beyond them for Mr. Munro, but he was not there. She hid a stabbing of disappointment. Had they not even invited him to tea? Or had he refused? There were still a few hours of daylight left. He could be well on his way to London before darkness fell.

Mr. Watkins cleared his throat. "Miss Gray," he said, bowing to her with at least a decent show of respect, "would you care to join the, ah, the gentleman belowstairs? He would like a word with you. He is in the library. The servant in the hall will show you the way."

She jumped to her feet, a smile on her lips, and realized too late that her reaction had perhaps seemed too eager a one, considering the suspicions the other four occupants of the room must have about her and Mr. Munro. But she did not much care.

"Horace—" Cousin Bertha said, also getting to her feet.

But Cousin Horace held up a staying hand. "No, Bertha," he said. "It is quite all right."

Stephanie left the room without a word and ran lightly down the stairs. She felt a fluttering in her stomach again at the realization that this was all hers—or would be hers if . . . But she did not spare much thought for that little problem. Her eyes sought out the servant, who was standing across the hall before a large doorway. He opened the door as she approached him and smiled at him. She stepped inside the library.

He was standing with his back to the fireplace, his hands clasped behind him. He was not smiling, but then he had not smiled a great deal during their journey. He looked more— oh, what was the word? He looked more *imposing* than he had during their days together, though she remembered the impression she had had of him at first as a haughty, rather bored gentleman. She remembered his gloved hand tapping rather impatiently on the window of his carriage before he had decided to take her up.

If she were seeing him for the first time now, she thought, she would be a little afraid of him. But she was not seeing him for the first time. She hurried across the room toward him, both her hands outstretched. He took them in his.

"Mr. Munro," she said, "I am so glad you did not slip away before I had a chance to speak with you. You cannot know how grateful I am to you. Words are not always adequate vehicles for the expression of feeling. You cannot know, perhaps, what it is like to be a woman stranded without money or friends far from either her place of origin or her destination. Frankly, it is terrifying. I might have died— or worse. I will repay you. I swear it. I will find a way. But I will not offer you money. It would be vulgar, would it not?" She smiled brightly at him.

"It would be vulgar," he agreed. "Miss Gray, you are in need of a husband—very soon. Sir Peter Griffin is, I believe, the man to whom you referred during our travels?"

"Yes." She would say nothing to make him feel the burden of her problem.

"He would make you a miserable husband," he said. "He would make you feel like some inferior insect. I do not doubt he would beat you."

She had not thought of that. But it might well be true. "He has not stopped frowning since he set eyes on my gorgeous plumes," she said, laughing. "Poor man, he was quite disconcerted by them, was he not? I will be kind to him. I will refuse his offer."

"Good," he said. "Then I have no rival. You will marry me, Miss Gray, if you will be so good."

At first she felt only incredulity. Then she understood. She laughed again. "Oh dear," she said, "have they been threatening you? Have they backed you into a corner? Have they persuaded you to do the honorable thing, sir? What nonsense. I shall say no. No, thank you very much. There. Now they must be satisfied. You have offered, and I have refused. I daresay they will find someone else for me within four months. I do believe I must be far wealthier than even I thought if this house and park are anything to judge by. I will attract fortune hunters if no one else."

She smiled reassuringly at him. How unpardonable of her cousin and her grandfather's solicitor to make him feel that he had compromised her and must offer her marriage. When he had been so very kind. When he had come out of his way in order to make sure that she arrived safely. When he had saved her life.

"Miss Gray." He had tightened his hold on her hands. "I think it unlikely that in four months you will find a husband to love—that one and only mate created for you in whom one is tempted to believe from time to time. You said yourself that you were prepared to accept an arranged marriage, that almost any marriage was preferable to you than the alternative. You have known me for only three days. It has been a very brief acquaintance, though the fact that we have spent every moment of each day together has perhaps made it seem longer. Do you have any violent objection to me as a husband? Can you not bring yourself to accept me?"

She could feel herself flushing. She was suddenly almost overwhelmed by temptation. In three days she had not once thought of him in terms of matrimony, except perhaps to envy the Mrs. Munro who clearly did not exist. But now that she *did* think of it, she could see that it was a very attractive idea indeed. Almost irresistibly so.

She frowned. "I told you so, did I not?" she said. "I warned you. I knew how it would seem if you brought me all the way here. But you were too gallant to allow me to travel the last short distance by stage, and I was too weak to insist. But you need not offer for me, you know, despite what Mr. Watkins and Cousin Horace may have said to you. Perhaps I have my chance to repay your kindness now, long before I expected to have any opportunity. I release you from any obligation you may feel, sir. You are free to leave and return to your life in London. There. It seems a small thing to do to repay such a debt, but it is really not so small, is it? Marriage is for a very long time—a lifetime. I once overheard one of Mr. Burnaby's guests refer to marriage as a life sentence. He was right." She tried to withdraw her hands from his, but he held on to them.

"Has it occurred to you, Miss Gray," he asked, "that I did it all deliberately? That I have developed an attachment to you during the past few days, that I knew you must find a husband soon, that I maneuvered matters so that you would choose me?"

"But why?" She searched his eyes and found no answer there. "Do you mean that you fell in love with me?"

"I spoke of an attachment," he said. "I have grown fond of you. *Will* you marry me?"

It was impossible. How could he have developed an attachment to her? She was a nothing, a nobody. Until a week ago she had been treated rather like dirt beneath the feet of her employers. It was six years since she had felt fully a person. How could he like her enough to wish to marry her? *He* was not obliged to marry within four months, after all. Then she had a thought.

"Are you impoverished?" she asked and then flushed painfully once more at the impulsive, dreadfully rude question. But she had the right to ask it of him under the circumstances, did she not? "Is it my fortune, sir?"

"I have made a tentative marriage agreement with your solicitor," he said. "I have insisted that none of your property or fortune will come to me in the event of our marriage. They are yours to enjoy while you live and to will to whom you choose. I have a quite adequate fortune of my own, thank you very much."

"You really wish to marry me, then?" she said. "It is not because of the pressure they have put upon you?"

"There has been no pressure at all, Miss Gray," he said. "*Will* you marry me?"

It was too wonderful to be true, she thought, feeling dazed. She had known him for only three days. Indeed, she did not know him at all. He had told her nothing about himself. But she had learned to like him, to trust him. And he was so—beautiful. She despised the thought, but she was honest enough with herself to know that it made a difference. She would have a handsome husband after all. And really, if she needed an argument to finally clinch the answer, she knew she was going to give anyway—there was no time in which to be cautious. Four months really was not a great deal of time at all.

"Yes, then," she said. "If you are quite sure, sir. Because I owe you so much. Everything, in fact."

He raised her hands one at a time to his lips. She felt his warm breath on her hands and realized something that self-discipline had kept from her conscious mind for three days. In addition to being handsome, he was *attractive*. He was going to be her husband. She was going to have an intimate relationship with him. She felt slightly breathless.

"It is time I introduced myself properly to you, then," he said. "I have told you only half. Alistair Munro, Duke of Bridgwater, at your service, Miss Gray."

Her stomach felt as if it whooshed up into her throat, whipped itself upside down, righted itself once more, and slid back down into its appointed position. The whole exercise left her breathless, wobbly-legged, and fuzzy-headed. She clung to his hands, which suddenly felt very much warmer than her own.

"No," she said.

"Yes." He half smiled. "I am afraid so. You will be nothing as mundane as Mrs. Munro, you see. You will be the Duchess of Bridgwater."

"No." She succeeded in freeing her hands. She turned her back on him. "Oh, no. That is quite impossible. I could not possibly be. I would have no idea— What would I even call you?" She turned to look at him in deep dismay. "What *do* I call you? My lord?"

He clasped his hands at his back. It was there plain to see now that she was looking for it. It was quite unmistakable. He was every inch the aristocrat.

"Other people address me—and will address you—as 'Your Grace,'" he said. "You may call me Alistair, Miss Gray."

"No," she said. "Oh, no, sir . . . Your Grace. This is bizarre."

"I am to be rejected, then," he asked, "merely because I had the misfortune to be born heir to a dukedom? Have pity on me."

"I grew up in a vicarage," she said. "For six years I have been a governess in the home of people who have only a small claim to gentility. I believed a short while ago that Sir Peter Griffin was the only titled person I have ever met, and I despised myself for almost feeling awe. But you are a *duke*. It is impossible, sir. You and I have lived in different universes."

"You are afraid," he said, "that you will be unable to fit into my world, Miss Gray? And yet you own all this?" He lifted one arm to sweep in a wide arc that seemed to include the room and everything beyond it. "Your grandfather has already moved you into a new world. My mother will help you move comfortably in mine—and my sisters. They will be delighted."

It was the first personal detail she had learned about him. He had a mother and sisters.

"I must return to London without further delay," he said. "But I will have Mrs. Cavendish bring you to town within the week. She and my mother will take you shopping. We will have the announcement of our betrothal and imminent marriage announced in the morning papers. My mother will take you about to all the correct social functions. And soon—well within the four-month limit—we will marry at St. George's, Hanover Square. Have you heard of it? It is where almost all the fashionable marriages of the Season are solemnized. And then you will be my duchess."

"No," she said. She was terrified—and terrifyingly excited.

"You said no to me on another occasion," he said, "and I believed you and left you. Must I believe you now too? Will you not marry me? Would you prefer Sir Peter?"

She bit her lip.

"Say yes," he said. "Please?" He smiled fully, an expression she had seen only once before. Usually he only half smiled, using his eyes more than the rest of his face.

"Yes then," she said. "You have been so kind from the start. You are the only one who has shown me respect and believed in who I am since I was forced to wear those embarrassing clothes."

"Splendid." His smile disappeared, and his manner became brisk and businesslike. "We will go to the drawing room, Miss Gray, and make our announcement and swift arrangements for your coming to London. I must be on my way then. You will find, though, I believe, that you will be treated here with considerably more respect than was accorded you on your arrival. If you are not, you must insist on it. And if you are still not, I will want to know the reason why of your relatives and your solicitor when they bring you to town next week."

She felt suddenly like a child who had no control whatsoever over her destiny. He swept into command as to the manner born. It seemed for the next half hour as if she said nothing except "Yes, sir," and "No, sir,"—she could not seem to bring herself to call him "Your Grace." And it seemed to her as if everyone else said no more than the same words, either, though they all addressed him correctly.

And then, long before she had worked the bewilderment from her brain, he had her back down in the hall, and he had both her hands in his again, and he was bowing over them and lifting them to his lips and reminding her that he would do himself the honor of calling upon her in London in one week's time.

"Yes, sir," she said.

His lips quirked briefly so that for a moment she was reminded of the man with whom she had traveled for the past three days. Her feeling of unease lifted. But then he straightened up and left the house without another word or backward glance.

Stephanie took a deep breath and held it for a long time. She felt as if she had been caught up in a whirlwind one week ago and was still spinning helplessly about, waiting to be dropped to earth again. She wondered if it would be a soft landing or if she would be dashed quite to pieces.

Somewhere along the way she seemed to have lost herself. It was a bewildering thought.

Chapter 6

The Marchioness of Hayden and the Countess of Greenwald were sitting with their mother, the Duchess of Bridgwater, in the drawing room of her town house. The Duke of Bridgwater was present too, though he was on his feet, pacing more than he was sitting down. They were waiting for the arrival of Mrs. Bertha Cavendish and Miss Stephanie Gray to take tea.

"Do sit down, Alistair," his mother said, looking up from her embroidery at him. "You remind me of a bear in a cage."

"I beg your pardon, Mama," he said stiffly, seating himself in the nearest chair.

"I still cannot believe what you have done, Alistair," the marchioness said, frowning. "A parson's daughter. A governess. And you a duke. You know very well that a duke rarely looks below an earl's daughter for a bride."

"But she *is* an heiress, Lizzie," the countess said gently. "A very wealthy one, apparently. And she is a gentleman's daughter. You speak as if she were entirely beyond the pale. I am sure she is quite lovely and quite refined. Else Alistair would not have offered for her."

"Thank you, Jane," the duke said dryly, getting to his feet again and taking up a brief stand before the fireplace.

"But we know very well, Jane," the marchioness said, "that he offered because he felt he had compromised her. How can a duke compromise a governess? I would like to know. Hayden says—"

"I offered," the duke said firmly, fingering the handle of his quizzing glass and looking rather haughtily at the elder of his two sisters, "because I wished to, Elizabeth. And I do not recall granting you—or Hayden—permission to question my wishes. Miss Gray is no longer a governess. She is, as Jane has pointed out, a considerable heiress, owner of Sindon Park. And she is soon to be the Duchess of Bridgwater. You will doubtless keep those facts in mind when she calls."

"The only significant fact," the duchess said, setting her embroidery on a small table beside her, "is that Alistair is betrothed to Miss Gray and that her cousin has brought her to town and is accompanying her here this afternoon to make our acquaintance. We will remember, all three of us, that within a month Miss Gray will assume my title as Alistair's wife, that she will be the leading lady of this family, superseding even me. I will be merely the *dowager* duchess. We will treat her accordingly, both this afternoon and for the rest of our lives. I trust that is understood?"

"Yes, Mama," the countess said, smiling. "I am sure I am going to love her. I have been despairing of you, Alistair."

"Of course, Mama," the marchioness said more briskly. "You can always count on me to behave with good breeding and to do what is correct. Hayden always says—"

"Ah," the duchess said as the drawing room door opened, "here is Louise at last."

Lady George Munro, the Duke of Bridgwater's sister-in-law, hurried into the room, bent over her mother-in-law to kiss her cheek, and smiled a greeting at everyone else.

"I thought I might be late," she said. "Caroline is cutting teeth and was fretting at being left with Nurse. But I would not have missed coming here for worlds. Alistair, you are looking positively green. George says he cannot understand what possessed you. You are always so very high in the instep—his words, not mine, I assure you." She laughed lightly. "We thought perhaps you were waiting for an available princess, having judged every other lady beneath your notice."

The Duke of Bridgwater's hand closed about the handle of his quizzing glass, and he raised it to his eye, pursing his lips as he did so.

"Ah," he said, "then you have been proved wrong, Louise, have you not? You and George both."

But she only laughed merrily. "Oh, do put the glass down," she said. "You cannot cow me with it, Alistair. Henry can imitate you to perfection, you know. He can have us in stitches with laughter."

The duke lowered his glass and raised his eyebrows. His eleven-year-old nephew was growing into too impudent a wag for his own good. And George and Louise were encouraging him in such insubordination? So much for favorite nephews and the gratitude they owed a doting uncle.

The ladies settled into a dull and cozy chat about children. Among the three younger ladies, there were enough children to provide topics of conversation to last a week or longer. But they were not content with just their own.

"Cora is in town with Lord Francis and the children," the countess said. "Did you know, Mama? I was delighted beyond anything when she called yesterday. Do you remember the Season when she stayed here with us and you brought her out? The year Charles and I became betrothed? The year she married Lord Francis? And what a famous heroine she was?" She laughed at her memories even before the others began discussing them.

"Dear Lady Francis," Lady George said fondly. "She saved Henry's life. How could I ever forget her? How are her children, Jane? Four, are there not?"

But Bridgwater was no longer listening. He had crossed the room to the window and stood looking down on the square below, waiting for the appearance of another carriage.

In his mind's eye he could see her rather tall, slender figure. He could see her auburn hair thick and wavy like a cloud about her head and shoulders, as it had been that first night, which he had expected to spend with her. He knew that her eyes were hazel with golden flecks. He remembered that she had a dimple in one cheek—the left?—and very white teeth. He remembered that her smile lit up her face. He knew that she was pretty.

But he could not for the life of him put the pieces together in his mind in order to form a clear image of her. He even wondered foolishly if he would recognize her when he saw her this afternoon.

It had been ten days.

Ten days since he had fallen into his great madness. It seemed unreal, looking back. It was hard to believe that it had actually happened—all of it. That strange journey south with a bright bird of plumage, whom he had mistaken for a ladybird with a vivid imagination. His insistence on seeing the adventure through to its end so that he might enjoy her discomfiture when all her lies were finally exposed for what they were. His sudden realization, after they had arrived, that everything she had told him was true, and the accompanying realization that he had hopelessly compromised a lady. His offer. His insistence that she accept it.

Yes, he had insisted. She had tried more than once to refuse. She had quite categorically released him from any sense of obligation he might feel. She would not have been ruined if she had. The other occupants of the house would have kept their mouths shut—even Sir Peter Griffin. Yes, especially. He would have kept his mouth shut in the hope of marrying her himself.

And yet the insistence. And her final acceptance.

He had not even corrected her on the assumption that had seemed to be at the heart of her acceptance. She had assumed that he had behaved throughout their acquaintance with the utmost gallantry. She had called him kind. She had thought his decision to take her all the way to Sindon had proceeded from his concern for her safety. She had said he had been the only person to treat her with respect for who she really was since she had acquired those atrocious garments. Lord, if only she knew!

He had not disabused her. It had seemed unmannerly to

do so. It would have hurt her. Besides—dared he admit it?—she would have thought the worse of him if she had known.

He felt a little guilty for not admitting he was not quite the hero she thought him.

Yes, it was hard to believe that it was all true. Except that the memories of shocked disbelief among his family were very fresh indeed and very real. His mother, who now appeared to have accepted the inevitable, had been worst of all. He could not possibly so disgrace his name. She would not believe it of him. But she had believed eventually and had decided to stand by him.

And now the female members of his family were gathered behind him, waiting to meet his betrothed. The announcement was ready to go into tomorrow's papers, and St. George's had already been booked for the wedding in one month's time.

He watched almost dispassionately as a plain carriage entered the square and drew to a halt before the doors of his mother's house. He watched the steps being put down and two ladies being helped to the pavement—one middle-aged, one young. Neither looked up. Both ascended the steps of the house and disappeared inside.

He had intended calling on them yesterday or this morning. Yet, when he had made inquiries late yesterday afternoon, they had still not arrived at the Pulteney. This morning Mrs. Cavendish had sent a card to his mother, and his mother had sent word to him. He was to come here this afternoon, she had written. Mrs. Cavendish and Miss Gray were coming to tea. And so he had waited for the afternoon. He wished now that he had made arrangements to call for them and to escort them here.

He had been very firmly head of his family for longer than ten years. No one, least of all he, had been in doubt about that. But today he felt like a boy again, unsure of himself, subject to his mother's will. He drew a deep breath and let it out on a silent sigh. The door had opened behind him, and his mother's butler was making the expected announcement. He turned. All the ladies were rising to their feet.

He stood at the window like a spectator. She and her cousin both curtsied. His mother hurried toward them, greeted the older lady courteously, and then held her hands out to the younger, who took them.

"Miss Gray," his mother was saying graciously, "what a pleasure it is to meet you. The past week has seemed interminable. I do hope you had a comfortable journey up from the country and that your hotel is to your taste? You must tell us all about it. Allow me to present you to my daughters and my daughter-in-law."

They buzzed. They talked. They laughed. Mrs. Cavendish buzzed and talked and laughed back.

And then his mother turned to him, a smile on her face. "Alistair?" she said.

He came forward at last. "Ma'am?" he said to Mrs. Cavendish, bowing over her hand. "Miss Gray?" He took her hand in his and raised it to his lips. It was cold, even a little clammy.

Her dress was pale blue rather than gray. Her hair, dressed in a simple knot behind, was slightly flattened from the bonnet she had left downstairs. Her face was pale, her eyes slightly shadowed. There was not a glimmering of a sign of her dimple or her white teeth.

"Your Grace," she said in a voice that was little more than a whisper.

She looked every inch a governess.

He felt the nervous urge to laugh. Where were the fuchsia cloak and the plumed bonnet? Without them she seemed to be robbed of identity.

"Alistair," his mother was saying, "you will show Miss Gray to a chair? Mrs. Cavendish, do take the seat beside Lady George. Here is the tea tray."

He seated her on a love seat. He should have taken the place beside her. The occasion called for it. He should have engaged her in a tête-à-tête conversation, as far as politeness would allow. It would be expected of him. Instead, he walked to the fireplace a short distance away and stood with his back to it, his hands behind him.

She was a stranger. She was a clergyman's daughter, a governess. He did not think of her as his social inferior—just as his social opposite. He was a duke. There was a whole way of life his duchess would be expected to fit into with grace and ease. This woman just would not be able to do it. She already looked like the proverbial fish out of water.

By insisting that she marry him, he had ensured her unhappiness—and his own. He pursed his lips and set himself to being sociable, the perfect host. The role was second nature to him.

Cousin Bertha and Cousin Horace had fawned upon her for longer than a week. Unkind as the word was, Stephanie could think of no more suitable one.

She was to marry a *duke,* the Duke of Bridgwater. They did not seem to tire of exclaiming over the fact and reminding her of her good fortune. How provident it was that they and Mr. Watkins and Sir Peter Griffin had all been at Sindon to witness her arrival with His Grace. Had there been no one but servants at home at the time, he would doubtless have withdrawn quietly and dear Cousin Stephanie might never have netted him. But he had seen how disconcerted they were, of course—how could they help but be outraged even if he *was* a duke and everyone knew that members of the aristocracy were a law unto themselves? For very decency's sake he had been forced to offer for dear Cousin Stephanie. She had done very nicely indeed for herself.

They had a week to get Cousin Stephanie ready to go to town and show herself worthy of being a duke's bride. Everything about her needed transforming. Gracious heavens, what must His Grace have thought of her in that dreadful cloak and bonnet? And in the even more dreadful gray dress? She needed new clothes, she needed to dress her hair differently, she needed to learn how to curtsy and how to converse in polite society. She needed to learn to *impress* people. How were they ever to be ready in time?

The village seamstress was brought to Sindon Park and

kept a virtual prisoner in an attic room until she had produced a number of new clothes, which would have to do
until Cousin Bertha had a chance to take Cousin Stephanie
to a more fashionable modiste in London. A former ladies'
maid, who had a reputation as an artistic dresser of hair, was
engaged and set to work to show what she could do with
Cousin Stephanie's unfortunately red and unfortunately unruly hair.

All the dresses except one—the one Stephanie had insisted upon for day wear—were so bedecked with ribbons
and frills and flounces at Cousin Bertha's insistence that
Stephanie swore privately she would never wear any of
them. They made her look as if she were masquerading as a
sixteen-year-old—a sixteen-year-old without any taste
whatsoever. And the curls and ringlets with which her new
maid loaded and decorated her head made her look so
grotesque that she always brushed them out as soon as she
was able and knotted her hair in its usual comfortable style.

"You have no *idea* how to go on, my love," Cousin Bertha
said in despair the day before they left for town. "You will
appear a veritable *bumpkin* to His Grace. I would not doubt
he will quietly dissolve the betrothal. You look like a *governess.*"

Perhaps he really would dissolve the betrothal, Stephanie
thought. Surely he would. He must have had second
thoughts—and third and fourth thoughts—by now. He must
have realized what a dreadful mistake he had made. As had
she.

She could no longer remember what he looked like. She
had only disturbing and vague memories of a tall, handsome, rather arrogant figure. The memories terrified her as
did the knowledge that he was a duke. Was a duke not next
to a prince in rank? Above earls and marquesses and barons?
How could she enter that world? Just a couple of weeks ago
she had been a governess.

Several times—usually during the nights, when she
awoke from disturbing dreams—she was on the verge of
writing to him, telling him that she had changed her mind,

telling him that she would release him from his promise, so hastily and rashly given. He would be as relieved as she, she told herself.

But always before she could write the letter—though once she actually started it—she remembered how little time she had. Less than four months during which to find a husband. Or else she must go back to being a governess. Sometimes the prospect of that familiar and drab life was less daunting than the one that actually faced her.

And now suddenly—it all seemed to have happened to her without her exercising any control at all over events— here she was. In London. At the Duchess of Bridgwater's house. Feeling numb and terrified all at the same time.

They were almost late. When she had gazed at her image in the glass at the Pulteney Hotel, and Cousin Bertha and her new maid had stood behind her, exclaiming on what a pretty picture she made, she had been almost paralyzed with horror. She looked grotesque! Despite the protests of her maid and the cries of dismay from Cousin Bertha, she had almost torn off the pink dress in her haste, and she had dragged a brush through her hair until tears stood in her eyes. And so at least she felt comfortable—oh, no, she did not!—in her plain blue dress and with her hair dressed as she had always worn it at the Burnabys'.

The Duchess of Bridgwater, his mother, was an elegant, gracious lady. She looked like a duchess. The ladies with her—his sisters?—all had illustrious-sounding titles. She felt overwhelmed, totally out of her depth. Suddenly, she was almost grateful for the six years of frequent humiliations she had been made to suffer. Those years had taught her always to be calm and dignified, never to crumble in a nasty situation.

She could not even remember the names of the ladies after the duchess had finished presenting her. Yet they were to be her sisters-in-law. The idea was so ludicrous that she almost laughed in her nervousness.

And then *he* was there before her—she had not even noticed him until that moment—taking her hand in his, bowing over it, kissing it. And she remembered in a rush that, yes, of course, this was how he looked. He was tall and elegant. His face was handsome and proud. He was not smiling. His pale gray eyes seemed cold. He had been *kind* to her, she thought desperately. For three days she had talked to him and felt at ease with him. But the thought was crowded out by the knowledge that he was a duke. This grand house belonged to his mother. These ladies—she seemed to remember that one of them was a marchioness, and all of them had titles—were his sisters.

She was his betrothed. No, it was impossible. As she allowed him to lead her toward a love seat, as she seated herself, she felt that the room was without sufficient air. She wanted nothing more than to jump to her feet and race from the room, down the stairs, and out the front door. She wanted to run and run and run. But where? Back to the Pulteney? There was nowhere else to run. London was bewilderingly strange and new to her. At the Pulteney she would have to wait for Cousin Bertha's return. Reality would have to be faced eventually.

Better to face it now.

Cousin Bertha had launched into loud speech. She was telling her audience about the expenses of their journey, about the high cost of rooms at the Pulteney and the exorbitant cost of meals there. She was telling them that she had brought her own bedsheets with her because one could never trust inns and hotels to have changed the linen after the last guests—not to mention the possibility of damp.

"One can never be too sure," she said, dropping her voice confidentially, as if whole armies of hotel servants might be standing with their ears pressed to the drawing room door to hear themselves maligned. "And I thought His Grace would thank me for protecting dear Stephanie from chills and fevers. He would not want to have a bride with the sneezes and a red nose on her wedding night, would he?" She simpered.

Someone had placed a cup and saucer in Stephanie's hand. She did not know quite how they had got there. The cup was filled with tea. She touched the handle with the fingers of one hand, but she knew that she would not be able to lift the cup successfully to her lips. The duke was commending Cousin Bertha on her careful nature and reminding her that the Czar of Russia had stayed at the Pulteney a few years ago.

"Miss Gray." One of the younger ladies—not the marchioness—was smiling at her. She had spoken up determinedly before Cousin Bertha could open her mouth again. "I understand from Alistair that you inherited Sindon Park only very recently and saw it for the first time less than two weeks ago. That must have been exciting. Are you pleased with the property?"

"Yes, thank you," Stephanie said. There was an expectant pause, during which everyone's eyes were on her, including *his*. There must be more to say. She could not think of a single thing.

"Of course she is pleased with it," Cousin Bertha said. "Are you not, my love? She is rather shy, you know. But how could she not be pleased? The furnishings and draperies alone are enough to pay a king's ransom."

"I understand that the park is somewhat celebrated," the duchess said. "Do you admire it, Miss Gray? How would you describe it?"

The park. For one moment she could not bring a single image of it to mind, though she had spent hours every day for a week strolling about it, drinking in the wonder and the beauty and the peace of it all.

"It is very pretty," she said. And then she remembered what she had missed. "Your Grace."

"The rhododendrons were planted there at great expense," Cousin Bertha said. "And the roses must have cost a minor fortune, I declare. There are two large rose arbors, Your Grace. Not one, but two. But then money is not lacking for such extravagant shows at Sindon. Mr. Cavendish always says that the visitors who come by the dozens every year to view the park should be charged for the privilege. But I always declare that those who are wealthy should be willing to share a little of their wealth free of charge. Would you not agree?" She smiled about at the ladies and at the duke.

The Duke of Bridgwater gravely agreed and mentioned the lime avenue at Sindon as a feature of the park he had particularly admired.

"Miss Gray," one of the younger ladies said—also not the marchioness, "do have a cake. Let me set your cup and saucer on this little table beside you so that your hands will be free." She smiled warmly.

"Thank you," Stephanie said, relinquishing the cup and saucer with some relief. And then the plate of cakes was offered. "No, thank you."

She had used to visit in the parish with her mother—and alone after her mother's passing. She had even visited frequently at the big house, where Squire Reaves had six daughters as well as a son, some of them older than she, some of them younger. She had never had problems conversing with people of any age or social level. Visiting had always been one of her greatest pleasures. Even during her years as a governess she had occasionally taken the children visiting or received visitors in the nursery. She had always accomplished both with the greatest of ease.

She sat now in the Duchess of Bridgwater's drawing room as if she had never learned any of the social niceties at her mother's knee. She could seem to volunteer nothing to the conversation. When questions were asked her in an attempt to draw her into the conversation, she could seem to make only monosyllabic answers. Her mind was blank and paralyzed with dismay—something that had never happened to her before.

She was horrifyingly aware of the ghastly impression they were making, she and Cousin Bertha. Cousin Bertha was embarrassingly loud and vulgar, but Stephanie could not censure her—at least she was making an attempt to converse. Stephanie, on the other hand, was saying almost nothing. She was painfully aware of her appearance in contrast with that of the other ladies, and of her muteness.

They were all being exceedingly polite. But what must they really think of her? And of the Duke of Bridgwater's betrothal to her?

She half raised her eyes to look at him, but found at the last moment that she did not have the courage to meet his eyes. Suddenly, she wished fervently that she was back at the Burnabys'.

He had actually kissed her once. His lips had touched hers.

And she was to marry him within a month. They were to live together in the intimacies of marriage.

And then Cousin Bertha was on her feet and signaling Stephanie with significantly raised eyebrows that it was time to take their leave. Stephanie half stumbled to her feet. The Duke of Bridgwater spoke at the same moment. "Miss Gray," he said, "perhaps you would do me the honor of driving in the park with me later this afternoon?"

"She would be delighted, Your Grace," Cousin Bertha said. "Would you not, my love? It is Hyde Park you speak of? It is only fitting that the future Duchess of Bridgwater be seen in London's most fashionable spot as soon as possible. You must wear your pink muslin, my love. You will have more frills than any other lady there, I do declare. But then the dress cost a fortune."

"Not today, Alistair," the duchess said, stepping forward with a smile and linking her arm through Stephanie's. "One can see that Miss Gray is still fatigued from her journey. And tomorrow will be a busy one for her. You will be moving here tomorrow, Miss Gray. It will be the best arrangement. It will give us an opportunity to get to know each other at our leisure before your wedding. I am sure Mrs. Cavendish will be delighted to be able to return to her husband far sooner than expected. You will, of course, return for the wedding one month from now, ma'am?"

Stephanie felt too numb to feel fully the dismay she knew she would feel soon. She could not do this. She just could not. Cousin Bertha exclaimed and protested and finally—

because she really had no choice in the matter—muttered something about Her Grace being too kind.

"I will walk you downstairs, Miss Gray," the duchess said, retaining her hold on Stephanie's arm. "Alistair will escort you, Mrs. Cavendish."

Stephanie wished desperately to redeem herself before leaving. She had never felt more like an utter dolt in her life. But the duchess spoke again before she could think of anything to say.

"I was the daughter of an earl," she said quietly. "But I had lived all my life in the country—a very secure but very sheltered existence. I can remember the bewilderment with which I faced my first Season in town and the courtship of Alistair's father. I thought I would never be able to measure up to the demands of being a duchess. But it is amazing what can be accomplished with a little courage and a little determination."

"I suspect that more than a little is needed, Your Grace," Stephanie said, beginning at last to find her tongue.

The duchess patted her hand. "You are quite right," she said. "Sometimes with the passage of time we belittle the efforts we once had to make. With a great deal of courage and determination, then."

"Yes, Your Grace," Stephanie said. When she tried to smile, she found her facial muscles obeying her will for the first time in what seemed to be hours.

The Duke of Bridgwater took her hand in his again as she was leaving and raised it to his lips once more. "Good afternoon, Miss Gray," he said.

"Good afternoon, Your Grace."

She wondered if it would be possible to write that letter to him after all this evening. Or was it too late? She had the feeling that she was being swept along by events quite beyond her control.

Chapter 7

Lord Francis Kneller was indeed in town. The Duke of Bridgwater met him at White's the following morning. He was looking healthy and sun-browned, just like a country squire, the duke noticed, though he had not lost his taste for brightly colored and exquisitely tailored coats. This morning's was lime green.

Lord Francis appeared quite happy to set aside his paper in order to converse with his longtime friend. "Bridge," he said, getting to his feet and shaking the duke heartily by the hand, "how are you, old chap? Er, do I congratulate you or commiserate with you?" He grinned a little uncertainly.

Bridgwater raised his eyebrows and fingered the handle of his quizzing glass. "I would hope for congratulations," he said. "Thank you."

They both sat down. "I can remember your saying," Lord Francis said, "that you were going to become a recluse. That you would never again so much as make eye contact with a single young lady for fear that somehow you would be trapped into a match not of your own choosing. It was just before I married Cora—and you were blaming yourself. But apparently it, ah, happened to you anyway."

His Grace paused to take snuff and ignored the last comment. "And how is Lady Francis?" he asked. "And the children? Well, I hope, after the stay in Yorkshire and the long journey home?"

"Blooming," Lord Francis said with a grin. "We were fortunate that the last one was a girl. Cora was beginning to wonder aloud if it was my ambition to produce a cricket team. And I must admit that one feels remarkably clever to have begotten a daughter. I will have to be very careful not to spoil her quite atrociously."

It was a marriage that had turned out remarkably well, considering its very inauspicious beginning, the duke thought somewhat gloomily. Lord Francis Kneller, son and brother to a duke, had been forced to offer for the daughter of a Bristol merchant after twice publicly compromising her—both times quite inadvertently. And Bridgwater *had* blamed himself. Cora Downes had been his mother's protégée at the time, and it was the duke himself who had presented Kneller to her and asked him to dance with her and bring her into fashion.

During the six years since then, His Grace had met them on a number of occasions, most recently in Yorkshire at the Earl of Thornhill's. There was no doubt that there was a fondness between the two of them and a contentment—and probably even that elusive something called love.

"We had been home at Sidley for only two weeks," Lord Francis said with a sigh, "when Cora began her annual rumblings. It was not right for her to force me to rusticate just because she is most contented in the country and the country is the best environment for the children. I must come to town for a month—and she must come too because she cannot bear to be a whole month without my company, and the children must come too because she could not possibly live through a whole month without them. I have learned from experience, Bridge, that one does not argue with Cora when her mind is bent on selflessness and sacrifice. It is pointless for me to argue that I am most happy when pottering about my own estate and partaking of my wife's companionship and romping with my sons—Annabelle is too young to be romped with yet." He sighed again and then chuckled.

"A month," the duke said. "You must come to my wedding then, Kneller. At St. George's, of course."

Lord Francis sobered. "Of course," he said. "Thank you.

Cora will be pleased. Your betrothed is in London, Bridge? Miss Gray, is it? Yes, of course Miss Gray. I read the announcement in the paper just before you arrived."

"She arrived two days ago," the duke said. "She put up at the Pulteney, but she is moving to my mother's house this morning." His mother had been going to fetch her. And no, it would be best if he did not accompany her, she had told him when he had suggested it.

"We will see her this afternoon, then?" Lord Francis asked. "In the park? I will be sure to be there with Cora. We are both eager to meet her—dying of curiosity is how Cora puts it. You will escort her to the Burchell ball this evening?"

"No," His Grace said. "Neither, in fact. She is, ah, still tired after her journey. And this morning's move will fatigue her further." It was not a convincing excuse to give, he realized even as he gave it. What sort of a delicate blossom would still be tired after a journey made two days ago— from Hampshire? And how fatiguing would it be to drive in his mother's carriage from the Pulteney to his mother's house? Servants would look after her luggage, after all.

Lord Francis looked uncomfortable. It would be general knowledge throughout the polite world of London by now, of course, that he was marrying in haste a woman he had met and compromised only two weeks ago, a woman who was a considerable heiress, but one who had been a governess for the past six years and a mere country clergyman's daughter before that. Curiosity about her and about their relationship must be rife. He wondered if it was also general knowledge that they had spent three days and two nights together on the road. He did not doubt that it was.

"As soon as she is receiving," Lord Francis said, "Cora will call on her at your mother's house. She will probably go with the Countess of Greenwald, her particular friend. Have you been to Tattersall's this week, Bridge? I wandered about there for an hour or two and was almost tempted to bid on a pair of cattle I have no need of whatsoever. That is what the tedium of town life does to a man."

The conversation moved into comfortable channels, until they were joined by a group of other gentlemen, all intent on congratulating the Duke of Bridgwater on his betrothal.

He walked home alone a couple of hours later. He would change and call on his mother—and on Stephanie Gray, of course. He drew a steadying breath. His female relatives had been swift in their judgments the afternoon before as soon as he and his mother had returned to the drawing room.

"Alistair," his sister Elizabeth had said, blunt and severe as always, "she is quite impossible. That dreadfully unstylish dress. And her hair! I have known governesses who are more elegant. And she has no conversation whatsoever."

"Oh, Lizzie," Jane had said reproachfully, "she was *shy.* And she really is rather pretty. I am sure she will acquit herself better next time."

"It must have been somewhat daunting," Louise had said, "paying her first call on Mother and finding all of us here too. But that dreadfully vulgar creature who came here with her! I was waiting for her to ask the cost of the tea service."

"You are talking," the duke had said, standing very still just inside the door, feeling fury clutch with cold claws at his insides, "about my betrothed. And about her relative. I will have nothing said against her. I will have her spoken to and about only with the respect due my future duchess. Is that clearly understood?"

Their faces had told him that it was. But his mother had come into the room behind him. She had proceeded unhurriedly to her chair and sat down. She had invited him to do likewise.

"It is not well-bred to criticize people behind their backs," she had said, "especially when they are people who are to have close ties with this family. On the other hand, Alistair, there are certain truths that cannot be swept under the carpet, so to speak. Miss Gray is not at the moment anywhere near fit to be your duchess. And Mrs. Cavendish is in no way fit to be her chaperon during the coming month. Do sit down, dear."

He had leapt to his feet at her words, ready to vent his

spleen once more. She had waited for him to overcome his fit of fury and seat himself once more before resuming.

"Miss Gray is Alistair's betrothed," she had said. "However rashly done it was, the fact is that he offered for her and was accepted. The announcement has already been delivered to the papers and will appear in tomorrow morning's editions. We cannot alter the facts, even if we wished to do so. Miss Gray is to be Alistair's wife, my daughter-in-law, and everyone else's sister-in-law."

"But Mama—" Elizabeth had said.

His mother had held up a staying hand. "The only thing we can do to alter the situation and make it more to everyone's liking," she had said, "is to make sure that by the time of the wedding in one month's time Miss Gray is fit to be Alistair's bride. She will move here tomorrow, and I shall take her under my wing. The task is not hopeless. She does have some beauty, as Jane pointed out. And I would also agree that she is shy, that perhaps it was a mistake to invite her to tea with all of us when she had never met even me and had not seen Alistair for a week and a half. I will see what can be accomplished during the coming month. I am confident that a great deal can."

"I will not have her changed, Mama," the duke had said stiffly. "I like her well enough as she is."

"Alistair!" Elizabeth had said in disbelief.

"For her own good there must be some changes," his mother had replied. "Even if you are too stubborn and too loyal to admit in public that she will just not do as she is, Alistair, you must surely see that she will be miserably unhappy if someone does not take her in hand. I will do that. You may trust me not to be harsh or contemptuous with her. She is to be my daughter-in-law, my son's wife, the mother of some of my grandchildren. I hope to have a relationship of affection and respect with her for many years to come. Go home, dear, and go about your daily activities as usual. I shall summon you when she is ready for you."

"I shall come with you to the Pulteney to fetch her here tomorrow, Mama," he had said.

"No, dear," she had told him quite firmly. "She will be bewildered. She is in a strange city and will be leaving a cousin who is still strange to her in order to take up residence with another stranger. She will not need the discomfort of your taciturn presence."

"I was *not* taciturn," he had protested, realizing even as he spoke that it should have been beneath his dignity to argue with his mother. "It seems to me that only I made an effort to converse with Mrs. Cavendish."

"And you virtually ignored your betrothed," his mother had replied.

Because he had felt horribly as if he had been on public display. How must she have felt, then?

"I will take her driving in the park tomorrow, then," he had said. "She will need to be introduced to the *ton*. That will be a fairly informal setting for her first appearance. Less intimidating than a soirée or a ball would be."

His mother had clucked her tongue. "Alistair," she had said, "how would the *ton* treat her if she appeared in the park dressed as she was this afternoon? Or in what I would guess to be the monstrosity of pink frills Mrs. Cavendish made mention of? We must be fair to her, dear. When she appears for the first time, she must look presentable. I look forward to seeing her lovely hair dressed properly—what a glorious color it is. Did you not admire it, Louise? No, Miss Gray will not appear in the park or anywhere else for at least a week. I would suggest that you stay away from her for that time too, Alistair, until she feels more the thing and can greet you with more confidence."

"No," he had said. "Absolutely not, Mama. She is my *betrothed*. I will call on her here tomorrow afternoon. You will wish to chaperon her, of course. But I would be obliged if you will contrive to leave us alone for a short while."

He had refused to allow her to shift him from that decision. And so now, walking home from White's, he planned his visit and wondered how awkward it would be to sit in his mother's drawing room and try to make conversation with

Miss Gray while his mother listened. Would she leave them alone?

He had been quite as dismayed as the ladies during yesterday afternoon's visit. She had appeared quite unlovely and quite without character, sitting mute and expressionless in her unstylish blue dress, her hair scraped back into an unbecoming bun. She had not eaten a bite or even sipped her tea. She had spoken only when questioned directly, and then had answered in monosyllables. She had not once looked into his eyes. She had given him no chance to converse with her, even if he had wanted to.

He had felt panic. *This* was the woman with whom he had committed himself to spend the rest of his life?

But neither the dismay nor the panic had lasted. He had been saved partly by the unfavorable reactions of his relatives. How dared they stand in judgment on her when he was the one who had trapped her into this and when she had so clearly been desperately uncomfortable? And he had been saved partly by memory.

He thought of her now as she had been during those three days—garish and vulgar in appearance, but refined in speech and manner. Oh, yes, he could see that clearly now that he knew the truth. The vulgarity had never extended beyond those unspeakable outer garments. He thought of her smiles, which he had interpreted as coquettish at the time, but which he now realized had been merely smiles. He thought of the stories she had told him, talking with warmth and animation about a very ordinary childhood and girlhood, talking with intelligence about books and about children and teaching.

How could he ever have made the mistake he had made? It seemed unbelievable now that he had based his whole opinion of her on a fuchsia cloak and on a brightly plumed pink bonnet. Was he to base his new opinion of her on an unstylish blue dress and a mute social manner—and on the vulgarity of her companion?

He owed her better than that.

And he remembered too—of course—the ravishing

woman he had glimpsed that first night, leaning back on her arms on the bed, her face lifted in ecstasy, her wavy auburn hair swaying from side to side against her back.

Oh, no, she was not unlovely. Not by any means. It was still easy to feel a stirring of the intense desire he had felt for her on that evening.

But who was the real Stephanie Gray? He did not know. But he must get to know. If his marriage was to stand any chance whatsoever of being a workable one, he must find out who she was, and he must learn to respect and even like what he found. His mother must not be allowed to change her too drastically.

He quickened his step. He was becoming distinctly nervous about this afternoon's visit, just as he had been about yesterday's.

She was wearing her blue dress again. The duchess had suggested that she wear something different today, but even Her Grace had agreed after inspecting her meager wardrobe that after all the blue was the only possibility.

"The gray is just too plain and even shabby," Her Grace said. "And the other dresses are . . . well, monstrous if you will forgive plain speaking, dear. Do I detect the hand of Mrs. Cavendish in the selecting of them?"

"Yes, Your Grace," Stephanie said. "She assured me that they were all the crack, though I loathed them even before they were made." She felt disloyal saying so, but she was appalled to think that the duchess might think they represented her taste.

"I have a few maids who will go into transports of delight over the prospect of owning them," Her Grace said. "And would you be more comfortable calling me Mother? Perhaps you would more easily forget that I am a person who inspires awe in you."

Stephanie was not sure a name would make any difference. It was the regal grace and the unconscious arrogance and the self-assurance of her future mother-in-law that awed her. "Yes, thank you," she said, "Mother."

"I will call you Stephanie," the duchess announced. It was not a question. "It is a pretty name."

And so only the blue dress would do until tomorrow, when she was to spend all day—the duchess had stressed the fact that it would be *all day*—at a fashionable modiste's, being outfitted from the skin out for every possible occasion that might present itself for the next six months or so.

"We will not look beyond that," Her Grace said in a quite matter-of-fact voice. "If all is as it should be, you will need larger, looser clothes for the following six months."

It took Stephanie a few moments to grasp her meaning. She blushed scarlet when she did so.

Her Grace was to hire a maid for Stephanie—the maid from home was paid handsomely and sent back there. In the meanwhile, the duchess's own maid was brought to Stephanie's dressing room to dress her hair. The curls and ringlets that resulted were not as grotesque as the ones produced yesterday had been. They actually made her look elegant and even handsome. The duchess viewed the final effect with her head to one side and a thoughtful look on her face.

"No," Stephanie said at last. She had vowed last night at the Pulteney, during a long and sleepless night, that she was not going to be awed into incoherence again. But that was more easily said than done, of course. She was trembling now. "It is very fine, Marie. Is it not, Your Gr . . . Mother? But it is not *me*. I . . . No, I cannot."

"Perhaps for a ball," the duchess said. "Certainly it shows off your finest feature to advantage. But if you would be happier with something a little simpler for the afternoon, then Marie will oblige you. But not yesterday's or this morning's severe knot, Stephanie. Let us compromise on something between the two extremes, shall we?"

They did so, and both seemed pleased with the result. Stephanie's hair was brushed smoothly but softly back from her face and curled simply behind.

"Yes," Stephanie said. "Yes, I like it. Thank you so very much, Marie. How clever you are with your hands. I am afraid I have given you a great deal of work, forcing you to change the very skilled style you gave me first." She smiled at the maid in the looking glass.

"It will do quite nicely," Her Grace agreed and nodded dismissal to the maid. She waited for Marie to leave the room and close the door behind her before speaking quite kindly. "There is no need to thank servants, Stephanie. A cool compliment now and then is quite sufficient. Certainly one does not need to be apologetic about the amount of work one is causing. Servants are hired and paid to work."

Stephanie, still seated on the dressing table stool, stared at her future mother-in-law's image. She flushed. How gauche she must seem. And yet she did not know that she could ever become oblivious to servants as many employers, even the Burnabys, seemed to be. Servants were people.

"I am sorry, Mother," she said.

Her Grace smiled. "You are to be a duchess, Stephanie," she said. "You will be expected to look and act the part. Much of it is nonsense, of course, but that is life. You must learn to tread the fine line between pride and conceit. You must expect to be looked up to by everyone except royalty. You will accomplish that by always being gracious but never being overfamiliar. It will be easier for you in future if you can cultivate the correct manner from the start. It will be a week before we can have enough clothes made for you to enable you to mingle comfortably with your peers. We will use that week to prepare you in other ways too. It will not be as daunting as you perhaps fear. Once you have accepted in your mind and your body and your emotions that you are no one's inferior—you are to be Alistair's *bride*, his *duchess*—you will no longer fear having to meet the *ton*. Most of the *ton* will be your social inferiors."

"You knew that I was afraid yesterday?" Stephanie asked.

The duchess raised her eyebrows. "I *hope* you were afraid," she said. "I would hate to think that you can do no better than you did then."

Stephanie grimaced.

"Even now," Her Grace said, "you are by no means a nobody. Your father was a gentleman and your mother a lady. And you are a wealthy woman—an independently wealthy woman, which is a rare distinction. There are not many women who are the sole owners of properties like Sindon Park. Alistair is coming to tea, dear. He will be here soon. He was brought up from birth to know that one day he would be a duke and head of his family. He has been both for almost eleven years since the death of my husband. He has all the pride of manner and all the stiff dignity that have been bred into him. He is very like his father. In order to please him, you must become his equal. You will not do that by cowering before him and being afraid even to look him in the eye. It will not be a good marriage, Stephanie, if it is an unequal one. I shall leave you alone for half an hour this afternoon. You must converse with him."

Her Grace had not mentioned until now that he was coming to tea. Stephanie had thought she would not see him again until she was deemed presentable. He must have been very displeased with her yesterday. His manner had been aloof, even though he had been perfectly polite, especially toward Cousin Bertha, whom the other ladies had all but cut.

Was it true, what the duchess had said? If she made herself into the person the duchess wanted her to be, would she please him? Would she find it easier to lead the life she must lead as his duchess? Would her marriage have a better chance of success?

But did she want to change herself? She had always been conscious of her imperfections—how could she not be as the daughter of a clergyman?—and she had always striven to become a better person. But on the whole she had been satisfied with the person she was. Was she now to make herself into an imitation of her future mother-in-law? Was she to think and feel and move and behave toward others as if she were superior to everyone but the royal family? Her father had always taught her to think of herself as the equal of everyone, but to behave as if she were the lowliest of servants even to the poorest of the poor. Her father had exaggerated the matter, of course, but even so—arrogance and the assumption of superiority seemed alien to her nature.

Did she want to change that much?

Did she want to please him? But she *must* please him. His kindness and his courtliness had led him to this—to having to marry a woman who was in no way suited to be his wife.

She would give anything, she thought—almost anything on earth—to release herself from this terrible mess. She felt as if she were living through a nightmare.

And yet the idea was laughable. She had been a governess and was now a wealthy, propertied woman. She had been a clergyman's daughter and was now to be a duchess. She had been a lonely spinster of six-and-twenty and was now to marry a handsome, influential man. And it was all a nightmare?

"Come, Stephanie," the duchess was saying, "we will go down to the drawing room and await Alistair's arrival. Lift your chin, dear? Ah, yes. Already you look more the part. Remember always to keep it raised. You are *someone*. You are going to be the Duchess of Bridgwater in just one month's time."

And she was going to see the Duke of Bridgwater in just a few minutes' time, Stephanie thought. She wondered if he would seem as much a stranger to her as he had seemed yesterday. She shivered and remembered to keep her chin up as she followed her future mother-in-law down the stairs.

Chapter 8

S he was wearing the same dress as she had worn the day before. Her face was still pale, and she still had dark smudges beneath her eyes, as if she had not slept well for several nights. Probably she had not, he thought. Neither had he. She was still unsmiling. Only her hair was different. Not a great deal, it was true. It was still combed straight back from her face and over her head and knotted at the back. Except that it was not scraped back quite so severely. It seemed softer and shinier. And the knot was composed of a few small, discreet curls.

She still looked like a governess.

But today she looked almost pretty again.

"Miss Gray." He bowed over her hand—it was as cold as it had been yesterday—and raised his eyes to hers. Today she looked back at him. Today he remembered those unusual golden flecks in her eyes.

"Your Grace," she said almost in a whisper.

They were no further forward than they had been yesterday at this time.

"Do show Stephanie to a seat, Alistair," his mother said. "And be seated yourself. You may stand and look impressively ducal when you are delivering a speech in the House of Lords, but here you are my son—and my guest."

Ah. So his mother was calling her Stephanie already, was she? It was more than he was doing. He wondered if his mother truly believed that the task she had set herself was a possible one.

They talked at some length about the weather, which was cloudy and chilly and no different from what it had been for the past week or more. They talked about the Pulteney Hotel, since it had been mentioned, and he and his mother told Miss Gray about the visit to which he had alluded yesterday. The Czar of Russia and his sister had stayed at the hotel while in London with other European dignitaries, celebrating Europe's first victory over Napoleon Bonaparte—before Waterloo. And he spoke of Waterloo until his mother fixed him with a sharp glance, and he remembered that a battle did not make suitable drawing room conversation for the hearing of ladies.

Stephanie Gray spoke today in more than monosyllables, though not significantly more. For half an hour his mother and he carried the weight of the conversation, until his mother got to her feet and he jumped to his. Half an hour and he was being treated as a guest. It was time to take his leave. But that was not his mother's intention.

"I have some business to take care of abovestairs," she said, smiling graciously. "Perhaps you will keep Stephanie company, Alistair, until I return. We would not wish her to feel lonely on her first day here, would we? I will be no longer than half an hour."

Ah, so she had remembered. He was glad of it, though he did not know what they would talk about. But good Lord, they had spent almost three days together not so long ago and there had been very few silences, and none of those had been uncomfortable.

He hurried across the room in order to hold the door open for his mother. She smiled reassuringly as she passed him. He closed the door and stood facing it for a moment, considering his next move. But when he turned, it was to find Stephanie Gray's eyes full upon him.

"It is just not going to work, is it?" she said. "I believe it would be better if I went back to Sindon and we forgot all about this disaster of a betrothal. It *is* a disaster, is it not?"

He walked slowly back across the room, resisted the temptation to stand before the fireplace, where he would feel in control, and took a seat close to hers. "It is because you are shy?" he asked. "This has been an ordeal for you?"

Her lips twitched, but she did not quite smile. "I have never been shy," she said. "No one has ever said it of me before. I just do not know this world, Your Grace. It is quite alien to me. Trying to live in it would be an embarrassment to me and worse than that for you. You have been kind to me. I still consider myself deeply in your debt and always will. I still feel responsible for this situation. But it just will not do. I will tell Her Grace so myself. I will explain to her that none of the blame must fall upon you. You have acted throughout as a true gentleman."

There was color in her cheeks again and light in her eyes. She looked more like his fuchsia ladybird again, though he must not encourage himself to think of her in those terms. Guilt gnawed at him for a moment. She was *not* responsible. The blame was his.

"You are awed by titles and fashionable dress and manners," he said. "It is understandable, but they are all superficial, you know. People are people when all is said and done."

"I think," she said, half smiling again, "you really believe that. You are wrong. You would not like having me as your duchess, Your Grace. And I would not like being a duchess. It would be foolish, then, to press on with this betrothal merely because at the time it seemed to you the honorable thing to do to offer for me. And because I was weak enough to consent."

Her eyelashes, he noticed when she lowered her eyes to look at her hands, were darker than her hair. They were thick and long.

"The betrothal has been announced," he said. "The notice was in this morning's papers."

"Yes, I know." She looked up at him again. "And so another notice must be sent correcting the first."

"There would be scandal," he said.

"I care nothing for scandal," she said. "And *you* will not be touched deeply by it. Your rank will protect you. I shall return to Sindon and be far enough away. I shall see if Mr. Watkins can find another husband for me within the next three months or so—one whose rank will not intimidate me."

"No one," he said softly, "will marry a woman who has just scandalized society with a broken betrothal."

She bit her lip. It was quite apparent to him that she had not known that. "Then I shall go back to my old life," she said. "I shall take another governess's post."

"Do you think," he asked, "that your former employers will give you a character when you walked out of their house early one morning without even giving notice?"

Her face was pale again. The shadows beneath her eyes were noticeable. Her eyes were fixed on his.

Why was he so diligently dissuading her from doing what she so clearly wanted to do? he wondered. He had felt the impossibility of it just as powerfully as she—especially since yesterday afternoon. Was it because he dreaded the scandal the breaking of the betrothal would bring on him? Or was it because, as he had just explained to her, she was in an impossible situation? He could *not* let her go.

She got to her feet suddenly and hurried across the room to stand facing one of the windows, where he had stood the day before watching for her arrival. He stayed where he was and watched her. She looked even more slender than she had during those three days. He wondered if she had been unable to eat as well as to sleep during the past week and a half. He remembered the trembling eagerness—though she had tried hard to hide it—with which she had eaten her soup on that first day.

He wondered briefly how innocence would feel beneath him on a bed on his wedding night. He had only ever known experienced women. And he remembered his assumption that she was very experienced indeed. If all had been as he had thought it was, she would have been his mistress now for almost two weeks. He would have been almost as familiar with that tall, lithe body as he was with his own. Well, in one month's time he would begin the lifelong acquirement of familiarity.

It was not by any means an unpleasant thought. If only that were all that was involved in his marriage!

"You will adjust to your new life," he said. "You have a lady's birth and education, after all. And my mother will be a good teacher. You can learn everything you need to know from her. She has not been . . . harsh with you today, I trust?"

"No," she said quickly, without turning. "No, of course she has not. She has been very kind. This must not be easy for her. She must be hating every moment. She must have had high hopes for her elder son."

He got to his feet and walked toward her. "She will be proud of you," he said, "and she will grow to love you. Over the coming week she will help you be fitted for clothes suited to your new station and she will help you learn some of the basic facts of a duchess's life. After that we will introduce you to Society between us. I look forward to it. You will take well. You are very lovely."

She lowered her head for a moment, but she did not immediately respond in words.

"Very well, then," she said at last. "I will learn how to dress and how to behave so that I will not shame you as I did yesterday, Your Grace. I will learn how to be a duchess."

He grimaced. "You did not shame me," he said. "I and my mother and sisters understood that you were somewhat overwhelmed by the occasion. It was thoughtless of me to have allowed it. I should have waited on you first at the Pulteney. I should have presented you first to my mother alone."

"You were not to know how it would be," she said, hunching her shoulders briefly. "Any lady from your world would have known what to expect and how to behave. She would not have been overwhelmed by the occasion."

He set his hands lightly against her upper arms. "You did not shame me," he said again. "And you will quickly learn to feel more comfortable in your new world. We will all help you—my mother and I, Jane, Louise . . ." He hesitated, but did not add Elizabeth's name.

She laughed and hunched her shoulders again. "Jane, Louise," she said. "I do not even know who they are. I do not even remember their titles or their other names. I am not even sure I would recognize them if I saw them again. I—"

"Give yourself time," he said.

She stood very still, her head down before nodding and turning to face him. "A week," she said. "We will have to hope that I am an apt pupil. We will have to hope that at the end of the week, when I leave this house to appear in Society, I will have learned enough not to disgrace you."

His hands had returned to her upper arms after she had turned. They were almost thin. "Promise me something," he said, looking into her eyes.

"What?" she said. "Have I not promised enough?"

"Promise me that you will sleep at night and eat at mealtimes," he said. "You have not been doing much of either, have you?"

She smiled fleetingly. "I wonder," she said, "how much Cinderella ate and slept in the weeks prior to her wedding."

"Try," he said. "Promise me that you will try."

"Very well," she said. "I promise."

He remembered touching his lips to hers briefly that first night at the inn, when he had expected that his kiss would be the mere prelude to the full feast, when he had thought that she had openly invited him to the feast. He remembered that he had been sexually aroused even before the kiss. She had looked so achingly lovely and so mouth-wateringly desirable arched back on the bed with her face lifted and her eyes closed.

"May I kiss you?" he asked.

Her eyes widened, and she flushed.

"We are betrothed," he said. "May I kiss you?"

He thought for a moment that she would not answer at all. Then she nodded almost imperceptibly.

Her lips were closed and immobile. Warm. She smelled of

soap, he thought as he lifted his own away from them. He had not realized until that moment how much he associated sexual passion with strong perfumes. He liked the soap smell. He preferred it.

Her eyes were on him. Wary.

He set his arms loosely about her before kissing her again, one about her waist, the other about her shoulders. She lost her balance and came swaying against him, her hands spread against his chest. There were no voluptuous curves, he thought, and yet she felt utterly feminine. She had long, slim legs. He kept his kiss light and undemanding, though he parted his lips to taste her and ran his tongue once slowly across the seam of her lips.

"You have never kissed before," he said as he lifted his head and released his hold of her. He wished immediately that he had not said it—he had done so only because the delightful novelty of it had somewhat dazed him. It was one more humiliation for her. He could see it as soon as her eyes dropped from his.

"The only chances I have had to kiss," she said, "have been with gentlemen who wanted a great deal more than just kisses."

He wondered if she too was remembering that first night.

"You will not be subjected to such indignities or to such humiliation ever again," he said softly. "My honor on it."

"This too," she said equally quietly, looking down at her hands, "I will learn in time with you as my teacher. I will try to be a diligent pupil, Your Grace. I am ignorant in so many ways, am I not?" Her voice sounded a little bitter.

"Ah, but it is ignorance," he said, "or rather innocence that a man hopes to find in his bride, Miss Gray. Do not apologize for yours. Yes, I will teach you. And you will teach me. We will each learn how to please the other. Now, I believe I will take my leave even before my mother returns. I believe you would appreciate some time to yourself, some time to sleep perhaps before dinner?"

"Yes," she said. "Thank you."

"Come," he said, "I will escort you to the stairs. I will leave word for my mother that you are resting."

He drew her arm through his and set his hand over hers. A few moments later he watched her climb the stairs to her room before he descended to the hall and left the house after giving his message to a footman.

He had no more idea than when he had arrived if this thing was going to be possible or not. All he did know was that it was impossible to go back or to try to change the situation. Like it or not, he was going to be a married man by this time next month. He was going to be married to Miss Stephanie Gray. She was an intelligent woman, he thought, with a natural refinement of manner, even if she had little confidence in her ability to be a duchess. His mother would see to it that she was brought up to snuff within the next week. And together he and his mother would polish the product and prune away its raw edges in the three weeks that would remain before the wedding.

Yes, she would take, he thought. He really did feel more confident than he had felt yesterday—considerably more confident. And there was something else too that helped him sit back in his carriage and relax against the velvet seats.

He was going to enjoy the intimate side of the marriage. As the flamboyant actress he had taken her for, he had wanted her. But as Miss Stephanie Gray, his betrothed, she was just as desirable. Perhaps more so. He really had found her innocence—her total lack of understanding of what a kiss could be—almost erotic.

Yes, today he felt considerably more cheerful.

She felt less cheerful than she had felt before his visit—if that was possible. Until then, she realized afterward, she had never been quite convinced that her betrothal was irrevocable. Bad as things had seemed, she had been able to tell herself that she could put an end to it, find herself another husband within the appointed time, or even go back to her old way of life as a last resort.

Now she knew that there was no going back. Only forward. But how could she go forward? It was impossible. Only by changing herself completely could she fit herself for her new life. And how could she change herself completely when she was already six-and-twenty? And when certain principles and attitudes and ideas were ingrained in her? And when she basically liked herself the way she was?

But change she must. And if she must change, then she would give herself a good reason for changing—a really good one. She would change for *him*. She would never forget how he had saved her from certain misery and terror and from possible death just two weeks before. And she would never forget how courteous he had been—except for that one small lapse when she had inadvertently tempted him. Of how he had treated her like a *person* even when others were looking askance at her because of her appearance. She would never forget how he had insisted on taking her all the way to Sindon Park, even though he had obviously realized that he was going to feel honor bound to offer her marriage. And she would never forget how he had urged her to accept and how he had continued to urge her today, just so that she would not suffer disgrace.

She owed him everything, even her life.

And yet, she was quite sure that he must be as reluctant about this marriage as she could possibly be. He was a young and a handsome man. He was a wealthy man and a duke. He had everything with which to attract any woman he cared to choose as a wife. Yet he had been forced—by his own gallantry—to take her. She wondered if he had ever had dreams of love. She did not know a great deal about men, but she imagined that they must have such dreams just as much as women did.

She would change for him then—in order to make him a worthy duchess. And in order to . . . please him. That was the term he had used. They would teach each other, he had said. They would each learn to please the other. She knew nothing about pleasing a man. But she drew comfort from the fact that he had told her men hoped for ignorance and in-

nocence in their brides. He would have both in full measure
with her. She knew nothing.

She had been shocked to the core of her being by his kiss.
His lips had been parted—she had felt the warmth and mois-
ture of his mouth against her lips. She had tasted him. And
he had touched her with his *tongue*. Perhaps what had
shocked her most, though, was her reaction. She had felt the
kiss not only with her lips. She had felt it with her body, with
a rush of strange sensation to her breasts and to the most secret parts of her body. Her legs had almost collapsed under
her.

Oh yes, he would have his innocent, right enough.

She would change for him—for his sake.

And so the following day—and again four days after
that—she stood uncomplaining for hours on end while the
duchess's own modiste measured her and pinned fabrics to
her and showed her endless patterns and bolts of fabric and
lengths of trimmings. She listened meekly to Her Grace's
advice and to the modiste's and only occasionally insisted
on disagreeing. She felt incredulity at the number of different clothes for all occasions that were deemed the bare es-
sentials for her during the next six months—of course she
was expected to be *increasing* by that time. But she said
nothing.

At home—at the duchess's home—she sat for more hours
on end unmoving while Patty, her bright and talkative and
skilled new maid, dressed and redressed her hair in a dizzying number and variety of styles. And she listened to Her
Grace's judgment on each and resisted the urge each time to
grab her brush and pull furiously at the elegant creations.

At home too she trailed about the house after the duchess,
listening to that lady's conversations with her housekeeper,
her cook, and her butler. She memorized both Her Grace's
manner of speaking and her way of taking command of her
own household. She genuinely admired the quiet firmness
with which Her Grace treated all her servants, but she wondered if there would be any harm in a little more warmth.
She quelled the thought. If this was how a duchess ran her

household, then she would learn the way. She would not disgrace him when the time came by trying to make friends of his servants.

In the duchess's private sitting room, where they often sat for long stretches of time stitching away at their embroidery—Stephanie preferred that to the endless piles of mending and darning with which she had been expected to occupy her evenings at the Burnabys'—she listened and learned about the *ton*, about Society manners and morals. She learned all the small details that would help her avoid embarrassment and awkwardness—like the fact that at a ball she must dance with the same gentleman, even her betrothed, no more than twice in one evening, or that the sort of curtsy with which she might greet a lady or gentleman of no title must differ from the one with which she would show respect to a dowager countess or duchess. And her curtsies now, when she was merely Miss Stephanie Gray, must be more deferential to all than they would be when she became the Duchess of Bridgwater.

She learned that after her marriage she must expect to see little of her husband. It would be considered bad *ton* if they lived in each other's pocket. Men had their own pursuits and did not appreciate clinging, possessive wives. If her husband chose to keep a mistress after his marriage—Her Grace spoke about it quite as matter-of-factly as she had spoken about everything else—then she must pretend not to know. It was ill-bred to be jealous. And if she chose to take a lover, it must be done with the utmost discretion and only *after* she had presented the duke with a son.

"It is my hope, of course," Her Grace added, "that Alistair will be faithful to you. But he is a grown man and head of this family. He will make his own decisions. I say these things only so that you will understand the rules, Stephanie. It is of the utmost importance that you know the rules and abide by them."

She learned the rules, carefully and meticulously committing them all to memory so that she would not make any gauche blunders when she appeared in Society herself. She would not make mistakes. She would not shame him.

He did not call upon her again during that week. Neither did anyone else. Apart from the two lengthy visits to Bond Street and Her Grace's modiste, she spent the week inside the duchess's home, seeing no one except Her Grace and the servants.

But the day finally came when a staggeringly large number of parcels was delivered to the house and the modiste arrived at the same time. Stephanie's new wardrobe was ready. She had to try on every one of the clothes while the duchess and the dressmaker looked critically at them and a few minor adjustments were made.

Stephanie, it seemed, was ready to meet the *ton*. There was to be a ball the following evening at the home of the Marquess of Hayden. It was a ball being given in honor of the Duke of Bridgwater's betrothal to Miss Stephanie Gray.

The Marchioness of Hayden, Stephanie remembered belatedly, was the duke's sister.

"I could have wished for some smaller, quieter entertainment for your first appearance, Stephanie," Her Grace said. "But it is as well to start this way, perhaps. And you are quite ready, my dear. I have seen during the past week that you learn fast and that you have made every effort to learn. I am very pleased with you. Alistair will be equally delighted. He will come tomorrow to escort us to Hayden's for dinner and the ball to follow it."

Stephanie drew a slow breath. She would not disgrace him, she thought. He would look at her and be pleased. He would watch her through the evening and be satisfied.

Oh, she hoped she would not disgrace him. She owed him so very much. She must repay him at least in this very small way.

The thought of seeing him again set her stomach to fluttering. It was neither a wholly pleasant nor a wholly unpleasant feeling.

Chapter 9

His mother had worked miracles in the course of a week. That was the Duke of Bridgwater's first reaction when he saw Stephanie on the evening of the Marchioness of Hayden's ball.

He was standing in the hall of his mother's house. He had been told that the ladies were almost ready to leave and had waited for them to come downstairs. His mother came first, looking her usual almost regal self in purple satin with matching plumed turban. He took her hands in his and kissed her on both cheeks.

"As usual, Mama," he said in all sincerity, "you look far too young and far too beautiful to be my mother."

"But," she said, "only a son of mine would have learned so to flatter me, Alistair."

She had come down ahead of Stephanie Gray, he knew, so that all his attention could rest on his betrothed as she descended the staircase. He looked up now to watch her come. And yes, he thought, definitely a miracle had been wrought.

She wore pale green. The underdress was cut low at the bosom and was high-waisted, with one deep flounce at the hem. The overdress was of fine lace. She wore pearls at her throat and about one gloved wrist. Her hair was dressed smoothly at the front and sides, though curled tendrils at her temples and neck softened any suggestion of severity. He could see elaborate curls at the back, even though he had as yet only a mainly frontal view of her.

He could recognize his mother's superb taste in both the deceptive simplicity of the gown and the style of her hair. She looked impeccable and elegant. She would far outshine any of those ladies at the ball—and there would be many of them—who would think to draw attention and admiration by the fussiness of their appearance.

But it was not just the hair and the clothes that made him think of miracles. There was something about *her* that had transformed her from a governess to a duke's fiancée. He had never thought of her as having poor posture, yet there was something now about the set of her shoulders and the straightness of her back that suggested almost a regality— like his mother. And she held her chin high in an expression of pride that stopped well short of conceit.

Her posture and her gown combined emphasized all that was best in her appearance—her tall slimness, her swanlike neck, her long slim legs, clearly outlined as she walked.

"Miss Gray." He waited for her to reach the hall before taking a few steps toward her and stretching out his right hand. When she placed her own in it and curtsied, he bowed over it and raised it to his lips. "I almost did not recognize you." He turned to look at his mother. "You have performed a miracle, Mama."

"Stephanie has been the easiest pupil any teacher could wish for," his mother said. "It is no miracle, Alistair. Hard work has done it."

He looked back to his betrothed. "You are nervous about tonight?" he asked her. She had been half smiling as she descended the stairs. The smile had vanished now.

"A little, I suppose," she admitted.

He squeezed her hand, which he had not yet released. "You need not be," he said. "You look magnificent, as I am sure your glass and my mother have both informed you. If you remember everything that I am sure she has told you during the past week, you will do very well this evening. If you feel a little uncertain at any time, remember who you are. Remember that you are my betrothed and that soon you will be the Duchess of Bridgwater."

"Yes, Your Grace," she said. "I will remember."

But he knew that she was still nervous. Her eyes had lost some of the sparkle they had had a minute before. Her face looked paler. He felt an unexpected rush of sympathy for her and of protectiveness too. This must all be very difficult for her. He did not doubt that the closest she had ever come to a grand ball was a country assembly when she had still been living at the parsonage. He hoped his mother had thought to brush up on her dancing skills. But he was sure she would not have forgotten something quite so elemental.

His mother led the way out to the carriage while he followed with Miss Gray, her arm resting along the top of his own. He looked reassuringly at her. "Do not fear," he said. "No one seeing you tonight would ever guess that until three weeks ago you were a governess. My sisters will be amazed and delighted by the transformation in you."

She looked up at him briefly before he handed her into the carriage, but she said nothing.

He would have to be careful, he thought. He knew that the temptation would be to hover over her all evening, to try to protect her from the ordeal he knew she would be facing. He must not do it. Nothing would be more certain to make her appear like a gauche rustic who had neither the manners nor the conversation required by the role she was about to assume in Society. He must not ask Elizabeth to seat him next to her at dinner. He must dance with her only twice, and he must not take up his place at her side between sets more than once or twice.

He must trust his mother to see to it that she got through the evening unscathed.

He listened to his mother talk as the carriage made its way through the streets of Mayfair and to Stephanie Gray replying more briefly. She addressed his mother as "Mother," he was interested to note. He did not himself participate in the conversation. He was feeling nervous about the coming evening, he realized—and just a trifle depressed. Why was it that good manners always ensured that one kept one's distance from the very people with whom one would most like to spend most of one's time?

He was surprised to find that in some ways he was beginning to look forward to being married. They seemed to be able to relax a little more when they were alone together than they could when in company with others. He wanted to hear her talk again as she had talked to him in his carriage. He wanted to get to know her. And—the thought seemed strangest of all—he wanted her to get to know him. He had always been a very private person. Nobody, he felt, really knew him. And he had liked it that way—until now.

The carriage slowed outside the doors of his brother-in-law's mansion on Berkeley Square.

The evening was going well. She had not yet set even one foot wrong, so to speak. She had done nothing to embarrass herself and nothing to shame either the Duke of Bridgwater or his mother. She had sat next to the Marquess of Hayden at the head of the table at dinner; her future brother-in-law, older than his wife by at least ten or fifteen years, was a man with an enormous sense of his own consequence. She had stood in the receiving line between the marchioness and the duke since the ball was in honor of her betrothal and had smiled and curtsied and tried to memorize the names of a seemingly endless stream of guests. She had danced the opening quadrille with the duke and every set thereafter with a different gentleman. She had remembered the steps of every dance and had executed them without mishap. Between sets she had stood with the duchess and a number of other ladies and gentlemen. She had never once been alone.

It was going well. Or so Her Grace assured her. The duchess was pleased with her. She was taking well, it seemed. She looked quite strikingly beautiful—Her Grace's words—and she looked poised and confident without in any way appearing conceited. It did not matter, the duchess assured her, that she had little conversation. The important thing was that she smiled at those who spoke to her and encouraged them with polite questions and responses. Shyness, provided it did not border in any way on muteness or sullenness, was no disadvantage at all in a lady. Quite the contrary. Everyone would know, after all, that she was being elevated on the social scale by her betrothal to Bridgwater. Her shyness would be considered becoming modesty.

All was going well. Except that she was not enjoying herself. She tried, whenever the demands of conversation were not occupying her mind, to understand why this was so. Did she feel uncomfortable? No more than was to be expected. In fact, she was finding that she need behave not very differently from the way she had behaved throughout her years as a governess. Quiet dignity, self-containment, the ability to listen while saying little—these had been a way of life to her for six years. Did she fear that she had failed, then, that she had somehow let the Duke of Bridgwater down? No, she did not feel it. And if she did, she could not disbelieve what his mother told her. Her Grace would have been fast enough to point out any glaring shortcoming.

Everyone had been polite to her. Many had been kind and even friendly. She had not been a wallflower as she had feared she might. She had not lacked for company between sets. No one had treated her with contempt or even noticeable condescension.

The ballroom, with its many mirrors and chandeliers, with its numerous floral decorations, was beautiful. It was filled with elegant, beautiful people. It was the perfect scene she had always dreamed of—the sort of setting she had always imagined for Cinderella's ball. And in many ways she was the personification of the fairy-tale heroine.

Why, then, was she not quite enjoying herself? Was it because after the first set the Duke of Bridgwater had not danced with her again or come near her between sets or even shown any sign that he was aware of her presence in the ballroom? He danced every set. He mingled easily with the company, conversing with people whose identities she had forgotten. He looked thoroughly at home in this, his own environment. And he looked exquisitely elegant and handsome in black evening clothes with gleaming white linen.

Was she hurt by his apparent lack of interest in her? No, she told herself. She had learned from the duchess during the past week—and she had partly known it before that— that it was not considered good manners among the *ton* for a man and his wife or betrothed to cling together as if they could not bear to be out of each other's company in order to enjoy that of others. His behavior was no personal affront to her, but merely evidence of his perfect manners.

She just wished perhaps that occasionally his eyes would alight on her, that he would perhaps smile at her. He had not smiled at her all evening.

She was not allowed to waltz. It seemed that no lady was allowed to perform the dance in London until she had been approved by one of a select group of ladies. It seemed absurd that the rule applied to Stephanie, since she was six-and-twenty years of age, but the Duchess of Bridgwater had told her during the week that it would be unwise to do anything that might raise polite eyebrows—at least until after her marriage.

And so she did not waltz. It was the only set before supper that she missed. But she was not left alone to watch everyone else dance. A lady to whom she had been introduced earlier as the wife of a particular friend of His Grace's—she could not for the life of her remember the lady's name—took her arm and smiled brightly and warmly at her.

"I can remember being wild with fury during my first few balls not to be allowed to waltz," she said, "even though I had already passed my majority. I still think it foolish beyond belief that a few social dragons can have so much power, but I have learned by now to laugh in private—or with only Francis for an audience—at such stupidities. Francis is dancing with Jane because he forgot this was a waltz and should therefore have been mine—I shall make him suffer for that later. Come, Miss Gray. You and I will stroll outside and pretend that we would not waltz even if our respective menfolk were on their knees begging us." She laughed heartily.

Francis, Stephanie thought frantically, allowing herself to be led away. He was Lord Francis Something. Lady Francis Something looked at her as they left the ballroom and crossed the terrace to descend the steps into the garden. She laughed again.

"Oh, that remembered look," she said. "That *who the devil are you, but I do not dare to ask* look. I am Lady Francis Kneller, Miss Gray, but I would far prefer to have you call me Cora. Titles used to terrify me, and so it is rather ironic that I married one. You did need rescuing, did you not? Just for a short while? I could see it. And of course the Duke of Bridgwater would never do anything as improper as spend the evening at your elbow. He used to awe me into incoherence—I lived at the duchess's home, you know, for part of one Season while she attempted to find me a husband. Not Francis—I am a merchant's daughter and could not think of looking so high. But Francis had the misfortune to decide to amuse himself by bringing me into fashion, and dreadful things happened to force him into offering for me. Can you imagine a worse fate?"

Stephanie felt rather as if she had been caught up in a whirlwind. Lady Francis Kneller was taller than she and far more amply endowed. She was not pretty—her features were too bold—but the word "handsome" leapt immediately to mind.

"No, I cannot," Stephanie said.

Lady Francis looked sharply at her. "Oh dear," she said, "I have opened my mouth and stuffed my slipper—my lamentably *large* slipper—into it, have I not? How Francis will shake his head ruefully and refrain from scolding me when I tell him what I just said to you. It is exactly what happened with you and His Grace too, is it not? We were quite incredulous when we heard. His Grace has always been very adept at avoiding matrimonial snares and fortune hunters. And so he was snared accidentally by a wealthy heiress who happened to be a governess before she inherited. You cannot imagine how *pleased* I am, Miss Gray—may I call you Stephanie? You are just what he needs. Someone to throw him slightly off balance, so to speak. He has always been just too perfectly *balanced* for his own good. That is why I have always stood in awe of him, though not so much lately. Francis has derived so much amusement over the past six years from the great dithers I go into when I meet a title—especially in light of the fact that he is himself a duke's son—that I have learned to laugh at myself too. It is either that or bash his head in, Stephanie, and how could I do that to my beloved Francis?" She laughed gaily.

The strange thing was that Stephanie found herself laughing too, with genuine amusement. How refreshing it was to find that there was someone human at the ball—she did not stop to ponder the strange thought. And she remembered now that Lord Francis Kneller was the gentleman with the coat of a delicate spring green satin and with the laughing eyes. He had been noticeable in a ballroom full of gentlemen who were wearing either black or dark sober colors. It was no wonder his eyes laughed if he lived with Cora, she thought.

Lady Francis squeezed her arm. "All will be well, you know," she said. "I promise you, though it is very stupid to do so when I cannot know the future. But when two people are forced into marriage, each feels guilty and apologetic to the other, and both make an extra special effort to make the marriage work. If you think a governess-turned-heiress and a duke an unpromising combination, as I am sure at present you do, then imagine what my situation was, Stephanie. A merchant's daughter and a duke's son and brother. But Francis and I are now the dearest of friends and hold each other in the deepest affection. You must not allow them to intimidate you, you see. The Duchess of Bridgwater is a wonderful lady—she was remarkably kind to me all because I had apparently saved her grandson's life—but she can be intimidating. I found her so, and I can readily believe that she is ten times more so to someone who is about to marry Bridgwater. She means well. But you must not allow it to happen. You must remember that there is nothing wrong—and nothing inferior—about being a governess or a merchant's daughter. I have no patience with snobbery."

Stephanie smiled. "You are very kind, Cora," she said. "I am much obliged to you for suggesting that we come outside for some air. I feel considerably better."

"There," Lady Francis said, squeezing her arm, "you will feel the better for getting all that off your chest. A person always does. I have been only too glad to lend a sympathetic ear. I will call on you, Stephanie, and you must call on me. I shall like it of all things. I sometimes feel a little lonely in town—lonely for adult company, that is. I have four children, you know, all below the age of six, and I dote on their company. But when in town I insist that Francis go about all those dull gentlemanly pursuits that gentlemen set such store by, even though he always tries to be noble and insist that he would be far happier with me and the children. One has to understand men, Stephanie. They do not understand themselves half the time, I do declare."

Stephanie was chuckling again. She found that for the first time all evening—perhaps all week—she was relaxing and even feeling a measure of enjoyment. But the music of the waltz wafting from the ballroom into the garden had ceased. That particular set was at an end, it seemed.

"Ah," Lady Francis said, cocking her head to one side and listening, "it is time to go inside again. Time for me to scold and sulk over the fact that Francis danced our waltz with Jane. No matter that she is one of my closest friends. He is not to be forgiven."

When they had entered the ballroom and Lord Francis joined them immediately, bowing and smiling at Stephanie and extending his arm for his wife's, the latter tapped the arm with her fan and scowled.

"I am in a towering rage," she said. "Am I not, Stephanie?" But she immediately gave the lie to her words by grinning broadly at her husband and linking her arm through his. "Stephanie is terrified of the Duke of Bridgwater, Francis. I have been consoling her."

"Oh dear," Lord Francis said and grinned back at his wife before looking a little uncertainly at Stephanie.

It was not clear to Stephanie whether his concern was over her mythical terror or his wife's consolation. But she caught the duchess's eye at that moment, smiled at Lady Francis, and made her way across the room. Now that she was inside again, though, she felt even more discontented than she had before. It was something Lady Francis had said, she thought. She frowned to bring back the relevant words. Lady Francis had said a great deal altogether.

You must not allow them to intimidate you.

There, that was it.

They were intimidating her. Both of them. Oh, they were both kind, just as Lady Francis had said. But intimidating too.

Suddenly, Stephanie could not bear the thought of standing next to the duchess for more endless minutes, smiling and listening to the conversation of those who came to make her better acquaintance. She could not bear the thought of dancing again just yet, nor could she bear to watch the duke, her fiancé, quite oblivious to her presence, converse with everyone, it seemed, except her and dance with yet another lady. It seemed to her that the evening was interminable, that it would never end.

"Excuse me," she murmured to Her Grace, "I shall be just a few minutes."

But she knew even as she hurried away to the ballroom doors and through them that she had no intention of returning until she felt she could avoid doing so no longer. It was the occasion that was overwhelming her, she thought as she tried to find a place in which to be by herself for a while. But all the small rooms on either side of the ballroom and the landing itself were occupied. She hurried down the stairs, trying to look as if she had a destination in mind. Perhaps, she thought belatedly, she could have gone back out into the garden. There had not been many people out there when she had strolled with Lady Francis. But she could not go back to the ballroom now and out onto the balcony without the risk of being seen. Perhaps she could find her way out from downstairs.

She did not find the garden door. But she did find something even better—a conservatory that was both dimly lit and deserted. She found a large plant almost as big as a palm tree and sank down onto a chair conveniently placed behind it, hiding her from the door.

All week she had been oppressed by a sense of obligation to the Duke of Bridgwater. She had felt deeply in his debt. She had thought to try to repay that debt at least in some small way by making herself into the sort of woman who could be his duchess. She had worked hard. Except in one or two very minor matters concerning her clothes, she had argued over nothing. She had accepted whatever the duchess had told her. She had absorbed everything and had adapted her own behavior and attitudes to what was now expected of her.

She had dressed earlier this evening in a flutter of nerves. Not so much nerves over the ball—though there had been that too, of course—as nerves over what he would think of her. She had imagined how he would look at her, what he would say. Surely, he would be pleased. She had tried so hard.

Had he been pleased?

Yes, he had. She had seen approval in his eyes when she was coming down the stairs. When he had taken those few steps toward her as she reached the bottom and stretched out his hand for hers, all had seemed worthwhile. She had been like a child waiting for a parent's coveted praise.

Miss Gray. I almost did not recognize you.

Praise would follow. He would applaud her taste in dress and hairstyle—both were slightly plainer than Her Grace had wanted, though her own wishes had been respected.

You have performed a miracle, Mama.

Yes, Stephanie thought now, staring ahead of her, oblivious to the beauty of the exotic plants about her. Yes, she had forgotten. But that was what had prevented her from enjoying the evening—just that—long before they had even arrived at the Marquess of Hayden's mansion. She felt hurt all over again, as she had felt hurt then.

It was his mother who was to be applauded. Just as if she, Stephanie, was an object. Just as if everything had been done *to* her and nothing *by* her.

You look magnificent. . . . If you remember everything that I am sure she has told you during the past week, you will do very well this evening.

Now she could not stop remembering.

If you feel a little uncertain at any time, remember who you are. Remember that you are my betrothed and that soon you will be the Duchess of Bridgwater.

Was that her identity, then? Her sole identity? She was his betrothed, his future duchess. But yes, of course. That was what the past week had been all about, had it not? Erasing everything else about her that was not that one thing. All her lowly and embarrassing past was to be blotted out as if it had never been.

And she had concurred in the transformation.

Did she regret it, then?

She sat for a long time without knowing the answer. She lost track of time. Although the music from the ballroom was clearly audible in the conservatory, she failed to notice when the one set ended. It was a voice that finally startled her back to the present.

"Miss Gray?" the voice said.

He was alarmingly close. Of course he would have to be. From the doorway he would not have seen her. He had come right inside, looking.

"Miss Gray?" the Duke of Bridgwater said again. "You have been gone from the ballroom for a long time—since well before the start of the last set. I grew concerned. So did my mother. This is not quite the thing, you know."

She drew a deep breath and looked down at the fan she had been clutching unconsciously in her lap. She had the choice between ripping up at him, or apologizing, she thought. It would be unfair to do the former—what he said was quite right. It was one of those rules that had been instilled into her all week. But she would not apologize. *You must not allow them to intimidate you.*

"No, Your Grace," she said, looking up into his eyes. "It is not, is it?"

Chapter 10

It felt strangely exhilarating to be at a large squeeze of a ball with his betrothed—to be at his betrothal ball. Though as a younger man he had dreamed of love and happily ever afters, and as a more mature man—just a few weeks ago—he had considered the necessity of making a dynastic marriage in order to secure his line, he really had not quite expected that he would marry. Marriage was for other men, not for him.

And yet here he was at Hayden's and Elizabeth's, betrothed. He was to be married in three weeks' time. And rather than feeling depressed or even panicked because he had been forced into a betrothal with a stranger—a woman almost from outside his own world—he was feeling exhilarated.

He no longer felt nervous. She was beautiful. He had known that before, of course, but now she was a beautiful ornament of the *ton*. She fit her surroundings perfectly at the same time as she outshone them. He had received a dozen compliments or more on her beauty before the evening was half over. More important, she had somehow acquired the poise and dignity to appear quite at her ease in the ballroom. She smiled at everyone, conversed with everyone, though he noticed that she did so more by listening and looking interested than by talking. And she danced with grace and confidence.

He felt enormously relieved. He had so feared that she

would look as out of place and behave as awkwardly as she had in his mother's drawing room a week ago. His heart would have bled for her. He would have felt forced to take her away and marry her quietly and keep her in the country for the rest of their days so that she would not have to face the humiliation of such ordeals again. It would not have been a situation conducive to happiness or contentment for either of them.

He felt so very guilty about the way his own stupidity had trapped her and given her no choice at all of husband. And about allowing her to go on believing it had been all her fault. She had had little enough choice as it was, time being so short for her. But he had taken away even that little. And he had brought her into a world she had never experienced before.

He was relieved to know that, after all, her birth and education had made it easier for her to adapt than he had feared. He was proud of her. Apart from his mother and perhaps his sisters and sister-in-law, only he knew how much effort it had taken for her to appear thus tonight.

Like a gauche and eager schoolboy he wanted to stay by her side all evening. He wanted to dance with her all evening. At the very least he wanted to watch her, to feast his eyes on her. But he could do none of those things, of course. He could not humiliate her by making it appear that she could not cope alone in a social situation.

But he watched her covertly. At every moment of the evening he knew where she was, with whom she talked and danced. It was a new feeling for him. Even when he was younger and had had flirts, he had never been so aware of them as he was of Stephanie. He was pleased when she stepped out of doors with Lady Francis Kneller during the waltz. He had been about to cross the room to her and take her walking himself. But he had engaged her for a set after supper. It would be too much to walk with her now as well.

He saw her leave alone after saying a few quick words to his mother. He watched for her return as he danced a country set and apparently gave his attention to his partner. His anxiety grew as the set progressed. Where was she that she was gone so long? Had she met someone outside the ballroom who had kept her talking?

His mother was worried too.

"I have just looked in the ladies' withdrawing room," she told him when he joined her at the end of the set. "She is not there, Alistair. And nowhere else that I can see."

He looked into all the rooms on the ballroom floor. He wandered out onto the balcony and down into the garden. She was nowhere to be found. Soon her absence would be noted, if it had not already been. He reentered the house through the garden door on the lower level and made his way to the hall, where a few footmen stood on duty.

"Miss Gray stepped this way?" he asked nonchalantly, his eyebrows raised, his hands clasped behind him. "The lady in green?"

"She is in the conservatory, I believe, Your Grace," one of the footmen said, bowing deeply and hurrying ahead of the duke to open the door for him.

It was not in total darkness, but it seemed quite deserted. He almost turned back to resume his search elsewhere. But it was clear to him by now that she was either hiding or had left the house altogether. And if she was hiding, she would hardly sit in full view of the conservatory door. He strolled inside.

She was sitting very quietly behind a potted palm, staring ahead of her. Apparently, she was quite unaware of his presence. She must have been here for longer than half an hour—quite alone and unchaperoned. Yet this was her betrothal ball.

"Miss Gray?" he said.

Her head jerked up, confirming his first impression, though she did not turn to look at him. He felt suddenly angry.

"Miss Gray?" he said again. "You have been gone from the ballroom for a long time—since well before the start of the last set. I grew concerned. So did my mother. This is not quite the thing, you know."

For a while he thought she was not going to answer him. She still had not looked at him. Rather, she directed her gaze at the fan she held in her lap. But finally she spoke.

"No, Your Grace," she said coolly, and finally she turned her head. "It is not, is it?" She spoke quietly. Why, then, did her words sound like a declaration of war?

He would not rip up at her, he decided, and then was surprised that he had even had to curb the urge. He never ripped up at anyone. He did not need to. He had learned as far back as boyhood the art of imposing his will by a mere look or quiet word. He must certainly not be angry with Stephanie. Doubtless she had been awed by the occasion. He moved to stand in front of her.

"You have been overwhelmed by it all?" he asked her gently.

She lifted her shoulders, but did not answer him. She was gazing at her fan again.

"You have done remarkably well," he said. "Your manner has been as poised as if you had been accustomed to this way of life for years. You are lovelier than any other lady present. I have had numerous compliments on your beauty."

She raised her eyes again. "Have you?" she said. There was an unidentifiable edge to her voice. He waited for her to continue, but she did not do so.

"Talk to me," he said. "How can I help you if I do not know what ails you?"

Again he thought she would not speak. He remembered the way she had talked and talked in his carriage, her face animated and framed by the foolish bonnet. Somehow it was hard to realize that this was the same woman.

" 'You have performed a miracle, Mama,' " she said so quietly that he thought he must have misheard.

"What?" he said, frowning.

" 'You have performed a miracle, Mama,' " she repeated a little more loudly. "It is what you said earlier, Your Grace. Almost your first words, in fact."

Oh, good Lord. She was right, was she not? That was what he had said. He had been so delighted at his first sight of Stephanie, so . . . dazzled, that he had spoken without thinking. Words of congratulation to his mother. None to Stephanie herself. Surely, he had congratulated her too? But he could not remember saying anything. It was his mother who had pointed out that the transformation was the result of hard work rather than of a miracle.

He went down on his haunches before her and rested his wrists over his knees. "You are quite right," he said. "I gave you no credit at all, did I? Will you forgive me? I know—I knew at the time—that it was you who made the miracle happen, that my mother merely guided and advised. You have worked incredibly hard during the past week. And I spoke as if it was all my mother's doing. Forgive me, Stephanie." It was, he realized, the first time he had used her given name. He had not asked her permission—another error uncharacteristic of him.

"Of course," she said. "Are you pleased then, Your Grace? Will I do? I have not embarrassed or shamed you tonight?"

"You know you have not," he said. "And you must know that I am pleased—even if I was doltish enough to phrase my pleasure quite wrongly at the start of the evening."

"Then the hard work has been worthwhile," she said. "I have done it for you, you see, because I am so very deeply in your debt. I believe I owe my life to you."

"No." He felt distinctly uneasy. He reached for her hands and held them tightly. He rested one of his knees on the floor. "You owe me nothing. I seem to have caused you more misery than anything else."

She smiled at him for the first time. He was startled anew by her dimple, by the sunshine of her smile. "There are thousands of women who would give all they possess for such misery, Your Grace," she said. "Have I been gone very long? I meant to sit here only until the set had ended. But I believe I lost track of time. You cannot know, perhaps, how bewildering this is for me. All my life I have been accustomed to quietness and even to solitude. I enjoy both and must have them occasionally."

He squeezed her hands. "I will remember that," he said. "But you will, of course, learn when solitude is appropriate and when it is not. It is not appropriate in the middle of a ball, especially when you are the guest of honor."

"Yes." She visibly drew breath. "I still have much to learn, Your Grace. I will try to achieve perfection. Will my absence have been remarked upon? Will I have brought disgrace on you?"

"By no means," he said, bringing one of her hands to his lips. "We will return to the ballroom from the garden and balcony, and it will be assumed that we have taken some time to stroll together. It is quite unexceptionable to do so since we are betrothed. And it will be understood why we have done so during this particular set. It is another waltz."

She listened to the music, which was quite audible. "Yes," she said. "So it is." It seemed to him that she sighed.

"Do you know the steps?" he asked.

"Yes," she said. "I was required to teach them to the eldest daughter at the Burnabys'. I always thought it would be wonderful to waltz with a real gentleman at a real ball."

"Am I real enough?" he asked her, getting to his feet and retaining his hold on her right hand. "Is this ball real enough?"

Her smile was rueful. "I am not allowed to waltz here," she said. "Her Grace said that perhaps it would not be quite improper since I am well past the age of majority, but she also said that I must be very careful not to give anyone even the slightest reason to frown."

"She is quite right, of course," he said. "You must never risk censure unnecessarily. But I meant here. Our own private ballroom. Shall we?"

Her smile grew slowly and caused strange fluttering sensations in the regions of his heart and stomach. He could not understand now why he had once thought it was the smile of a coquette. There was too much of pure joy in the expression for it to proceed from anything else but innocence. He was beginning to find innocence far more alluring than experience had ever been.

He took her hand in his and set his arm about her slender waist.

Waltzing with a pupil while playing the role of the male partner, and waltzing with a gentleman were two entirely different experiences, Stephanie realized immediately. His shoulder was well above the level of her own and felt solidly muscled beneath her hand. His hand was large and warm. She could feel his body heat, smell his cologne. He held her very correctly so that she touched him only at the hand and shoulder. But she knew instantly why so many people had been dubious about the morality of the waltz not so many years ago.

It was an intensely intimate dance.

He waltzed expertly. After the first few moments she found that she no longer had to concentrate on counting steps and following his lead. All she had to do was move her feet and float and enjoy the moment.

She did not believe she had ever enjoyed any other moment as she was enjoying this one. She closed her eyes and trusted that he would prevent them from colliding with plants and chairs.

"Come," he said after several minutes, "confession time, Stephanie. You have not been a teacher of general instruction for the past six years. You have been a teacher exclusively of the waltz. You dance it superbly."

She was so very susceptible to praise from him, she thought as she opened her eyes to smile up at him. Just as she had been easily hurt by his unintentional slight at the start of the evening. But perhaps the reason was that her life for so many years had been starved of praise or even approval.

"I am merely good at following the lead of a superb partner," she said.

He laughed, and she realized how rarely he did so and how very attractive he was when he did. Not that he was unattractive even when he was at his most poker-faced, of course.

"Touché." He stopped waltzing even though the music continued from somewhere above their heads. "When we are seen entering the ballroom from the garden, you know," he said, "it will be assumed that I have stolen at least one kiss from you. I would be thought a remarkable slowtop if I had not tried."

She had dreamed all week about his kiss, about what he had done with his lips and tongue. She had relived, with some guilty shame, the effects his kiss had had on her body. She had wanted to be kissed again. She had wondered what the intimacies of the marriage bed would feel like.

"May I?" he asked.

She nodded.

She had grown up in the country. She knew what happened between male and female, though she was not quite sure how exactly it was done between man and woman. For years she had longed to find out and had expected never to do so. In three weeks' time she would know finally—with this man. Unsuspected muscles deep inside her contracted and left her shaken and breathless.

He kissed her as he had kissed her the week before, briefly and lightly on the lips before lifting his head and looking into her eyes. Instinct told her that she wanted to feel him with her breasts, that tonight she did not want her hands to be trapped against his chest. She slid them upward and clasped them behind his neck. She let her body sway against his as his arms came about her waist. She could feel him from her shoulders to her knees. All warm, solid masculinity. She closed her eyes.

Yes, the kiss continued as before—his slightly parted lips, his tongue touching the seam of her own lips, the sizzling sensations in other parts of her body. But she wanted more. She parted her own lips tentatively and felt his tongue come through them to stroke the soft, sensitive flesh behind. She opened her mouth.

After that her mind ceased making a running commentary of what happened. It was only afterward when she thought about it—she spent all night thinking of nothing else—that she remembered sucking inward on his tongue until he moaned. And his mouth against her throat and her breasts, which his thumbs had bared by drawing her dress down beneath them. And his hands spread firmly over her buttocks, holding her against masculine hardness. It was only afterward that she thought to feel shock—and shame.

He was breathing hard, his face turned in against her hair, when his hands covered her breasts with her gown again. He held her by the shoulders for a few moments and then put her away from him and turned his back on her.

"The music has stopped," he said, his voice sounding quite normal, if a trifle breathless. "Thank God. Miss Gray, did your mother never warn you against situations like this? Or my mother?"

A pail of cold water flung in her face could not have more effectively brought her back to the present.

"Yes," she said. "And experience has taught me how to handle situations like this. A governess is often prey to lascivious attempts at seduction, Your Grace. I thought this was different. I thought I need not fight. You are my betrothed." If truth were known, she had not even considered fighting.

"We are not married," he said. "It would be folly indeed to anticipate the marriage bed, Miss Gray. What if I should die before the day? What if I should leave you with child? Even failing that, what if I should leave you a fallen woman?"

Hurt and anger—and shame—warred in her. And confusion about which was uppermost held her silent.

He turned to look at her. "I am sorry," he said. "Deeply sorry. The fault was all mine. I asked a kiss of my betrothed and then proceeded to use you as I would a—" He stopped to inhale deeply. "Forgive me. Please forgive me. It will not happen again."

"No." She brushed past him on the way to the door. "It will not, Your Grace. It seems I have more to learn than I have realized. It seems I have more in common with a whore—that *is* the word you stopped yourself from saying, is it not?—than a true lady. But I will learn. By the time I am your duchess, I will behave like a duchess. I will remember that kisses are meant to be brief and decorous."

"Stephanie—" he said, coming after her.

"We must return, Your Grace," she said, "before the next set begins. If we leave it longer, the *ton* will no longer think that you have been stealing a kiss. They will think you have been tumbling me, and my reputation will never recover. You and your mother will be disgraced."

"Stephanie," he said again, drawing her arm through his even though she tried to resist, and leading her out through the garden door she had been unable to find earlier. "What I said was unpardonable. I was horrified by my own lack of control and blamed you. I seem to have done nothing but insult you this evening. It was unpardonable. I will not even ask your pardon. I will bear the burden of my own guilt. But please do not blame yourself. Not in any way. When you look back later, as you surely will, you must take none of the blame on yourself."

He was leading her quickly up the steps onto the balcony and across it to the French doors into the ballroom. Almost without thinking she smiled. She was on view again.

The point was, she thought, that she would not have considered their embrace in terms of guilt or shame if he had not made her see that both were needed. It had felt right. They were betrothed, soon to be married. Attraction—physical attraction—between them had seemed desirable. Without ever thinking of it in verbal terms, she knew that she had embraced him with a feeling close to love. She had believed, naive as she was, that he had felt the same. There had been no question—surely there had not—of anything happening that might have left her ruined or with child. That was for the marriage bed. They had been standing in the conservatory.

But it seemed that there was guilt and there was shame. Such things as physical attraction and passion were quite inappropriate between a duke and his duchess—they were acceptable only between a duke and his mistress. And of course the word "love" was probably not even in the ducal vocabulary.

Well then, she thought almost viciously as His Grace led her toward his mother and they all smiled as if nothing untoward had happened all evening—well then, she would learn.

If it was the last thing she ever did in life, she would learn.

She seemed less shy today, he thought. Less shy with other people, that was. He was driving her in his curricle in Hyde Park during the fashionable hour, and she seemed in no way intimidated by the crush of people that the sunshine had brought out—not that the *ton* needed sunshine in order to gather for the daily ride or stroll and for the polite gossiping and ogling. Only a downpour of rain would keep them away.

She was looking extremely lovely in a pale blue muslin dress of simple, elegant design and a cornflower-trimmed straw bonnet. Her blue parasol was the only article that was in any way fussy. She twirled it above her head as they drove along. She smiled.

In the park she spoke to everyone who stopped to pay their respects. Unlike last evening she did not merely listen and encourage more talk with her smiles. Today she participated fully in the conversations. He knew that she was succeeding in charming the gentlemen and perhaps making the ladies faintly envious. She was far more lovely than anyone else there, after all. He did not even pause to wonder if it was partiality that led him to such a decisive conclusion.

He had been foolish to worry that she would just not be able to learn in time what she would need to know to be his duchess. There would be a great deal more, of course, than merely to look fashionable and to converse with ease and charm. But those things certainly helped. And if she could learn those so quickly and so thoroughly, then surely she could learn everything else too, given a little more time.

He was pleased with her. He was proud of her.

And he was uncomfortable with her and still ashamed of

himself. He had scarcely slept during what had remained of the night after he took her and his mother home from the ball.

If the cessation of the music in the ballroom had not somehow penetrated his consciousness when it had, he thought, he might not have brought that embrace to an end until it had reached its logical conclusion. He had been drawing up the skirt of her gown, bunching it in handfuls about her hips when he had realized what was happening— and what had already happened.

If one thing had characterized his life for the past eleven years, and even longer, it was control. He had always felt fully in control of other people and events and—most important—of himself. Last evening had bewildered him. He had insulted her right at the start in a way that was inexcusable, especially since he had not even realized it until she had pointed it out. And later, he had insulted her in such an unpardonable manner that he had shuddered over it all night and all morning—he had blamed her for his own loss of control.

The trouble was that his dream—his long abandoned dream—had leapt to life for a few mindless minutes while he held her and kissed her. For those few minutes she had been that dream of love. She had felt like the other half of his soul—the half he had always known was missing, the half he had always yearned to find.

It had been a ridiculous feeling. All that had happened was that he had lusted after her, his own betrothed. He had behaved unpardonably.

And so today he was uncomfortable with her. And today her bright charm seemed more like a shield than anything else. She talked to him incessantly on the way to and from the park—about the weather, about the flowers she had received from various gentlemen who had danced with her last evening, including his orchids, about the kindness Lady Francis Kneller had shown her last evening and the amusement she had provided, about a hundred and one topics that held back the silence between them.

Silence, when there had been silence between them in his carriage during that journey, had been a comfortable thing. No longer. Not that either of them put it to the test today.

"Miss Gray," he said when he had lifted her down from his curricle and led her inside and refused his mother's invitation to come upstairs for tea, "I told you last evening that I would not ask your pardon for what was unpardonable. I have changed my mind. *Will* you forgive me?"

"Of course, Your Grace," she said, smiling warmly. "I believe you were right to put at least part of the blame on me, though you were gallant enough to retract what you had said. I am gradually learning the rules, you see. I hope to have them all by heart by the time of our nuptials."

She offered him her gloved hand, and he took it and raised it to his lips.

"Until this evening, then," he said, "and the theater."

"I am looking forward to it," she said.

He knew what was wrong as soon as he stepped out of the house and climbed back to the high seat of his curricle. Although she had smiled and although her voice had been warm, there had been no gold flecks in her eyes. Strange, ridiculous notion. How could eyes change?

But hers had. There had been a certain blankness in their smiling depths.

Chapter 11

S he had become two different people—she was uncomfortably aware of that realization during the three weeks leading up to her wedding—two quite distinct people.

When she was alone—but how rarely she was alone during those weeks—and during her dreams at night she was Stephanie Gray, vicar's daughter. She was the girl and young woman who had kept house for her father. She was the general favorite of the villagers and even of the squire's family. She visited everyone and was a friend of everyone, young and old, rich and poor alike. She took gifts of baking and needlework to the sick and elderly. She refused a marriage offer from Tom Reaves, the squire's only son, though they had been playmates all through their childhood and friends in more recent years. She refused because she knew he had offered out of pity, for her father had died and left her poor and she was compelled to seek employment elsewhere. Friendship seemed not a strong enough basis for marriage.

When she was alone and when she dreamed, her life at the vicarage became idealized. It was always summer there. The sun always shone. The flowers in the garden always bloomed. The villagers always smiled. Tom always seemed a little dearer than just a friend. And his sisters seemed more like her sisters too.

When she was alone, she liked who she was. She was the

woman her parents had raised her to be. She was the woman she wanted to be. She was herself.

But when she was not alone—most of the time during those weeks—she was the betrothed of the Duke of Bridg-water. She dressed the part, always expensively elegant. And she lived the part, every word, every action, every reaction consciously chosen. There was no spontaneity at all in this Stephanie. She seldom made a mistake. After the gentle scolding meted out by the duchess following that first ball— "Everyone feels the occasional need for solitude, Stephanie. But a duchess recognizes that she is a public person. She learns to live without solitude"—after that there were no more scoldings and only the occasional reminder. Like the time she apologized and smiled too warmly at a milliner's assistant who had patiently taken out more than a dozen bonnets from their hat boxes only to find that she had not after all made a single sale—"A duchess *never* apologizes for giving a servant work, Stephanie."

With her betrothed she behaved as a future wife should behave. Never again would he have cause to compare her to a whore—though he had stopped himself from using that word at the Marquess of Hayden's ball, she knew it was the word he had almost said. She conversed with him when they were alone together on any genteel topic that leapt to mind. When they were not alone, she gave her attention to other people. No one would ever accuse her of clinging to the coattails of her husband.

He did not kiss her again during those weeks, except for her hand. Had he asked for another kiss, she would have of-fered her lips while keeping her hands and her body—and her emotions—to herself. When they were married, she would offer her body. But only as a genteel wife would. She would offer herself for his pleasure—never her own— though she knew that he would probably get most of that elsewhere. Most important, she would offer herself as a bearer for his legitimate offspring. She would give him his heir. Her Grace had already told her that this would be her primary duty.

She would give him a son, God willing, she thought. A life in exchange for a life. She would give him a son and heir, and perhaps then she would feel it possible to take back her own life. Perhaps she would feel that she had repaid the huge debt she owed him.

Perhaps . . . Oh, perhaps one day she could be herself again. Or was self always lost in marriage? Even when one did not owe one's life to one's husband, one became his property after marriage. All that one possessed became his.

No, that was not true in her case. He had insisted in the marriage settlement he had made with Mr. Watkins and Cousin Horace that Sindon Park and all her inheritance was to remain hers. He had been kind to her even in that—unbelievably kind.

She was constantly aware of his kindness. Had she merely owed him her life, she might have come to hate him during those weeks. She might have rebelled, despite herself. But in saving her, he had been kind to her. And *after* saving her, he had continued kind. And had given up his own freedom in order to take her safely home.

When she was not alone, she was the person she had been trained to be by her future mother-in-law. She was the person she had chosen to become, because of an obligation that lay heavily on her. But she felt like a stranger to herself.

Only occasionally and all too briefly did she break free.

They were at the Royal Academy art gallery one afternoon in company with Lord and Lady George Munro and the Earl and Countess of Greenwald, her future in-laws. Her arm was drawn through the duke's. They were all sedately viewing the crowded tiers of paintings and commenting on their various merits and demerits. Stephanie judged with her emotions. If a painting lifted her spirits, she liked it. She did not try to analyze her feelings.

But His Grace smiled when she explained this to him. "Then you miss a whole area in which you might exercise your mind," he said. "You do it with books, but not with paintings, Miss Gray? You surprise me." And he went on to analyze a Gainsborough landscape she had admired in such a manner that she was enthralled and felt that she had simply not seen the painting at all before.

"Oh," she said, "and I thought it was merely pretty. How foolish I feel."

"I must confess," he said, "that I react to music much as you do to painting. I suppose sometimes we need to allow our intellects to rest in order that we may merely enjoy."

She smiled at him.

And then beyond him, she spotted two couples standing before a canvas, absorbed in viewing it. Her eyes fixed on them and widened. It could not be—but it was. She forgot everything but them. She withdrew her arm from the duke's, took a few hurried steps across the gallery, and stopped.

"Miriam?" she said uncertainly. "Tom?"

She had not seen them for six years. For a moment she thought she must have been mistaken. But when all four people turned their heads to look inquiringly at her, she saw that she had not. Tom Reaves stood before her—and Miriam, his sister, the one closest to Stephanie in age—looking hardly any different at all than when she had last seen them.

"Stephie?" Miriam questioned, her eyes growing as wide as saucers. *"Stephanie?"*

And then they were in each other's arms, hugging and laughing and exclaiming.

"Steph?" Tom was saying, loudly enough to be heard above them. "Good Lord!"

He caught her up in a bear hug, swinging her off her feet and around in a complete circle. She was laughing helplessly.

"What on earth are you doing here?"

"You look as fine as fivepence—as *seven*pence."

"I cannot believe it!"

All three of them spoke, or rather yelled, at once. All three laughed.

"I cannot believe it," Stephanie said again. "To meet my dearest friends again, and in London of all places. How very wonderful!"

"Steph, you look . . . like a duchess," Tom said, his eyes sweeping over her from head to toe.

"What on earth are you doing here?" Miriam asked again. "You are supposed to be in the north of England, teaching. What a *fortunate* coincidence to run into you here, Stephie."

"We are here for a month of sightseeing," Tom said. "With our spouses, Steph. This is my wife, Sarah." He smiled at the young lady standing beside him. "And Miriam's husband, Perry Shields. Stephanie Gray, my love. She grew up close to us at the vicarage. The best female cricketer it has ever been my misfortune to know. She had a formidable bowling arm."

They all laughed merrily. And then the two couples looked inquiringly beyond Stephanie's shoulder. She was brought back to reality with a sickening jolt. Oh dear, she thought. She had abandoned him in the middle of the gallery and had proceeded to shriek and laugh like a hoyden—or a country bumpkin—with people who were strangers to him. She had hugged Miriam with unbecoming enthusiasm. She had allowed Tom to sweep her right off her feet and swing her around.

The Duke of Bridgwater was looking at her with raised eyebrows when she turned.

"Oh." She felt herself flushing. And then the part of her that no longer did anything impulsively or spontaneously felt the awkwardness of a dilemma. If one should meet an acquaintance while in company with someone else, the duchess had taught her just a few days before, one ought to avoid introducing the two people unless permission has been granted beforehand by the socially superior of the two. Thus one avoids putting that person into the regrettable situation of having to acknowledge an unwanted acquaintance.

But she had no choice in the matter now. He had followed her across the gallery room, as his sister and brother had not. That meant, surely, that he wished to be presented. Or did it merely mean that he had come in the hope of preventing her from making a further spectacle of herself?

"Your Grace," she said, "may I present Mr. and Mrs.

Shields and Mr. and Mrs. Reaves? Miriam and Tom are dear friends from my girlhood."

He bowed his head in acknowledgment of the introductions.

"May I present His Grace, the Duke of Bridgwater?" she said, looking at her friends. Their faces registered an almost embarrassing degree of surprise.

"I am pleased to make your acquaintance," the duke said. "You are in town for long?"

"For ten more days, Your Grace," Tom said. "We have come to see the sights. The ladies have come also to shop."

"Oh, and the gentlemen too," Miriam said, "though they hate to admit it."

"Perhaps," the duke said, "you can be persuaded to extend your stay by a few days. Miss Gray and I are to be married in two weeks' time. Yet it seems that the guest list consists almost entirely of my relatives and friends."

Miriam's eyes had widened still further if that was possible.

"Oh, Stephie," she said, "is this true? I am so happy for you. *May* we, Perry?" She looked eagerly at her husband.

"Will you like it, my love?" Tom was asking his wife at the same moment. "Shall we stay?"

It was all arranged within the next couple of minutes, before His Grace took Stephanie's arm in a firm clasp and led her back to their companions, who were discreetly viewing another portrait, their backs to the other group. Miriam and her husband and Tom and his wife were to attend the wedding. The duke had asked for their direction—they were staying at a hotel not frequented by the elite of the beau monde—and had promised that an official invitation would be sent there the same day.

Foolishly, although they went to Gunter's for ices after leaving the gallery and then walked home so that there was all the time in the world for conversation and even for some private words since the six of them did not all walk abreast in the street, Stephanie talked determinedly on a number of topics, but did not once mention the meeting with her friends.

She felt a little like crying. It was almost as if her dreams of her youth had conjured up Miriam and Tom. She felt a huge nostalgia for those days, for her parents, for the vicarage, for the simplicity and happiness of her first twenty years.

But she felt embarrassed too. She had forced the duke into an acquaintance that was not of his choosing. By describing Miriam and Tom as her dearest friends, she had perhaps made him feel obliged to issue the invitation to their wedding. Surely, he could not want them there. Although of gentle birth, they did not move in *ton* circles.

And she felt unhappy at the implied snobbery of her embarrassment. Was she ashamed of her friends? No, of course she was not. They were most dear to her because they had filled her childhood with friendship and happiness. She was merely concerned that they would be treated with condescension and even perhaps downright contempt at her wedding. And yet even that thought suggested uncomfortably that she *was* perhaps ashamed of them. Would she have preferred it if they had refused, if they had used their planned departure for home as an excuse not to attend?

She realized afresh how wide apart her two worlds were, the one to which she was about to belong, and the one to which her heart cleaved.

It was the Duke of Bridgwater himself who mentioned them as he was taking his leave of her in the hall of his mother's house.

"I shall send the invitation to your friends as soon as I return home," he said. "They seem pleasant people."

"Yes," she said. "Thank you, Your Grace."

He held her hand silently for a few moments longer, gazing into her eyes as he did so. Then he raised her hand to his lips and took his leave of her.

Her uninhibited exuberance had probably disgusted him, she thought as she climbed the stairs wearily. She should have excused herself quietly, talked with Miriam and Tom quietly, and then returned to her group quietly. Quietly and decorously, in a manner to embarrass no one. That was what Her Grace would have expected of her. But she had spied her friends and had forgotten everything she had learned in the past two weeks.

She would not forget again, she vowed.

But she did forget again only a little more than one week later.

The Duke of Bridgwater had been delighted to hear that this closest friend, the Marquess of Carew, was on his way from Yorkshire with his wife and children. The wedding invitation had been sent, of course, but the duke had not really expected that they would come. They rarely came to town, claiming that life was too short to be spent going where one *ought* to go when one loved no place on earth better than one's own home.

But they were coming to his wedding. So were the Earl of Thornhill and his family.

"We have all been telling one another to the point of tedium that we really ought to join you and Francis and Cora in London for a few weeks of the Season," the marquess had written. "And then your announcement and your invitations arrived. There is to be no keeping us away now, of course. Expect us to arrive in plenty of time to look over your bride and give our approval. Samantha declares that it is high time. I leave you to interpret that comment for yourself. She has persuaded me to allow her to travel, by the way, despite the almost-imminence of the event that must have been obvious to you when you were here."

They arrived, the four of them plus their families, true to their word, one week before the wedding. The Earl of Thornhill had opened his town house. He and his countess invited the Duke of Bridgwater and his betrothed to dine with them two days later in company with the Carews and Lord and Lady Francis Kneller. It felt like a reenactment of a few weeks before except that circumstances had changed. And Stephanie had not been in Yorkshire.

It was an awkward evening, though Bridgwater was not sure that anyone but him felt the awkwardness. Stephanie looked beautiful in a gold evening gown with a simplicity of design he was beginning to recognize as characteristic of her. She was poised and charming and apparently quite at her ease in the company. His friends treated her warmly. Conversation throughout dinner was lively.

"A beauty, Bridge," the Earl of Thornhill said when the ladies had retired to the drawing room and the gentlemen had settled for a short while with their port. "And she certainly knows what to wear to show off that hair."

"And a charming lady," the marquess added. "I hoped she would not be intimidated by us all as I remember Cora was when she first met us."

Lord Francis grinned. "I still see that twinge of panic in Cora's eyes when there is a new title to meet," he said. "She is fond of Miss Gray, Bridge. She has kept Cora company a few mornings in the park with the children after I have been banished to enjoy myself at White's. The children even refer to her as Aunt Stephie, for which familiarity I was advised not to scold them. It seems that Aunt Stephie requested it."

The rest of the evening progressed just as smoothly as they conversed and played cards and took tea in the drawing room.

But the Duke of Bridgwater found the evening uncomfortable. Actually, he found every day and every evening uncomfortable. He had hurt her and insulted her on the evening of his sister's ball, and he knew that she had not forgotten, even though he had apologized—with deep sincerity—and she had given her forgiveness. There had been a barrier between them since that evening that had proved insurmountable.

It was not that she was sullen or even silent. Quite the contrary. She never lacked for conversation. He could not fault her on any detail of her behavior either with him or with society in general.

But there was not the slightest hint of anything personal in their relationship. The warmth and the smiles he remembered from those days on the road—how long ago they seemed now—were gone. The shy uncertainty of those first days in London and the hints of feeling, even of passion, had disappeared.

He had tried to make their conversation more personal when they were alone. He had tried to get her to talk about her girlhood again. He had failed utterly. She always turned the conversation. He had hoped when they met her friends at the Royal Academy—how totally enchanted he had been by the bright vivacity of her manner there—that perhaps he had found the answer. He had hoped she would talk about them, suggest that they call on them at their hotel. But there had been nothing.

She had shut him out of her world. He was being punished, he thought, for daring to criticize her behavior at his sister's ball. How he longed for a repetition of that behavior. And now that it was too late to go back and do things differently, he wondered why he had been so alarmed and so ashamed. She was, as she had pointed out, his betrothed. It was to be hoped that as man and wife they would find each other desirable, since for the rest of their lives they would find that sort of pleasure only with each other or not at all. They had found each other desirable three weeks before their wedding—and he had accused her of wantonness and himself of an unpardonable lack of control.

But it was too late to go back. And there was no chance to repeat the embrace and do it all differently. She gave him no chance. She behaved so correctly that sometimes it seemed to him that she was inside an invisible casing of ice.

Having seen his friends again, he felt the hopelessness of his own case. They had overcome the odds against contentment and even happiness, all three couples. It seemed impossible, just too good to be true, that the same might happen to him. And yet seeing his friends had made him realize how desperately he wanted to capture that dream he had had as a young man.

How he longed to love her. To have her love him. To become her closest friend. To make her his. To live with her in companionship and intimacy and contentment for the rest of his days.

He remembered the disorienting impression he had had during that notorious embrace that she was the missing half of his soul. He had been wrong, of course. They were two strangers about to spend the rest of their lives together. They were of two worlds that would only rarely touch and perhaps never would.

But perhaps he could make things a little easier for her, he thought. She appeared to like his friends, and they seemed to return the feeling. She already had a personal friendship with Lady Francis. She must like the children if she had asked them to call her aunt. And she was from the country. She must miss it after three weeks spent in London, moving from one fashionable drawing room or ballroom to another.

"Will you all join Miss Gray and me for a picnic in Richmond Park tomorrow afternoon?" he asked before they took their leave. "The children too, of course. I shall have my cook provide sufficient food."

"Cricket," Lord Francis said. "I shall provide the bats and balls and wickets. Splendid idea, Bridge."

"Trees to climb," Lady Francis said in a voice of mock gloom, "especially for the youngest, who will be able to climb up but not down again."

"We will allow you to rescue them all, Cora," Lord Thornhill said dryly.

They all knew that Lady Francis was terrified of heights, though neither that nor her fear of water had ever daunted her from rushing to the rescue of anyone she perceived as being in distress.

"The outdoors again almost before we have arrived in town," Lady Carew said. "Bliss. What a wonderful idea, Alistair. Thank you."

"We will be there," the Countess of Thornhill said. "I hope you realize, Miss Gray, that you are going to be surrounded by no fewer than nine children. And none of them, except Samantha's Rosamond, can be described as shy."

"Not by any stretch of the imagination," the marquess said with a laugh.

"I shall look forward to meeting them all tomorrow," Stephanie said. "I am fond of children."

"I can vouch for that," Lady Francis said. "A picnic. How we will look forward to it. Will we not, Francis? Though it will deprive you of one of your precious days in town."

Lord Francis grinned and winked at the Duke of Bridgwater as soon as his wife turned her head away.

It was settled then, the duke thought. A picnic might be just the thing—with his friends and their children—in the rural surroundings of Richmond Park. Perhaps he could get past that barrier with her again. Perhaps he could get their relationship onto a more workable footing.

There was so little time left. Only five days.

His stomach lurched at the thought. In five days' time they would be man and wife. They would be irrevocably bound together. But then they already were. A betrothal was quite as binding as a marriage.

Chapter 12

Richmond Park. It was close to London, and yet it was pure countryside. There were even deer grazing among the giant oak trees. And there were long stretches of grass. Stephanie loved it. It helped too that after the gloomy weather of much of the past month the sun shone from a cloudless sky.

She felt relaxed and happy almost from the start of the afternoon. The Marquess and Marchioness of Carew and their children traveled with them in the Duke of Bridgwater's carriage. Despite their somewhat daunting titles, Stephanie had found both of them to be sweet and kindly the previous evening. And the marchioness immediately set her at her ease during the afternoon.

"Oh," she said after Stephanie had greeted them, "do I have to be 'my lady' all afternoon? It sounds so pompous for a picnic. And does Hartley have to be 'my lord'? I am Samantha, Miss Gray. And you are Stephanie?" She smiled. "You will hear Jenny call me Sam, but Hartley prefers what he calls the more feminine form of my name."

It was agreed, as it was later with the Earl and Countess of Thornhill—Gabriel and Jennifer—and with Lord Francis Kneller, that they be on a first-name basis. Stephanie felt warmed, as if she had been accepted and welcomed by the people who were perhaps her future husband's closest friends. She also felt a little awkward. His Grace had at one time told her that she might call him by his given name, but she had never done so. He had called her a few times by hers, but not during the past two weeks. Were they to be formal today only to each other?

The marquess and marchioness's little girl, three-year-old Rosamond, a blond and pretty replica of her mother, was extremely shy. But Stephanie sat forward in her seat and had soon won the child's confidence sufficiently to draw her onto her own lap. They played at counting fingers while five-year-old James told the duke how his riding skills had improved during the weeks since His Grace had left Highmoor. His father rested his left hand on the boy's head and gently ruffled his hair. He smiled sweetly.

"He has wanted to ride during every waking hour since you told him he had a splendid seat, Bridge," he said. "We have a famous equestrian in the making."

The other carriages were close behind the duke's with the result that they all arrived together at the park, and all spilled out together to great noise and confusion and much laughter.

"Michael," the countess said to her eleven-year-old son, "remember that you are the oldest. I am trusting you to behave responsibly and not lead the younger ones into trouble."

"Yes, Mama," he shouted over one shoulder as he raced for the closest tree.

"Francis," his wife called. She was holding baby Annabelle, who was squirming to be put down. "Andrew is off."

"Ho!" Lord Francis shouted, and he sprinted after his two-year-old, who had already covered an admirable distance for one with such short legs.

"Andrew has never yet heard of curves or corners," Lady Francis explained to Stephanie, "or of walks either. He runs—and always in a straight line."

"Yes." Stephanie laughed. "I had noticed once or twice before."

"Papa," five-year-old Jonathan demanded of the earl, "I want to play cricket. You said Uncle Frank was bringing the things."

"My dear lad," his father said, "might we at least wait five minutes? Might we be permitted to catch our breath?"

"Yes, cricket!" five-year-old Paul Kneller cried with enthusiasm. "I want to bat first. I get to go first because the bats are mine."

"And the manners are decidedly not," his mother said sharply. "Oh, thank you, Stephanie. She is *such* an armful." She flashed Stephanie a smile as Annabelle was lifted from her arms. "You may pull Aunt Stephie's hair for a change, sweetheart."

"You can bat first, Paul," Jonathan conceded magnanimously. "But I get to be on Uncle Frank's team."

"It looks as if your afternoon has been mapped out for you, Frank," the earl said as Lord Francis returned to the main group, tossing his shrieking son up in the air and catching him as he came down.

"While we ladies are relegated to watching the toddlers," the marchioness said with a mock sigh. "The world never changes."

But the duke had other ideas, and soon enough order had been restored to the scene of cheerful chaos. Those who wished to play cricket were to gather about Lord Francis and be organized into two teams of near enough equal strength and skill. He himself had no intention of being drawn into the game, and he believed he spoke for the earl and the marquess too.

"They are all yours, Frank," he said. "Hart, you had better take Rosamond since she will doubtless not come to either me or Gabe. Annabelle can go with Gabe. Andrew, my lad, you may ride on Uncle Alistair's shoulders if you promise not to pull my ears. When you grow tired, you may run to your heart's content or until you have exhausted me. Ladies, I will spread the blankets on the grass before I leave, and you may relax and enjoy the game or a quiet conversation."

"Well!" the countess said. "A man after my own heart. Gabriel—"

"I was about to suggest the exact same thing," the earl

said, winking at the duke as he took Annabelle from Stephanie's arms and immediately had his hat knocked to a decidedly rakish angle. "But Bridge spoke faster."

"I do believe," the marchioness said, "Alistair is tactfully taking note of my condition. I shall be eternally grateful."

The gentlemen set off on their walk with the younger children as soon as the blankets had been spread for the ladies. But Lord Francis had a problem on his hands. Every prospective cricketer wanted him on their team, but as he pointed out, he could not divide himself in two.

"And even if I could," he said, "someone would have to take the left-hand side and therefore the useless side."

"But—"

"But—"

The chorus came from all sides.

Stephanie got to her feet and coughed for their attention. "If it is an adult who is wanted on both sides," she said, "I could offer my services."

Everyone—including Lord Francis to his discredit— turned to stare at her as if she had two heads.

"I was the champion bowler of my county for years," she said rashly. "Of the girls anyway," she added more quietly. "I shattered more wickets than anyone could possibly count."

"I can count to a hundred, Aunt Stephie," four-year-old Robert Kneller announced.

"More than that," she said. "Well, here I am. Take me or leave me."

"Stephanie," the countess said with a grimace, "you really must not feel obliged—"

"I am going to sleep with the sun on my face," Lady Francis announced, stretching out her full length on the blanket and determinedly closing her eyes.

But Stephanie was in the game—on sufferance, she realized when she saw the glum faces of her team members. Lord Francis, of course, was on the other team.

Gloom turned to exuberance when her turn at bat came and she hit a four off the first ball Lord Francis bowled at her. She suspected that he had thrown it deliberately slowly, as he had done for Robert and Jennifer's Mary. She laughed and whooped as she hitched her skirts and ran between the wickets. Her team cheered wildly. The other team looked accusingly at their hero. Samantha and Jennifer applauded.

"Oh, very well done, Stephanie," Jennifer called.

After that success Stephanie threw herself even more wholeheartedly into the game. She cheered and coaxed and coached her own team; she jeered and taunted the other team—the oldest member of it, anyway. She pulled off her bonnet and tossed it to the blanket. She tucked her dress a couple of inches up beneath the ribbon under her bosom so that she would not trip over the hem as she ran. She lost hairpins. She gained color.

She had not enjoyed herself so much for ten years or more.

And then came her moment of greatest triumph. Her team was leading by only two runs, and Lord Francis, the final batter for the other side, came in to bat.

"Move your fielders back, Aunt Stephie," he called, taking the bat in both hands and flexing his wrists. "Here comes a certain six."

Cheers from his side.

"Stay where you are, fielders," Stephanie commanded, "so that you may have a better view of the wickets shattering."

Cheers—considerably more halfhearted—from her side.

But it happened just as she had predicted. Luck was with her, of course, as she would have been the last to admit. The ball took an awkward bounce on the grass before the bat and hopped over it, while Lord Francis sawed at the air. It sent the wickets toppling with a satisfying thud.

"Yes!" Stephanie pumped both fists in the air and then fell backward as her team threw themselves at her, all shrieking enough to break eardrums. She laughed and hugged them and wrestled with them. Lord Francis, she noticed as guilt suddenly struck her, was also prone on the grass with his team on top of him. Considerable laughter came from their direction.

A few minutes passed before the children dispersed, intent on sharing their triumph with mothers. Stephanie, still laughing, struggled to her feet and brushed ineffectually at the grass clinging to her muslin skirt. Her hair must be similarly full of it, she thought, lifting her hands to the ruin of curls that Patty had created just a few hours before.

And then she saw that the children were talking excitedly at the blankets not only to mothers, but to *fathers* too. And Annabelle was crawling on the grass, trying to pull the head off a daisy.

Reality came crashing back as she found him at last with her eyes—leaning against the trunk of a tree a short distance from the blankets, his arms folded across his chest, his eyes focused on her. In his dark green superfine coat and buff pantaloons and black Hessians, he looked about as immaculate as a man could possibly look. He was not smiling. *Of course he was not smiling.*

An hour or so ago he had left the ladies to sit on the blankets. Being decorative. Being dignified. Behaving as ladies should behave. And the other three ladies had done just that.

"Bravo, Stephanie," the earl called to her.

"Francis may never forgive you, Stephanie." Lady Francis was laughing gleefully.

"Oh, Stephanie, your poor dress," the marchioness called.

"We thought only Cora ever acted above and beyond the call of duty," the countess said, and everyone laughed, including Lady Francis herself.

Stephanie scarcely heard them. She swallowed. He was coming toward her. He stooped to pick up something from the blanket as he passed it—her reticule. He looked at her unsmilingly.

"Your friend, Mr. Reaves, did not exaggerate about your bowling arm," he said. "That was quite a show."

"It was a game," she said. "For the children's sake." In a sense it was true. It had started out that way. But quickly enough she had become one of the children.

Her dress was still tucked up awkwardly and covered with grass. She could see tendrils of her hair that had no business being visible. She felt hot and flushed. Goodness only knew how long he had been standing there, watching her. His words suggested that he had seen her bowl out Lord Francis at the least. That meant he had also watched the exuberant aftermath of the win. He had seen her roll and wrestle in the grass, laughing helplessly.

She could not feel more at a disadvantage if she tried for a thousand years, she thought.

"Your reticule," he said, handing it to her. "Come. We will take a short walk."

So that she could be scolded privately, she thought, taking his arm and not even looking back when he called to the others that they were going to take a short stroll before tea. To be informed that her behavior had just fallen far short of what was expected from any lady. That it was totally unacceptable in a lady who was to be a duchess within one week.

She wondered if he would turn her off. No, she thought immediately, he would not do that. It was too late. There would be too much dreadful scandal, for him as well as for her. Besides, he was far too kind to turn her off.

She was beginning to hate kindness.

And she was beginning to hate herself for hating it.

He was feeling rather as if he had been slapped across the face—the same sort of shock and humiliation—and pain.

He had scarcely been able to believe his eyes when he had returned from the walk with the other men and with the younger children, who would have given the ladies no rest if he had not devised a plan for taking them out of the way for an hour.

One of the ladies was playing cricket with Kneller and the children.

It was Stephanie, of course. The words that damnably good-looking old friend of hers had spoken at the Royal Academy had returned immediately to mind. It was Stephanie with her elegant muslin dress pulled up to show far too much ankle for propriety, with no bonnet and auburn hair in an untidy halo about her head. It was Stephanie, flushed and exuberant and laughing and totally absorbed in the game.

He had never seen a woman look so startlingly beautiful.

And she was his. All that beauty and vitality and uninhibited joy in life was his. He had felt a rush of pure lust for her. Though he had realized as soon as the word formed in his mind that he was doing himself an injustice—and her too. It was more a feeling of delighted possessiveness. No, even that was not quite accurate.

He was in love with her, he had thought at last—delighted with her and proud of her. Proud that his closest friends were looking at her too and seeing what a very *right* choice of bride he had made.

He had imagined her playing thus with his children—with *their* children. And this time the feeling really was pure lust.

He had arrived toward the end of the game and had got himself positioned a little apart from the others just in time to see the lucky result of the rather wild over-arm pitch she made to Kneller. Kneller had been showing off too, of course, hitting out when he should have been protecting his wickets. Bridgwater had propped one shoulder against a tree and watched the children of Stephanie's team bowl her right off her feet onto her back and pile on top of her. He watched her laugh and hug them and roll good-naturedly on the ground with them, making for them a perfect afternoon. He had even noticed her glance at Kneller and his losing team to make sure they were not dejected.

How wonderful she was, he had thought. He could not imagine any other lady of his acquaintance risking her appearance and her dignity for the sake of children who were not even her own. And for the sake of her own enjoyment too, he suspected. It saddened him somehow to think that exuberance, spontaneity, even laughter were stamped ruthlessly out of the lives of children of gentle birth as soon as they began to grow up. Gentlemen and especially ladies were expected to behave with quiet dignity at all times.

He had, he realized, quite without any merit to himself, found just the right bride. Perhaps she would help him relax the habit of years. Perhaps she would help him enjoy life again. Perhaps she would teach him to laugh in public.

And then the children had scattered, abandoning their heroine in order to take the glory to themselves by boasting to their parents. She had got to her feet, had begun to brush herself off—and then had seen him.

She had changed in a flash. At one moment she was vibrant with laughter. At the next she was frozen-faced and tight-lipped. She looked incredibly untidy.

That was when he felt as if he had been slapped.

He had taken all the joy out of her day.

How she must hate him.

He could think only that she was also going to be embarrassed in another moment to be seen as she was. She needed to tidy up. She needed some privacy in which to do it. He acted from instinct, walking toward her, picking up her reticule as he passed the blankets—perhaps she carried a comb inside it.

He wanted to tell her how splendid she had been, what a good sport. He wanted to tell her how proud he was that she had made the children so happy. He wanted to tell her how beautiful she looked to his partial eyes. He wanted to tell her that he loved her. But he was hurt. He felt bruised. She did not like him. He merely commented on her bowling skills and took her arm and led her away toward some of the ancient oaks.

He felt stiff and uncomfortable. Rejected. Hated.

"You will wish to tidy yourself before tea," he said.

"Yes." They were already out of sight behind the trees. She slipped her arm from his and pulled at the waist of her dress. He could see then why so much of her ankles had been showing. She had tucked up some of the fabric behind the ribbon under her bosom. She looked up at him briefly as he stood a foot away watching, his hands clasped at his back. It seemed to him to be a look of pure hatred.

"No *lady* would ever dream of doing such a thing, would she?" she said.

"Turn," he said. "Your back is covered with grass."

She turned obediently, and he brushed firmly with one hand, trying to make the action as impersonal as possible, but feeling her warm curves with every stroke.

"Your hair needs attention," he said when she turned again. "Do you have a comb in your reticule?"

"Yes," she said, more tight-lipped than ever. Perhaps she was embarrassed even with him, he thought. She probably was, in fact. Perhaps that was all this was—embarrassment, not hatred. He watched her take the pins from her hair and set them between her lips before combing quickly through her hair—thick and wavy. He remembered it from that first night at the inn and swallowed convulsively. She kept her eyes lowered.

"You have made the children very happy this afternoon," he said.

"The *children*, yes," she said around the pins in her mouth. She was knotting her hair at the base of her neck with sure, practiced hands, and he was reminded that she was a woman unaccustomed to the attentions of a maid. She slid the pins deftly into place.

He could not quite read her expression. He did not know quite what point she had been making with the three words. But they did not encourage him to continue.

Ah, God, and they were to be man and wife within a week.

She looked up at him with expressionless eyes. "Will I do now, Your Grace?" she asked him.

He could hear the hatred quite clear in her voice this time. Despite the pretty lemon muslin dress, she looked like a governess again—a hard-eyed governess who would stand for no nonsense.

"Yes," he said. "You will do."

And he felt suddenly and unaccountably angry. Though perhaps not quite so unaccountably either. What had he done to incur her hatred? He could think of a few things, perhaps, but they were in the past, and he had apologized for them and had tried to make amends. They were not the only couple the world had known who had been forced into a marriage not quite of their own choosing. She might give them a chance. She might try to like him at least. She might surprise herself and find that it was not altogether impossible. He was no monster, after all.

Without pausing to ponder the wisdom of what he was about to do, he took a few steps toward her, backing her up against the trunk of a tree. He set his palms against the trunk on either side of her head, brought his body hard against hers, and found her mouth with his own. It was not a gentle kiss. Unashamedly, he used his expertise to demand with his lips that she part her own, that she open her mouth. When she did so, he thrust his tongue inside to its full length and stroked back over the roof of her mouth with its tip.

And he lifted his head.

"Perhaps," he said, and he was amazed and a little alarmed to hear the cold haughtiness in his voice, "you would do well, Miss Gray, to reconcile your mind to the fact that you will be my wife in less than one week's time. The Duchess of Bridgwater. I will expect your attitude to change."

He did not know where the words came from. He certainly had not planned them. He listened to their echo as if they had come from someone else. He was, he realized, quite out of his depth. He had always been in perfect control of his own life. It was the fear of losing that control that had driven him into virtual hiding for the past six years. But it had happened anyway.

His dream had happened too, but it was a nightmarish parody of the dream with which he was to spend the rest of his waking life.

Her lips looked just kissed—itself an irony. "It will, Your Grace," she said, her head still back against the tree, her arms and hands pressed against it at her sides. "I will not forget again."

Her eyes brightened with tears, and he turned away, deeply ashamed. He seemed to have behaved at his worst with Miss Stephanie Gray right from the first moment.

"Come," he said. "We must return to the others. I am supposed to be the host, yet I have abandoned my guests before serving them tea. You and I must learn to rub along together somehow. Shall we resolve at least to try?"

"Yes, Your Grace," she said, taking the arm he offered.

He would give anything in the world, he thought foolishly, to hear her call him Alistair.

Chapter 13

She had rarely worn white. White, she thought, was a young girl's color. Yet as a young girl she had worn more practical colors as the busy daughter of the vicar. Between the ages of twenty and six-and-twenty she had worn only gray and brown and black. In the past month she had worn colors that both she and the duchess agreed looked good with her hair.

Today she wore white—white satin, made heavy and stately with its pearl decorations. But no frills, no flounces, no bows. White flowers and green leaves were twined into her hair. She wore white gloves and slippers. She carried a posy of gold rosebuds.

The duchess looked her over carefully from head to toe and nodded. "You will do very nicely, indeed," she said. "You are a bride fit for a prince, Stephanie."

"Mother—" She was cold all the way through to the heart. Cold with terror—with the certain knowledge that she was doing the wrong thing. But that it was quite, quite unavoidable. Foolishly and suddenly, she wanted her own mother and her father too. She wanted to be hugged, cried over. She was so cold. She was surrounded by coldness and had been for a month. With kindness and ice, an unlikely but all too real combination.

But it was only her nerves that made her imagine such things. That was obvious even as panic threatened to engulf her. Her Grace's lips twitched, her eyes grew unexpectedly bright, and she stepped hastily forward—the only time Stephanie had ever seen her do anything that might be called impulsive.

"Oh, my dear," she said, hugging Stephanie and laying a cool cheek against hers. "Make him happy. He is so very dear to me, my son. And be happy yourself."

And then she was standing apart again, looking cool and regal once more. "There," she said, "I risked squashing your flowers. Forgive me. Your cousin will be waiting downstairs, and I must be on my way to the church. In less than two hours' time you will have my title, Stephanie. Carry it as proudly as I have. But I am sure you will. You have worked hard during the past month. You have surpassed all my most optimistic hopes."

And with a half smile she was gone.

Cousin Horace exclaimed over the transformation in her appearance and reminded her of her extreme good fortune in having netted a duke for a husband. His Grace had shown her the sort of condescension for which she must be grateful for the rest of her life. And she must not forget too that from this morning on—once the wedding ceremony was over and the register signed—she would be secure in her inheritance. She would be an independently wealthy woman.

She should, she was told, consider herself the happiest and most fortunate woman in the world.

She felt cold to the heart.

And colder still when they reached St. George's on Hanover Square and walked through the path left clear by the curious gathered outside to watch a Society wedding. And even when they were inside and the organ began to play and she became aware of the pews filled with all the cream of the beau monde. Somewhere in the crowd—she did not even try to find them with her eyes—were her own two friends, doubtless feeling awed and perhaps even intimidated by the company in which they found themselves. The only two friends of her own present. Yet since she had met them two weeks ago, she had not even tried to see them again.

And then she saw him. He was waiting for her at the altar rail. He was watching her walk down the aisle on Cousin Horace's arm. Straight and tall and proud, he looked as cold as she felt. He was dressed all in white and silver. She had never seen a man dressed all in white before. He looked magnificent. And cold.

But his eyes, his silver eyes, when she was close enough to see them burned into hers with cold fire.

She stood beside him, quietly dignified as she had always been as a governess, proud of bearing as she had been taught to be by the duchess. She spoke the words she was told to say. She listened to him say what he was told to say. She felt his hand hold hers—warm and steady in contrast with his icy appearance. She watched as he slid the bright and unfamiliar gold wedding ring onto her finger; he had to coax it over her knuckle. She lifted her face for his kiss—warm, closed lips pressed firmly against her own while an almost soundless murmur passed through the congregation behind them.

She was his wife.

She was the Duchess of Bridgwater.

Her inheritance was safe.

She felt as cold as the marble floor of the church.

She realized why she had so dreaded her marriage for the past week and even longer than that. It was not just that she was losing her freedom to a man who did not want her, but was marrying her out of a sense of obligation. It was not just that she felt she was losing her identity in that of his duchess. It was not just that she felt bound and confined to the point of suffocation by the rules that she must not on any account break. It was not just that she was being rushed at dizzying speed from a dull but familiar world into a frighteningly new one. It was not just any of those things.

It was that she loved him—and was unloved in return.

If she could have remained indifferent to him, she thought, merely grateful to him and under an obligation to him, she could have borne all the rest. What freedom had she known for the last six years, after all? And what happiness and self-respect?

But she had not remained indifferent.

And then the rest of the service was over and the register signed, and she was walking slowly back up the aisle again, her arm resting along the top of her husband's. There were smiling faces wherever she looked. Cora, sitting almost at the front, was red-faced and openly sobbing and taking a large white handkerchief from Francis's hand. Jennifer, beside her, was smiling and teary-eyed. Gabriel was winking. Miriam, almost at the back, was wet-faced and brightly smiling.

And then they were outside and being greeted by the rowdy cheers and the bawdy comments of the small crowd gathered there. Her husband led her through it to his waiting carriage, handed her inside, and climbed in beside her. The carriage lurched into well-sprung motion as the first guests began to leave the church. The wedding breakfast was to be at the duke's town house—Stephanie had never yet been there, though her trunks and her maid had been taken there even before she had left for the church. The duke and his duchess must be there ahead of their guests in order to receive them as was proper.

As was proper.

"My dear," her husband said, taking her hand and setting it on his sleeve again—her bright new wedding ring shone up at them—"you look more beautiful today than I thought it possible for any woman to look. I wish you to know how proud I am of you."

Yes, she had learned her lessons well—with one or two rather nasty lapses. They would grow fewer and fewer as time went on, until they disappeared altogether.

"I have tried," she said. "I will continue to try so that you may continue to be proud of me, Your Grace."

His free hand covered hers. "Stephanie," he said quietly, "my name is Alistair."

"Yes." She closed her eyes for a moment, beguiled by the

intimacy of the carriage interior and by the softness of his voice, imagining that she heard tenderness in it. "Alistair."

"There is nothing improper about a man and his wife sharing the intimacy of their given names," he said.

"No." She opened her eyes again. "If it is not improper, it may be allowed, then." She hoped he had not heard the bitterness she tried to keep out of her voice.

Everything by the rules.

Very well, then. Everything by the rules.

He had intended to remain in London with his bride until the end of the Season. It was the proper thing to do, after all. As the Duchess of Bridgwater she would need to be presented at court to the queen. His mother would act as her sponsor. And she would need to establish her new position as his duchess and his hostess. They would need to entertain—dinners and soirées and one grand ball. Besides, she had a position of her own to establish. She was now undisputed and independent owner of Sindon Park and the fortune left her by her grandfather.

The proper thing to do was stay. It was what he had planned. But London appeared to be suffocating her. It was suffocating him. Suddenly, he wanted to be away from it, away from the social obligations. He wanted to take her into the country. He wanted to be alone with her, perhaps rashly. She hated him. She had not once smiled at him, though it was their wedding day, and she had smiled at everyone else. Even when she had come to stand beside him at the church rail she had not smiled.

Had he? He could not be sure he had. He had felt choked with a deep emotion he had been forced to keep under control. Half of the beau monde was looking at him—or at her. Probably at her. Everyone looked at a bride. Who was interested in a mere bridegroom? But he could not be sure anyway that he had smiled.

When he rose from his place at the wedding breakfast to speak to his guests, he announced that he would be taking his duchess to Wightwick Hall in Gloucestershire on the morrow. He did not look at either his wife or his mother to observe their reactions. He thanked his guests for attending both the wedding and the breakfast and for making the day a special one.

"I will send instructions without delay to your maid to leave your trunks as they are," he said quietly to Stephanie after he had sat down again. "She will unpack only what you will need tonight and tomorrow."

Tonight she would become fully his wife, he thought, watching the slight flush of color that stained her cheeks.

"Yes, Your Gr . . ." she said. "Yes. Thank you."

He wondered if he had been very foolish. The summer alone at Wightwick would be a long one if they began it this early. They could invite guests to join them there, of course, or they could take themselves off to Brighton for a few weeks. But for a while at least they would be virtually alone together. Was there any chance at all of making a viable marriage out of what they had begun? He doubted it. Their relationship seemed to have deteriorated steadily through the month of their betrothal. For the past four days—ever since the day of that wretched picnic—there had been nothing at all between them except cold formality.

It was his fault, he knew. There had been his dream, his longing for a marriage that would bring love and warmth and companionship and happiness into his life. But there had never really been the possibility of anything but the dream. All his education had been designed to make him into a dignified, controlled figure of authority. There had been love—certainly a fondness between him and his parents, between him and his brother and sisters. But love had always been a cool thing in his life, and for most of his life it had taken second place to dignity and duty.

He was capable of feeling love. He had always known that, and he knew it now with painful force. But he had never been taught a way of showing love—or of inspiring it.

He had inspired gratitude and respect and obedience in Stephanie, under largely false pretenses. But there was nothing more. She hated him, though he guessed that she must feel guilty at her feelings and would spend the rest of her life fighting them. He did not doubt that he had married a dutiful duchess.

He did not want duty. He wanted love.

Perhaps, he thought, at Wightwick . . .

But there was no further time for dreaming. There were guests to entertain for the rest of the afternoon and on even into the early evening. He scarcely saw his wife and had no chance to exchange even a single word with her. He glimpsed her talking with his relatives, his friends, her friends. She had acquired a great deal of the regal manner that had always characterized his mother, but to it she added her own brand of beauty and charm. He spoke with as many people as time permitted.

It was, of course, the correct thing for his wife and him to remain apart as they entertained guests. It was the way things would have continued if he had not made the impulsive decision to leave for Wightwick in the morning. A rider had already been sent, he gathered, to gallop hell-for-leather to his country seat to warn the staff there of his imminent arrival. There would be panic there for a few days, he did not doubt.

The thought brought a smile to his face.

But finally he was alone with her. They dined alone together; both had changed from their wedding clothes into evening dress. They conversed as smoothly as any well-bred couple might. They continued the conversation in the drawing room both before and after she had played for him on the pianoforte and he had played for her. They drank tea together.

And then he escorted her upstairs to the door of her dressing room, bowed over her hand, and told her he would do himself the honor of visiting her half an hour later.

He went into his own dressing room and flung himself into the closest chair. He propped his arms on the rests and steepled his fingers beneath his chin. He closed his eyes.

And remembered her as she had been that night at the inn. Warm and beautiful and inviting and willing—or so it had appeared. He wondered what would have happened if she had been what she had seemed. She would have been his mistress for a month now. They would be comfortable together, contented together. Would he have tired of her yet? Would he have ever tired of her?

Foolish, pointless thoughts, of course. She had not been as she had seemed. And he could no longer think of her in terms of sexual gratification alone. She was his wife, his life's partner.

He drew a deep breath and let it out slowly. It was time to summon his valet. He must not keep her waiting beyond the appointed time. She was probably nervous.

She was not afraid. It would be foolish for a woman of six-and-twenty to fear a physical process that would probably become almost as familiar as breathing to her over the coming months and years. She reminded herself that she was fortunate it was to happen at all. For years she had not expected that it ever would. But she had always wanted it to happen. She had always wanted children of her own—quite passionately.

He was a man she found physically attractive. He was a man she loved. She was not afraid.

She just wished that he could have stayed simply as Mr. Munro. She had liked him. He had been so very kind. He would have been of her own world. She would not have had to change. She would not have had to consider her every word and action to be sure that everything that was proper was said and done. She would not have come almost to hate him because she lived constantly in fear of shaming and disappointing him.

She did almost hate him. She also loved him.

Tonight she would be the duchess he expected—calm, gracious, unimpassioned. She would not find it too difficult. She was not afraid, after all.

She looked up with cool welcome when he tapped on her door and came inside. She stood still and relaxed as his eyes moved down over her loosened hair and her white silk and lace nightgown to her bare feet.

"Come in, Alistair," she said. "Let me pour you a glass of wine." She had thought to have some sent up. She poured a glass for herself too and handed him his. She wanted him to see that her hand was steady, that she was no shrinking bride unworthy of her position.

"So that we may toast our health?" he said. "And our happiness, Stephanie? To our health, then, and our happiness." He raised his glass.

She touched hers to it, and they drank. He held her eyes with his own as he did so. She wished he would smile at her. She longed to smile at him. But she would not risk appearing coquettish.

"Perhaps," he said, "we will be happy. Will we?"

To hide her longing from him, she took his empty glass and set it down with her half-full one on the tray.

"I shall try," she said, "to make you happy, Alistair. Always. Tell me how."

He half smiled at her then. One side of his mouth lifted. It was an expression she had not seen on him before.

"Ah, yes," he said. "You will too, will you not, Stephanie? We will make the best we can of it, then. And I will try to see to it that you never regret the events of this morning—and tonight. It will be my recipe for happiness. We will both try."

"Yes." She wanted suddenly to reach out with one hand to cup his cheek. But it was not the sort of thing one did with the Duke of Bridgwater. Even if he was her husband.

"Come, then." He reached out a hand for hers, his eyes probing hers at the same time. "Come to bed, Stephanie."

"Yes," she said. She moved too fast toward it and deliberately slowed her pace. She was perhaps a little nervous, after all. Since it was his mother who had instructed her, she had not liked to ask questions. Perhaps she would not have anyway. Should she raise her nightgown herself or wait for him to do it? Should she touch him with her hands or rest them on the bed? Should she say anything afterward or keep quiet? It was embarrassing at her age to know so little.

She decided on total passivity. At least she could do no real wrong that way. Perhaps he would tell her what he wanted. She learned fast; she had proved that to him in the past month. Soon enough she would learn what was expected of her in their marriage bed. At least she knew what he did *not* want. She had not forgotten the lesson learned in Elizabeth's conservatory.

He blew out the candles after she had lain down. She was glad of that. She was a little embarrassed as well as nervous. Her body had been so very much her own private property all her life. Even the presence of a maid during the last month had embarrassed her. But a maid was at least her own gender.

He lay down beside her, leaned over her, and kissed her. In the way he had kissed her twice before—she did not even want to remember that last kiss against the oak in Richmond Park. She should have been prepared for the same results. Her breasts tightened almost instantly, and she felt a rush of raw aching pain to her womb. She had disgusted him at Elizabeth's ball by giving in to her passion. She reminded herself of the fact, deliberately verbalizing it more than once in her mind. Not again. It would not happen again. She pressed her palms against the mattress and fought her body's needs.

Should she part her lips? His tongue pressed through, and the decision was taken out of her hands. Should she open her mouth? *Tell me what to do*, she pleaded silently. She opened her mouth.

She had never had a nightgown that buttoned down the front. Both her mother-in-law and her modiste had guided her to ones that did for her wedding clothes. In her naivete she had not realized why until her husband began to undo the buttons while he kissed her. The front opening was a long one.

His hand came inside against her bare flesh. He brushed his palm and his fingers over her very lightly. He touched her breasts. They already felt swollen and sore. She bit her bottom lip hard when his thumb touched and pressed lightly upon her hardened nipple. The ache that had been in her womb and between her thighs had become an insistent throbbing.

And then his hand was there too, and his fingers were probing—very gently. She could not have borne the pain of a firm touch. She shut her eyes very tightly and pressed her fingertips hard into the mattress. She wanted to squirm and cry out. She wanted to throw her arms about him and beg him to stop or to— But she did not know what. She held her breath. And through it all she felt embarrassment and humiliation. She could both feel and hear wetness.

"Let your breath out," he said quietly against her ear. "Relax. You will soon grow accustomed to it."

She felt so ashamed. That she had had to be told! Her breath shuddered out of her quite audibly. But he had moved over her and was lowering himself onto her body. It was almost a relief to feel his knees between her own. She did not resist as he pushed her legs wide. Her nightgown, she realized, was already up about her waist. She need not have worried about that either. There had been no awkward moment.

Despite herself, she drew in her breath and held it again. His hands were beneath her. She could feel him position himself.

And then he came into her. She had prepared herself for pain. But pain did not come immediately. She had not expected the incredible stretching sensation, the sense of being invaded, of having her body taken over by someone else. Then came the pain, the momentary panic. And the hard deep occupation of her secret depths.

She let out her breath slowly. This was it, then. What she had yearned for for so long. The completion of her femininity. The uniting with man. The hope of being fruitful. The pain had gone and the panic and the strange, unexpected outrage at being violated. Wonder replaced them all. Wonder that such a thing could be. Wonder that she held him so much deeper inside than she had expected. Wonder that there was no sense of embarrassment or humiliation. She relaxed completely.

It felt wonderful.

She knew what was to come. Or had thought she knew. She lay still, allowing it to happen, holding herself open to his pleasure, taking to herself as much secret pleasure as she dared without losing herself in passion as she had in Elizabeth's conservatory. She wanted to tighten inside muscles as she had during that embrace. She wanted to tighten about him and feel her pleasure. She lay relaxed and still as he pumped firmly and repeatedly into her. She could feel the heat of him—all over her, inside her. She could hear his labored breathing against her hair. She could smell his cologne and his heat and his sweat.

She wanted to lift her legs and press her inner thighs hard against his lean hips. She wanted to tilt herself so that she could bring him deeper. She wanted to wrap her arms about the firm muscles of his chest and waist. She lay still, spread-eagled beneath him, giving herself in marriage.

When his pace quickened and deepened and then he sighed and relaxed and she felt the heat of his seed inside her, she swallowed and fought tears. She lay very still. She had been told that she might find it unpleasant. She had been told that she might in time find it pleasant. She had not been told that it would be the most wonderful feeling in this world. And she had not been told that she would want to cry when it was over because she would want it to go on and on until . . . Oh, she did not know until when.

She felt cold when he moved away to lie beside her. She felt his hand lower her nightgown and raise the bedcovers. She felt his hand take her own; his was very warm and damp. He was still breathing rather heavily.

"Did I hurt you very badly, my dear?" he asked her.

"No." Her voice sounded high-pitched. She brought it back to normal. "Hardly at all, Alistair. I hope I pleased you." She was pleased with the calm, matter-of-fact tone she had achieved.

He did not answer for a few moments. "You pleased me,"

he said at last. "I thank you. You will find it less painful tomorrow and perhaps a little less . . . overwhelming."

"I was not overwhelmed," she said quickly, turning her head toward him. But she could not see him clearly in the darkness. "I tried. I . . . I liked it." Perhaps she ought not to have said that. Perhaps it was the wrong thing to say. "I hope I can bear you an heir within the year, Alistair."

He sat up on the edge of the bed, his back to her. His back seemed hunched. She guessed that his elbows were resting on his knees. She could see his fingers pushing through his hair. And then he was on his feet and bending over her. She felt the backs of his fingers light beneath her jaw.

"I will leave you to your sleep," he said. "You have had a busy day, and tomorrow we will be traveling all day. Thank you for today, Stephanie—for marrying me, for entertaining our guests, for . . . this. I shall try to be a good husband. Good night."

"Alistair—" she said as he moved away. But when he stopped and turned back to her, she could not think what to say. *Please come back to bed? Please let me admit to you how wonderful it was for me? Please let me love you?* "I will try too. All my life I will try."

"Good night, my dear," he said.

"Good night, Alistair." *Good night, my love.*

She could feel the soreness and the discomfort that the consummation of their marriage had left behind. She felt cold with his body heat removed. She could smell him on her pillow and on herself.

At first the sound of a noisy sob startled her. Then she turned her face into the pillow and indulged in a good self-pitying weep.

There was no one to see her loss of dignity and control, after all. She was tired to death of dignity and control.

She wondered how an act of such unbelievable intimacy could leave her just a few minutes later feeling lonelier than she had ever felt in her life.

Chapter 14

They were traveling in the same carriage as they had during that other journey. He tried to feel the sameness. He tried to feel relaxed, amused, totally in control of the situation as he had felt then.

Of course, she had sat on the seat opposite him during those three days. He had been able to watch her the whole time—the accomplished actress, fully aware of the lure of her beauty and charm. Spinning him a tale that was so unbelievable and yet so full of predictable clichés that he had enjoyed vastly the exercise of anticipating what she was about to say—and being right almost every time.

He had fallen in love with her as far back as then, he thought now in some surprise. Though there was nothing profound about falling in love, of course. Loving was a different matter altogether. He wondered which applied to him now. Was he merely in love with her? Or did he love her?

He half turned his head to look at her. She was dressed all in light spring green, even down to her slippers and gloves, which were lying on the seat opposite. She looked quiet and composed. She had been a bride just yesterday, he thought. She had lost her virginity last night. There was no sign in her bearing that such momentous events in her life had happened so recently. She smiled calmly back at him. She met his eyes, but did not blush.

He had hoped for blushes this morning, for lowered eyes, for some sign that she remembered their intimacy of the night before. But she had arrived at breakfast only moments after him. And she had sat and conversed easily with him and had eaten a breakfast of respectable size. There had not been even a tremor in her hands.

Of course she had behaved much the same way in bed. There had been none of the passion he had hoped he might rekindle, though her body had responded at least sufficiently to minimize the pain of his entry. There had been only the slight nervousness, which had caused her to tense just before she had been mounted for the first time—and the dignified, unresisting acquiescence in the performance of the marriage act.

He, of course, had been fiercely aroused by her tall, shapely slimness. By the almost athletic firmness of her body—a strange word to think of in connection with a woman.

"Tell me about your friends," he said. "The Reaveses, that is." Perhaps somehow he could recapture the charm of that other journey. He almost wished, absurdly, that she were wearing the flamboyant plumed bonnet again—and sitting opposite him.

"There are seven of them," she said. "Six girls and Tom. I am closest in age to Miriam and so was most friendly with her. And with Tom."

She had sat with Thomas Reaves and his wife for almost fifteen minutes yesterday, talking animatedly with them before moving away to mingle with their other guests.

"I was encouraged to be friendly with them," she said. "Mrs. Reaves said it was because only I could keep peace among the girls. Mama said it was because I was better born than they and Mrs. Reaves had social ambitions. But I think not. They were far wealthier than we were. None of that mattered to us when we were children, anyway. We played and played. We used to climb trees and swim in the stream and dive in the lake—all forbidden activities. I was . . . Mama once called me a hoyden. I am afraid she was right."

"Anyone who plays cricket as well as you must have been

a hoyden," he said. Absurdly, he wished he had known her then. In the month of their acquaintance he had had only a few tantalizing glimpses of the daring, exuberant girl she must have been.

"When I grew older," she said, spreading her hands in her lap and looking down at them—her wedding ring looked startlingly new and bright—"Papa suggested that I redirect my energies. And so I worked with Mama for as long as she lived and then alone in performing parish duties. But I did not mind. I loved the life."

She had talked about all this during that other journey, but he had listened in a different way then. He had thought then that she was spinning an amusing yarn.

"And the friendships faded?" he asked.

"Not really," she said. "They matured. The hardest thing to accustom myself to when I took employment with the Burnabys was the loss of those friendships. I was not allowed to receive personal letters at the Burnabys more than two or three times a year. I missed them, my friends. I missed Miriam."

"And Tom?" he said. "Was there never a romantic attachment between the two of you?" Surely, there must have been. They must be close in age. They were both handsome people. He wished then he had not asked the question.

"Not really," she said. "We had been friends all our lives. It would have been difficult to see each other differently. Of course it was hard saying good-bye and knowing that we would probably never meet again. And he felt bad about my having to become a governess—they all felt bad."

"But he did not try to stop you?" he asked.

She smiled at her hands. "He offered me marriage," she said. "I refused."

"Why?" he asked.

"Because he offered out of kindness," she said. "He did not love me. And I did not love him. It would not have been the marriage I had always dreamed of."

He felt uncomfortable suddenly. She might have been describing their own marriage. Except that she had been unable to say no to him.

"What was the marriage you had always dreamed of?" he asked almost unwillingly.

She looked up at him suddenly with cheeks that were at last slightly flushed. It was as if she had just realized the turn their conversation had taken.

"Oh." She laughed. "It was the dream all girls and very young women dream, I suppose. It seems foolish now and would appear even more foolish to a gentleman—to a duke in particular. I dreamed of romantic love. I believed in that quite ridiculous notion that somewhere for all of us there is that one perfect match, that . . . Oh, it does not matter. But I am glad I did not marry Tom. I would have always felt that I had"—she winced and caught at her bottom lip, but she had no choice but to complete what she had started to say— "that I had coerced him into it. I would always have felt th-that I owed him an obligation I could never fully repay. I . . ." She foundered to a halt after all.

It was how she felt about him, of course. She believed she had coerced him into marriage. She believed she had an obligation to him she could never repay. Her marriage was a burden to her. She could never be happy with him.

What would she say if she knew that he had mistaken her for an actress and a whore? That he had taken her all the way to Sindon not out of kindness and concern, but . . .

"Tell me more," he said, "about those games you played, about the exploits and the mischief." He was hungry to know her. Although she had told him a great deal more than he had ever told her, he still felt that she was a stranger—a stranger who was his wife and his duchess, a stranger with whom he had been intimate last night and would be intimate tonight and tomorrow night and so on through their lives.

"They were not dignified," she said, smiling quickly at him so that for a moment he had a dazzling glimpse of her dimple and gold-flecked eyes. "Some of them were downright dishonorable, like the time we all crept out at night— Tom, Miriam, Agnes, and I—because Tom had heard and believed the strange story that fish swam on the surface of the stream at night and might be caught in the hands. I believe I was eight years old. We did not see a single fish, let alone catch any, of course."

He smiled. She told him several more of her adventures that he had not heard before. It was clear that Tom Reaves had been the leader, with Stephanie a close second. He thought of his own childhood. He had been much like Tom, only perhaps considerably worse, until his father, despairing of ever grooming him to take on the ducal title and responsibilities eventually sent him off to school at the age of ten. It seemed to him that he had spent a large portion of his childhood bent over his father's desk trying not to hear the whistle of his father's cane, which was always the harbinger of stinging pain.

Let George be the damned duke, he could remember yelling once, dancing from foot to foot in a vain attempt to alleviate the stinging of his rear end. *All I want to be is a damned soldier or a damned sailor.* All he had got for his act of shocking defiance, of course, had been a thunderous order to bend over again. And school very soon after that. He had wondered how many people, knowing him now, would guess that he had been such a child.

Would his own eldest son be such a rebel? And would he handle the problem in the same way his father had handled it? His father had been stiffly dignified and humorless, though not lacking entirely in love. Was he like his father? His mother and his sisters said that he was.

He reached out suddenly and took Stephanie's left hand in his own. It was something he had been wanting to do for an hour or more. She had beautiful hands, with long slim fingers. He set a thumb and forefinger against her ring and twisted it on her finger.

"I believe you will like Wightwick Hall," he said. "The park is so large that you need hardly be aware of the farms unless you ride out to them."

"I am sure I shall like it," she said. She made no effort to reclaim her hand. "I suppose it is much larger than Sindon Park. I shall do my best to fulfill my duties there, Alistair."

"It is a safe, spacious place for children to grow up in," he said. "Six generations of my family have grown up there. Our children will be the seventh."

"Yes," she said. "I know that the Dukes of Bridgwater have not been without a male heir in all that time. There is a portrait gallery, is there not? Your mother told me that there are portraits of all your ancestors. I look forward to seeing them. And I shall try to see to it that the tradition is not broken. I hope to bear you an heir within the year."

It was coolly said, without a blush. He wished she would blush, thinking of how the begetting of an heir was to happen. She had shown passion once in Elizabeth's conservatory. There had been times since when he had wished he had carried that embrace to its conclusion, dangerous as it would have been in an unlocked room during a ball and grossly improper as it would have been when they had been merely betrothed. Their relationship might have taken a wholly different course if he had not remembered propriety and then reminded her of it in a particularly insulting manner.

He wondered what last night had meant to her. He wondered how she had felt, not just in her body, but in her emotions. He wondered what thoughts had gone through her mind as he had first fondled and then mounted and then worked in her. He wished he could ask her. Why could he not? But there was no point in asking himself the question when he knew that the answer was simply because. Because there was no closeness between them and he did not know how to bridge the gap.

"My mother will have told you," he said, "that that is your main duty as my duchess—at least until it has been accomplished." He half smiled at her, but she had looked away. He still thought George would make a quite creditable Duke of Bridgwater, and George already had healthy sons. He wanted children with Stephanie because he wanted a family. His dream was beginning to revive, though it would doubtless have to be a dream based on reality. She did not love him.

"Yes," she said. "I will begin my other duties as soon as

we arrive, Alistair. You must not fear that I will be inadequate to the task. I shall be a diligent mistress of your home.
I will visit all your tenants and laborers. And once you have
presented me to your neighbors, I will entertain and call
upon them as is proper. I believe you will not be displeased
with me."

He brought her hand to his lips and held it there for a few
moments. "I am not displeased," he said. "I am confident
you will acquit yourself admirably."

"Your mother mentioned a summer fête," she said. "With
games and exhibits both in the village and in the park. And
an evening feast and dancing. She described my responsibilities there. I shall look forward to fulfilling them."

He made sure he was at home each year for the fête. He
never particularly enjoyed it since it was an entertainment
designed entirely for the local people, and he was no longer
able to mingle with them as he had done as a boy. He had
been a duke for longer than ten years. He was too far sepa-
rated from his people socially, even though he was fond of
them and he believed that they in their way were fond of
him.

It had been different when he was a boy, of course. Even
though school had quelled much of his rebellious high spirits and he had learned to be his father's son even when at
home for the holidays, there had still been moments of escape. It had been at one of the fêtes, late in the evening,
when his seventeen-year-old self had lost his virginity. He
had gone into the hay barn—he was still not sure who had
done the leading and who the following—with a merry
widow eight years his senior and had emerged three or four
hours later with his virginity several times gone, if that were
possible. He had been swaggering, thinking himself one
devil of a virile fellow, though the memory now of his four
vigorous performances during those hours brought a rueful
smile to his face.

"The fête is to be enjoyed, Stephanie," he said.

"Oh." She turned her head and smiled dazzlingly at him.
"I shall see to it that everyone does enjoy it, Alistair. I shall

begin planning it as soon as we arrive, though I know there are numerous traditions regarding it that I must follow. You must not worry about it. I shall plan it all myself. You will find that you have a competent duchess."

He had heard very little. The smile had dazzled him. He acted without thought. He leaned across her and set his mouth to hers. She was his bride of two days and one night, he thought, and they had traveled side by side for almost a whole day like polite strangers. He had plied her with questions, and she had spoken cheerfully about duty. About bearing his son, as if doing so meant no more to her than a duty that was expected of her.

He lifted his head and looked into her eyes. She was perfectly composed, her hands clasped lightly in her lap. She smiled placidly at him. She was being his dutiful duchess. She was fulfilling an obligation she believed would never quite be fulfilled.

"How do you feel about me?" he asked her.

Her eyes widened. "Alistair," she said, "you are my husband."

As if that was an answer.

"What do you wish me to say?" she asked when he continued to search her eyes with his own. "I have learned during the past month what will be expected of me as your duchess. But I realize that something has been missed. No one has tried to tell me how to please you personally, except for a few general principles." She blushed more rosily this time. She would have been told to be obedient and submissive, he thought—particularly in bed. "I want to please you, Alistair. Tell me how. I owe you everything."

"Perhaps," he said, "I have only one request, Stephanie. That you stop thinking that. It is untrue, you know. You owe me nothing." Words that were being spoken one month too late.

"I had enough money left to buy a small loaf of bread," she said. "During that one night I spent alone outdoors I very narrowly escaped having everything stolen—even my virtue. I was not so innocent that I did not realize they would have taken that too before leaving with my meager belongings. I would have faced other such nights. Looking as I did when you first saw me, I would not have escaped again. I saw the way everyone looked at me—everyone but you. You were the only one who treated me with respect as well as kindness. And you took me all the way home rather than abandon me to the risk of danger again. Even though you knew that in doing so you would sacrifice your own freedom. I owe you my life and, just as important, my virtue. And you must ask how I feel about you?"

"No," he said, sitting back again so that he would not have to look into her face. He drew a deep breath "This will not do."

"I have tried and am trying," she said, her voice unhappy now. "I did not please you, did I? But I knew nothing, Alistair. Tonight perhaps I will do better. Please tell me how I may better please you. Pleasing you is the dearest wish of my heart."

"Stephanie," he said, "I felt no more respect for you than anyone else. I saw the abominable bonnet and the tasteless cloak and I saw nothing else. And heard nothing else. I thought you were at best an actress and at worst a whore. Probably both. I will not say I intended from the start to have you. I did not. I kept you with me because the parcel of lies I thought you were telling me amused me no end, and I wanted to see your embarrassment when I finally backed you into a corner and exposed you for what you were. That first night I thought you a clever tease and out of my own boredom decided to play your game. But before we reached Hampshire and Sindon Park, I fully intended to have you for my mistress—after I had taken you there and watched to see how you would handle the situation. I trapped myself. *Now* tell me how much you owe me. Now tell me that pleasing me is your dearest wish."

It was something he had thought never to tell her. He had convinced himself at first—perhaps with some compassion—that doing so would only humiliate her. But he had seen since that his silence had actually caused something worse. She had been trapped, suffocated, made intensely miserable by the debt she had thought she owed him. He had released her at last. Too late? How was she going to react? But he could not feel sorry that he had spoken the truth.

He turned his head to look at her when she did not immediately speak. Her body was quite rigid. Her hands, still clasped together in her lap, were white-knuckled. Her face had lost all vestige of color. Her eyes were closed.

"It would be absurdly inadequate," he said, "to beg your pardon. But I am the one, you see, Stephanie, who has atonement to make. You did not have a great deal of freedom anyway, but I took away even the little you had."

"You believed nothing I said?" She was whispering.

"No," he said. "A bright bird of paradise standing on a dusty and deserted road told me that she was on her way to Hampshire to take up her inheritance, and I was amused."

"I was not shown to the wrong room that night, was I?" she said. "It was the right room. I was to share it with you."

"Yes," he said.

"I was to share the bed with you too," she said. "You were going to do to me what you did last night."

"Yes," he said.

He heard her draw a sharp breath and hold it. It shuddered out of her after a while.

"Why did you not?" she asked. "Two nights in a row it happened, then. I had narrow escapes twice. Why did you let me escape?"

"For the reason I mentioned a short while ago," he said. "I thought you had outmaneuvered me, and I chose to humor you."

"It was not simply because I had said no?" she asked. Her voice was so soft that he could scarcely hear her.

He thought for a moment. "Yes," he said, "for that reason too. I would never force myself on a woman who had said no."

"Does your wife qualify as a woman?" she asked.

Oh, good Lord! He thought about it. "Yes," he said at last,

as softly as she. "Are you going to say no tonight? And to-morrow night?"

She said nothing for so long that he thought perhaps she intended never to speak to him again. But she spoke at last.

"I suppose," she said, "I must be thankful for that bonnet and that cloak. If I had been my usual gray self—gray like my name—you would not have afforded me even a second glance. You would not have stopped to take me up. I would have starved and perhaps died. I would probably have been ravished. Your error saved me." Bitterness was heavy in her voice. "But despite that, I need no longer feel beholden to you. I believe, when I have recovered from my shock, I may find that fact enormously freeing. Why did you tell me? You might have kept it secret for the rest of our lives. I would never have suspected. I would have been your willing slave for a lifetime."

His own voice too was bitter when he spoke, though he knew he had no cause for bitterness. "Perhaps I do not want a slave," he said. "Perhaps I want a wife."

"Oh, you have that," she said. "I married you yesterday, if you will recall. We shared a marriage bed last night. I tried so very hard to please you, because I thought you were like a god. I might have better spent the time pleasing myself."

"By sending me away?" he said. "By saying no?"

"No," she said and laughed harshly. "Oh, no, not that."

They must be nearing the inn where they were to spend the night. He looked out through the window for familiar landmarks. He had traveled this road hundreds of times. Neither of them had spoken for several minutes. He wondered why he was feeling strangely calm. And he realized with a grim smile that it was because he now for the first time had a real relationship with her. A disastrous relationship, perhaps—no, probably. But real, nonetheless. It was better than what he had had with her before.

He would rather live without her than have her as a slave. It was a surprising and quite bleak realization.

"We will be at the inn soon," he said. "I have had a suite of rooms reserved. You will have your own bedchamber.

You will be under no compulsion to receive me there. You will not be relegating me to a distant attic if you say no."

She said nothing. She was sitting straighter than before. She was less relaxed.

"May I come to your bed tonight?" he asked.

"No," she said after a slight hesitation. "Not tonight, Alistair. Maybe not tomorrow night either. I do not know. I need some time."

He nodded. "I will ask again tomorrow," he said.

His carriage was making the turn into the large stable yard of the Bull and Horn, and ostlers and grooms were converging on his familiar carriage.

Chapter 15

It was a relief to arrive at Wightwick Hall, principal residence of the Duke of Bridgwater in Gloucesterhire. If they had arrived just this time yesterday, Stephanie thought, it might have been no relief at all. If she had been amazed at the sight and size of Sindon Park a little over a month ago, she would have been awed to incoherence by Wightwick with its massive stone gateposts and wrought iron gates, its twin gatehouses, which seemed almost small mansions in their own right, by the seemingly endless curved driveway flanked by oak trees, by the three-arched stone bridge over a river or stream, and by the long, sloping lawns and groves and flower arbors leading past the large stone stable block up to the stately Palladian house.

She would have been awed by the sight of grooms in livery lined up on the terrace—far more than would be needed to tend the four horses and the carriage, and by the almost regal figures, dressed all in black, of the butler and housekeeper, standing at the foot of the marble steps leading to the main entrance doors. She would have been overwhelmed by the high domed grand hall and by the sight of two motionless lines of house servants awaiting her inspection.

She was not awed—only relieved. Relieved to be away from the oppressive silence of her husband's presence. Not away exactly, of course. He walked slightly behind her right shoulder, presenting her to his head groom, who had handed her down from the carriage, and then to the butler and housekeeper. He followed her along the lines of servants and spoke quietly to a few of them as she had a word and a smile for each one.

He and his wife had scarcely spoken all day. After she had assured him that yes, she had slept very well, thank you—she had not—and that yes, the sky did look overcast but no, it did not look quite as if it would rain, there had been no further conversation at breakfast. Through the day in the carriage he had tried a few times to draw her into conversation, but her monosyllabic answers had discouraged him each time.

It was not that she was being deliberately sullen. It was just that she was totally bewildered. All the worlds she had ever known, and now this new one into which she had tried so hard to fit—all of them had crumbled. She no longer knew who she was or where she belonged.

"You will wish to see your apartment, Your Grace," the housekeeper murmured when the inspection had been completed, "and freshen up. I will have tea served in the drawing room in half an hour's time."

Stephanie smiled at her.

"Her Grace has had a tiring journey, Mrs. Griffiths," her husband said. "She will take tea in her private sitting room. Parker will bring something more appropriate to me in the library."

Stephanie expected that he would remain downstairs. But he stayed just behind her as Mrs. Griffiths led her up four flights of marble stairs and along a wide carpeted corridor toward what must be the ducal suite at the front of the house. He followed her while the housekeeper showed her the large, luxuriously appointed sitting room, which was, it seemed, exclusively hers, and the spacious dressing room in which Patty and two other maids were already busy opening trunks, and the bedchamber, the largest, most luxurious room of all.

"I shall leave you to your maid's care, then, Your Grace," Mrs. Griffiths said, inclining her head with gracious respect. "I shall have tea sent up."

"Thank you." Stephanie smiled and watched the house-keeper leave the room. Her husband remained behind.

She turned to look at him, her chin raised, her hands clasped loosely before her. He looked so very handsome, as he always did. She was very aware of the large canopied bed behind him. What would happen now that they were—home? She was, after all, his wife. She had vowed to be obedient to him. She would not break her vows. Would he break his?

"Welcome home, my dear," he said softly.

The words took her by surprise and almost took away her control. She had not realized until that moment how close to the edge of control she had been living for the past twenty-four hours.

"Thank you." She drew a slow breath and smiled at him. "It is magnificent, Alistair. More so even than I expected."

"It is my pride and joy," he said.

The old cliché touched her in some strange way. But she did not want to be touched in any way. Not yet. She needed to think. But so far even her mind had deserted her. She had been unable to think for a night and a day. She lowered her gaze and said nothing.

"Stephanie," he said, "will you answer one question before I leave you to rest alone?"

"Yes." She looked up at him again.

"If I had told you," he said, "on that day in Sindon Park, would you have married me?"

No, of course not. But she held back the words. Would she? The arguments in favor of their marriage would have been just the same. Her options would have been just as limited. How could she know what her answer would have been? The point was, he had not told her. He had allowed her to believe in his kindness and gallantry—in his self-sacrifice.

"I do not know," she said. But she had to be honest with him. Only through honesty now could she hope to regain herself. "Yes. I believe I probably would have. I had tasted something better than what I had known for six years, you see, but to keep it I had to marry soon. It is difficult deliberately to give up something desirable once one has tasted it. I wanted wealth. I wanted Sindon Park."

He nodded.

"I would probably have married you anyway," she said, "but perhaps I would not have sold my soul if you had told me everything at the start."

"What do you mean by that?" he asked.

She lifted her chin. "I wanted to be worthy of my savior," she said. "I have spent the past month changing myself into someone worthy to be your duchess. There was nothing equal in our union, Alistair. All the giving, all the stooping, all the condescension were on your part. I was totally inferior—in every conceivable way. It did not need to be that way. I could and should have been your equal in everything except rank. You took that away from me."

"I did not want to humiliate you by telling the truth," he said.

She smiled. "Or yourself?"

He hesitated. "Or myself," he admitted.

They stood looking at each other. She wondered if she still loved him. Or if she ever had. How could one love a god? One could only serve a god. But he was not a god at all. She did not know what or who he was. He was a stranger to her. She touched her wedding ring with the thumb of her left hand. And her mind touched on the brief and secret pleasure she had known in her marriage bed. He had been inside her body.

But he was a stranger.

"Where do we go from here?" he asked. "Is this the end, Stephanie? Is there no chance for our marriage?"

She had not faced such a stark question yet. It frightened her to hear it thus put into words. Surely, it was not this they were facing? Two days ago had been their wedding day.

"I do not know," she said. "Alistair, I do not know you. I know only a few things *about* you, and not even many of those. I do not know you at all. You have told me nothing. You are a stranger to me."

"And do you wish to know me?" he asked. "Or is it too late?"

She wanted to know him, she realized suddenly. Now that he was no longer a god, he was knowable. Despite his impressive title and his wealth and his enormous dignity, he was a man. A man just as she was a woman. She wanted to know him. She wanted to know whom she would reject—or accept. But was it too late to make such a decision after their marriage? He was standing still and quiet, waiting for her reply.

"I want to know you," she said.

She could see him draw breath. "Then you will know me," he said. "For the next days and weeks, Stephanie, I will do the talking. It will not come easily to me. I have been accustomed to self-containment, you see. It was part of my upbringing. It has been the dominating fact of my adulthood. But for you I will talk. I will try to teach you who I am."

"Is this marriage so important to you, then?" she asked.

"Yes."

He answered without hesitation, but he did not explain in what way it was important, though she waited. It would be humiliating for him to have a broken marriage almost before it had begun. It would be dreary for him to be locked for life into a non-marriage. It would be disastrous for him to be in a marriage that offered no possibility of an heir—unless he intended to break his promise. Or perhaps the marriage was important to him in some other way, some more personal way. She did not know. She did not know *him*.

She would not wait for him to ask the one remaining question, she decided. "Alistair," she said, "you may come to me tonight if you wish." No matter what happened, no matter what her final decision, she realized, she would give him his son if she was physically capable of doing so.

"Thank you," he said. "You are tired, my dear. I shall leave you to rest. I shall come to your dressing room to escort you down to dinner."

"Yes," she said.

He took a couple of steps toward her, took her right hand in both of his, and raised it to his lips.

Then he was gone.

She understood one thing during the couple of minutes she stood where she was before going to her dressing room. It was the first really clear thought that had formed since his staggering revelation of the day before. She was glad he had told her. A great deal had been destroyed. She was not sure if anything could be rebuilt. She was not sure of anything— except one realization. She was glad he was no god. She was glad he was merely a man.

She brushed the fingers of her left hand absently over the back of her right hand, where his lips had just been.

Conversation came easily to him. It was a necessary accomplishment for any lady or gentleman of *ton*. It was an art, perhaps, but one he had practiced for so long that he no longer had to give it conscious thought. He knew almost by instinct to whom he should speak about books or ideas or politics or economics or fashion or gossip. By the same instinct he knew with whom he must lead the conversation and with whom he could merely follow.

He had never feared silences. Sometimes silence could be comfortable and companionable. And when it was not, he always knew how to fill it.

The silence throughout this day had suffocated him. It had been something loud and accusing, something painful and impenetrable.

Conversation at the dinner table, though there was scarcely a moment of silence, was equally uncomfortable. One topic had never been part of his conversations, he realized now that he had committed himself to it for the coming days and even weeks. He was quite unaccustomed to talking about himself. It was as if, in becoming reconciled to the very public nature his life must take as the Duke of Bridgwater, he had shut away the private part of himself, hidden it away so that no one would take that too away from him.

"George was my dearest friend and my worst enemy," he

told her, beginning abruptly without stopping to consider exactly where he should start. He could hardly begin with his birth, after all, though in more ways than one that had been the most significant event in his life. "I loved him and I hated him."

"It is something I have always found perplexing," she said, "but it is something that seems quite natural. I longed and longed to have sisters and brothers. Yet it seems that those who do, spend their childhoods fighting with them."

"I resented him quite bitterly," he said. "He was born barely eleven months after me. I never forgave him for waiting so long. If only he had been born eleven months before me. I am not sure I still do not resent him."

Her place had been set at the foot of the long table in the dining room. They would have had to raise their voices to converse. He had had her moved beside him.

Her knife and fork remained poised over her plate for a moment. "Is it not usually the other way around?" she asked. "Is it not the younger son who is supposed to resent the elder? Eleven months cut your brother out of the title and the fortune and Wightwick Hall."

"Even as a child," he said, "I felt the bars about my cage and knew that for George there were no bars, no cage. Ungrateful wretch that I was, I raged against my bars. Yet strange as it may seem, I do not believe that my brother ever raged against me or the fate that made him the younger."

He knew that he had started in the right place. If he had told her all the facts of a happy, carefree childhood—and the facts were there in abundance—he would not have told the essential truth. He would not be enabling her ever to know him.

She leaned a little toward him, her food forgotten for the moment. "I cannot picture it," she said. "You and your title and position seem to be one and indivisible."

"They are now," he said. "I am talking about my childhood—my rebellious childhood. I knew very early that life would offer me no choices, you see. Now who would complain about that when he could be secure in this for a future?" He indicated with one hand the room about them. "Only a foolish child, of course. A man learns to accept his fate, especially when it is a fate that brings along with it such luxury and such security and such power."

"But who can blame a child," she said, "for wanting to be free? For wanting to dream."

Ah, she understood. No one else ever had. No one. Not that he had talked about such things for eleven years. No, longer than that. Not since boyhood. He had never really entrusted himself to anyone. He felt suddenly vulnerable, almost frightened. He concentrated on his food for a while.

"Very few people are free," he said. "Almost no one is, in fact. It is something one learns as one matures. Something one comes to accept. Yet many people's cages are poverty or ill health or—other miserable factors. My father was right to call me an ungrateful cur and to squash my rebellion as ruthlessly as he did. He must have been bewildered by me. We must hope that our eldest son will not be so perverse."

"If he is," she said, "we must hope that his father will give him the benefit of his understanding."

He smiled at her. They spoke as if there were a future. Was there? The future was in his hands, he suspected. He had to help her to get to know him. He had to hope that she would like him, that she would wish to spend the rest of her life with him. She must already know that he would never force her either to live with him in the intimacy of marriage or to remain with him in the facade of an empty marriage. She was independently wealthy, with a sizable home of her own.

And he had begun by pouring out the foolish, ungrateful self-pity of his childhood self.

For the rest of dinner, and for a while in the drawing room afterward, he told her happier stories of his childhood, choosing the amusing ones involving mainly him and George. Elizabeth and Jane had been born some years after them and had never really been playmates. He was rewarded with smiles and even with laughter.

"Tomorrow," he said finally when he could see that she

was tired, "I will show you the house, Stephanie, including the state apartments and the portrait gallery. If the weather is fine, I will show you the park too. We will take tomorrow for ourselves. The day after you can begin being the Duchess of Bridgwater here if you wish."

"Yes," she said, "I do wish, Alistair. But tomorrow we will spend together. It is important that we do so."

He was leading her up the stairs. He paused outside her dressing room door. "I may come to you tonight, then?" he asked.

She nodded, and he opened her door and closed it behind her when she had stepped inside.

He had not told her what a dreamer he had been. There had been the two totally different sides to his nature—the mischievous, energetic, rebellious boy on the one hand, and the lone, moody dreamer on the other. Both had infuriated his father. Both had been quelled, totally repressed.

He was not sure he could share the second aspect of his nature with Stephanie. He was not sure there were the words. He was not sure he could so bare his soul even for her. And yet, he thought bleakly as he prepared for her, something told him that his only chance with her was in total honesty. Was he capable of it?

She was standing at the window, looking out, though her head turned back over her shoulder when he came inside the room. It was not a studied pose, he realized—he knew far more about her innocence than he had known on his first acquaintance with her. But if it had been, it could not have been more provocatively done. Her auburn hair, caught by the candlelight, lay in heavy waves down her back. The turn of her body, clad in a fine silk and lace nightgown, emphasized its lithe slimness.

She turned completely as he crossed the room toward her, and her hands reached out for his. She had said he might come, and she was not going to stint her welcome, he saw. She lifted her face to his.

He tried to keep his hunger in check, but she opened her

mouth as his lips lightly explored hers, and he slid his tongue into moist heat and gathered her closer. She came, arching her body to his, bringing her hands up to rest on his shoulders. He wondered if it was merely duty, but he could feel the heat of her body through his nightshirt and her nightgown.

He kissed her throat, her ears, her temples, her eyelids. Her mouth again.

He had hurt her, he thought. He had admitted to her that at first he had believed the evidence of his own eyes above the story she had told him. He had told her in effect that she had been a toy to him, a creature of fun. One he had used for his own amusement and had planned to use for his sexual pleasure. He had denied her personhood.

And now she had the power to hurt him, to bring shattering down about him the house he had built for himself over the years so carefully that he had not even fully realized it himself. The house inside which he had hidden so that no one would find him and reveal to him the emptiness of his existence.

Stephanie had found him, whether she realized it or not.

"Come and lie down," he said.

But he stopped her when she was beside the bed and about to lie down on it. He lifted his hands to the top button of her nightgown.

"May I?" he asked her, looking into her eyes.

For a moment she glanced aside to the single candle that burned beside the bed. There was a whole branch of candles on the mantelpiece. She nodded almost imperceptibly, and he undid the buttons one by one until he could lift the gown away from her shoulders. She did not even try to hold on to modesty by bending her arms at the elbow. She held them loosely at her sides so that the single garment slithered all the way to the floor.

She was all slim, taut beauty. She watched him, her face calm, her chin high, as his eyes roamed over her. He pulled his nightshirt off over his head and tossed it aside.

"Lie down," he said.

He hesitated for only a moment. But he did not extinguish the candles. And before joining her on the bed, he stripped back the bedclothes to the foot of the bed. Perhaps he was sealing his own doom, he thought, but if she was going to allow the continuation of their marriage, then perhaps it was as well that she understood the full physical, carnal nature of what they would do together in her bed. He rather suspected that on their wedding night she had hidden behind darkness and closed eyes and beneath bedcovers and inside the instructions on duty that his mother of all people must have given her.

There could be no more hiding for either of them. Every day now, he realized, and every night, he would risk losing her. But he could only come out into the open with her and take the risk.

He slid an arm about her shoulders, but did not draw her close. He raised himself on his elbow and leaned over her to kiss her. With his free hand he explored her and fondled her. After a while he lifted his head away and watched what he did. She watched his face.

He could see and feel and hear her body's response. Her nipples hardened. She grew almost hot to the touch. She was breathing quickly and rather raggedly. But she lay still and relaxed and continued to watch him.

He slid a hand beneath her leg and lifted it. She followed his unspoken direction and raised both legs, setting her feet flat on the bed. When he slid his hand between her knees, she let her legs drop open. He fondled her with his hand, parting, stroking, teasing with light fingers while he leaned forward to kiss her breasts and her flat abdomen. He would not move his head lower. Not yet. She was not ready for that kind of extreme intimacy. Perhaps she never would be.

She was slick with wetness. Ready for him. He slid a finger in and out and listened to the erotic sucking sound. When he looked into her face, he found that she was still looking at him. But her eyes were heavy-lidded, and her lips were parted. He knew that she was listening too and that tonight she was not embarrassed by the sound.

She would not hide from any of it, he decided. She would not use his body as a blanket. When he moved over her, he knelt between her thighs and lifted her legs up over his and positioned himself. Her eyes dropped from his eventually when he paused and waited for her. She watched. He pushed himself slowly inside until he was fully embedded. And drew out again almost his full length and pushed inward once more. She was watching.

"Touch me," he said to her as he leaned over her and set his hands on either side of her head, holding himself above her with straight arms. "Put your arms about me." Her arms were lying flat on the mattress beside her as they had on their wedding night.

She set her hands on either side of his waist. He watched her swallow and move them to his hips and around to touch his buttocks briefly. She rested them against his waist again and closed her eyes at last as he resumed his movements in her. She was soft and hot and wet. He closed his own eyes and held himself above her while he worked. He could smell her. Pure woman.

He waited for her body to move beyond arousal into the beginnings of fulfillment. He stroked her firmly for a long time, holding back his own pleasure. But he knew finally that it was not going to happen. There was no tension in her, only relaxed acquiescence, even though her legs were still twined about his and she was rocking to his rhythm. He could have moved her on to the next stage by sliding his hand between them and caressing a part of her she was probably unaware of. But he sensed that she did not want to abandon control. Control at the moment must be more important to her than almost anything else.

But she was not even trying to hide her quiet enjoyment of what was happening. She liked what he did to her, as she had two nights ago. It was enough. For now it must be enough.

He lowered his weight onto her and thrust deeply and quickly and repeatedly until release came and his seed spilled into her. He heard himself sigh against her hair.

He set his hand over hers after he had uncoupled them and moved to her side. She drew her legs together and lay quietly on her back.

"Thank you," he said.

She turned her head to look at him. "It is very pleasant, Alistair," she said. "I always expected it would be, but it is even more pleasant than I imagined. I want you to know that it was for myself that I said yes tonight. Not just because of duty and not because of . . . of you. It was for me. I decided to be selfish. So I must thank you too, you see."

He leaned over her and kissed her mouth. He was surprised to find that he was feeling almost amused, almost lighthearted. Did she realize that she was turning the tables on him? That she was making him her slave? That she was punishing him most effectively? Should he tell her?

"You may be selfish any time you wish, my dear," he said, "if the results for me are so very pleasurable."

She smiled at him tentatively as he smiled back. It was enough. Hope was born in him as he kissed her again and then reluctantly removed himself from her bed to return to his own room.

Chapter 16

Life became so busy for Stephanie over the following month that she had blessedly little time for thought. She was mistress of Wightwick Hall, a daunting task even for a bride who had been brought up to expect such a life. The only experience she had of running a home had been gained at the vicarage after her mother's death. It was pitifully inadequate as preparation for what faced her now. The month-long training given her by her mother-in-law helped a great deal. But she found that she had to learn to do the job in her own way. She had been taught to remember who she was and refuse to be intimidated by a regal housekeeper and a despotic cook. Yet she forced herself to remember too that her servants were people, that they had lives and dignity and pride of their own. She had to learn to command through a combination of firmness and kindness.

Sometimes she envied her husband, who needed to use neither. His word was everyone's command. He never raised his voice, never spoke harshly to anyone. Often he did not even have to speak at all. A lifted forefinger at the table would bring a footman smartly hurrying with the coffeepot. Raised eyebrows would send the instant message that a door should be opened or that one course of a meal might be removed and the next brought on.

But she could not be like him. She had to learn to live her new life her own way. She no longer needed to feel guilty about deviating from some of the instructions she had been given.

There were neighbors to meet, visits to make, entertainments to plan. There were tenants to be called upon and laborers too. There were the sick and elderly and very young to identify so that she might learn to give them extra attention. There were the rector and his sister to be seen and parish concerns to be discussed.

There were letters to write. After the restrictions imposed upon her by the Burnabys, writing and receiving letters were among her greatest pleasures. But there were so many. The dowager duchess wrote to her as did Cousin Bertha, her sisters-in-law, Jennifer, Samantha, Cora, Miriam, and Tom's wife.

There was her own estate with which to concern herself. She summoned her steward to Wightwick and spent hours with him over four separate days, asking questions, looking at ledgers, listening to advice, making decisions. She was very tempted to ask her husband to oversee the estate for her since she knew that he was more than competent with his own. And she knew that he waited to be asked, even though he said nothing but merely entertained their guest with his usual correct, rather austere courtesy. But she did not give in to the temptation. It was her property, and perhaps she would wish to live there one day—perhaps soon.

And there was the summer fête to organize. There were to be stalls and competitions and maypole dancing in the village, and cricket and races in the park. There were to be refreshments all day in the park and a grand ox roast there in the evening to be followed by an outdoor dance. All the celebrations in the park for years past had been organized by the dowager duchess. Now the task fell upon Stephanie's shoulders. The fête was the biggest event of the year in the neighborhood. She knew she would be judged harshly if it was poorly organized.

She might have busied herself with her tasks as Duchess of Bridgwater from the time of her early rising until bedtime, she sometimes thought, and still not feel that everything was done. But there was another major area of her life too, and it took at least half her time. She had a new marriage to work on.

Strangely, it was not difficult. It might almost have been idyllic if she had wanted it to be, she thought. Her husband made time to spend with her, though her mother-in-law had warned her that she must not expect to see a great deal of him once the marriage had been solemnized.

He was the one who showed her the house the day after their arrival, though Mrs. Griffiths seemed somewhat taken aback. He took her through the state apartments, rooms that awed her with their size and magnificence. He took her to the portrait gallery on an upper floor and spent longer than an hour there with her, pointing out his ancestors to her, telling her their stories. He paused longest before a portrait of his mother and father, painted soon after their wedding. His mother was beautiful then as she still was now.

"Oh," Stephanie said, going one step closer, "you are very like your father. You might almost *be* him." The former duke stared back at her from the canvas, proud, aloof, almost arrogant—and very handsome.

"Yes," her husband said quietly. "Perhaps that was part of the trouble. Because I looked so like him, I was expected to be like him in all ways."

She turned to look at him. "You did not love him?" she asked incautiously.

"Oh, yes," he said, "I loved him. And he loved me. Perhaps that was part of the trouble too."

He did not elaborate, but he was not silent with her. He talked to her almost constantly, telling her about his life, about his heritage.

He loved his home, she thought. Perhaps more deeply than he realized, though he had once described it as his pride and joy. If he had wanted none of it as a child, he certainly loved it now.

"You love Wightwick," she said to him, smiling at him.

"If you had been the younger son, it would have been George's now."

"Yes." He looked about him. "Yes, and so it would."

He walked about the park with her, showing her its most obvious attractions, taking her on walks that had been carefully laid out to give both a picturesque route and unexpected and glorious prospects of greater distances. He took her on a shady walk through a grove of trees until they reached a small, secluded lake she had not suspected was there.

"Hartley—Lord Carew—redesigned the park for me several years ago," he said, "before his marriage. He has great talent as a landscape gardener. Indeed, when he and Samantha first met, she mistook him for the gardener of his own estate."

"Oh," she said, "I hope he disabused her as soon as he realized what had happened."

"No." He smiled ruefully. "We men do not always do what we ought, Stephanie."

He took her riding. She had ridden as a girl, though not a great deal since her father had kept only one horse and that exclusively for the cart. She had not ridden as a woman. But he chose a gentle mare for her and rode patiently at her side while she cautiously walked the horse and eased it into a canter until the world seemed to be flying past at a dangerous pace to either side of her. Once she caught him laughing at her—it was when she had taken her horse to a canter for all of thirty seconds across a perfectly level meadow and then hauled back on the reins before blowing out her breath from puffed cheeks.

He looked like a mischievous boy when he laughed. She wondered how he had looked when he was nine or ten—when he had got up to some of those wild escapades he had told her about. She could not imagine his doing anything wild.

He always attended her in the drawing room when she was entertaining, even if it was just some of the ladies to tea. He made pleasant, courtly conversation with them. He always accompanied her on visits, even to his tenants. She suspected that he drank more tea during the first month of their marriage than he had drunk in the whole year previous to it.

He came to her bed every night. She was sometimes alarmed by the thought that she might be becoming addicted to what happened between them there. She found herself anticipating it with eagerness all day long, and willing it not to end while it was happening, and then fighting bleakness after he had returned to his own room at the thought that there was the rest of the night and all the next day to live through before it would happen again. The marriage act was the most enjoyable activity the world had to offer. She was convinced of it.

She was disturbed by her enjoyment, felt guilty about it. Sometimes she wondered if she stayed just for that. How would she live without it now that she had experienced it?

How would she live without *him*?

On the surface the marriage was not an unhappy one. Their neighbors and acquaintances had a way of looking at them—with a sort of amused indulgence—that suggested they were seen as a newly married couple living through a honeymoon. And in many ways they were. Stephanie found that even her need for quietness and privacy was waning. A couple of times during the evenings after dinner she had retired to her own sitting room with a book, feeling the need to be away from his eyes and his voice. Feeling the need to be herself. And yet the second time it happened, remembering how the first time she had been unable to concentrate on her reading or do any constructive thinking either, she took her book and went back downstairs. She found him in the library, also reading.

"May I join you?" she asked.

He had got to his feet as she entered; he always stood when she came into a room. He was always the perfect gentleman.

"Of course, my dear," he said, indicating the comfortable-looking leather chair on the opposite side of the fireplace from his. He waited for her to seat herself before resuming his own place.

At first she was self-conscious and read and reread the same paragraph without comprehending a single word. But after a while she looked up with a slight start, wondering for how long she had been absorbed in her book. He was reclined in his chair, looking very comfortable, clearly absorbed in his own reading. They sat, silently reading, for a few hours before he put his book down and suggested that she ring for the tea tray.

It had been a strangely seductive evening. They had not spoken, and yet his very presence had relaxed her and enabled her to enjoy one of her favorite pastimes.

"It is getting late," he said and half smiled.

She glanced at the clock on the mantel. They would drink their tea, and it would be time for bed. Within the next hour . . . She felt the now familiar aching sensation in her womb and between her thighs.

"I am sorry," she said, getting to her feet. "I have been neglecting my duty." But his words had not been scolding, and her answer had not been apologetic.

Sometimes she wondered why they were not completely happy. She would look back on her life with the Burnabys and shudder inwardly. She would picture life alone and free and independent at Sindon Park—she knew he would not try to stop her from going there if she decided to do so—and felt a bleak chill.

By her own request their marriage had continued to be a real marriage. She was proving both to her husband and to herself that she was capable of being his duchess. They communicated. She knew that she pleased him in bed. He pleased her there too. It was too soon to know whether she had conceived during this first month of their marriage—she had had her monthly period only just before her wedding and did not know yet if the next one would happen. But he had come to her each night except the second. She loved perhaps best of all, although it came at the end of what she never wanted to end, the heat of his seed passing deep inside from him into her.

Yet there was in both of them at the end of their first month together a sense of waiting—a sense of a decision yet to be made. It was strange, perhaps. They were married. The decision had been made. She was his property, to do with as he wished. She had vowed obedience and would not break her vow. But she knew that there was a decision to be made and that he would allow her to make it and would live by whatever she decided.

She was perhaps unique among women.

She was married, yet she was free.

She did not have that freedom by right. He had given it to her.

It was a thought that made her angry at first. Why could women not be free as men were free? Why did they have no right to freedom?

But it was also a thought that began to dominate her thinking, that began to haunt her night and day. He had her in his possession. All the forces of law and religion—as well as his superior masculine strength—were behind him to back up his claims. No one—*no one*—would ever blame him for holding on to her for the rest of their lives and forcing her into submission to his will. Yet he had given her her freedom. He had exposed himself to the possibility of censure and ridicule—he would receive both in plenty if he allowed her to leave him—and given her freedom.

He had treated her during that journey to Hampshire with contempt veiled in courtesy. He had been no different from anyone else she had seen while dressed in those clothes. He had judged by appearances and had dismissed everything she had said, everything she *was*, with an amused cynicism. He had been quite prepared to amuse himself with her during their nights on the road and to set her up in some love nest for his future pleasure.

Her shock at being so dismissed as a person deserving a hearing, deserving some respect, was still deep.

But he *had* helped her. And he *had* been courteous. And

he had *not* tried to force himself upon her once she had uttered that one word—*no*. And finally, when he had fallen into his own trap, he had taken the consequences with his characteristic courtesy and sense of honor.

And now he was *still* giving her the choice of saying no. No to whatever he wished to do to her or with her. No to being his wife in anything but name. No to living with him.

And even when they were still at Sindon Park, he had insisted that the marriage contract state that her inheritance remain independently hers.

Sometimes it seemed foolish and childish—and even downright insane—to refuse to forgive him.

Sometimes when his body was joined with hers in her bed, she would hold him with tenderness and try to persuade herself that it was merely with pleasure and that it was a pleasure she took for herself without regard to the pleasure he might be taking too.

But it was tenderness.

She was not sure that she could allow herself to feel tenderness for him. She was not sure she could respect herself if she did. But it was something she had to work out for herself.

It was a lonely feeling. Freedom is a lonely thing, she thought with some surprise.

The summer fête had never been his favorite day of the year even though he had always made it a point to be at Wightwick for the occasion. He had always felt it important to watch his people celebrating, to stroll among them, talking with them, encouraging the participants in the various contests, congratulating the winners, commiserating with the losers, eating with them. Even dancing with them. His mother, of course, had done all the organizing and had busied herself throughout the day, going from the village to the park, making sure that she was always available to judge the contests in baking and needlework and to hand out the prizes in all the races and other competitions. It was something she had done with grace and apparent ease and with perfect, unruffled dignity.

This year was to be different. He knew it almost before he had swallowed the first mouthful of an early breakfast. Fortunately, he had seen from the window of his bedchamber, the day promised to be sunny and warm, a luxury this year. Stephanie came hurrying into the breakfast room, smiled quickly at him, smiled more dazzlingly at the footman beside the sideboard, and asked him if he would please bring her two eggs and two rounds of toast. Oh, and some coffee, please, James.

She always smiled at their servants. She always said please and thank you. She always sounded genuinely grateful for their service. She often asked the servant—by name—about a particular detail of his or her health or of his mother's health or that particular item he had been looking to purchase. She knew each of their servants personally, he was sure. His mother would be alarmed. He was charmed.

"Alistair," she said, turning her smile on him, "you are to be captain of one of the cricket teams this afternoon. You did know? I did remember to tell you?"

"No, actually, my dear," he said. "Are you sure you would not prefer to do it yourself?"

"No." Her smile was almost a grin. "I have to be busy about other things. I have to make friends of a few women by awarding them prizes for their embroidery and netting and cake-making and so on, and make a few dozen enemies at the same time."

He had never joined in the cricket match, which was the highlight of the day for many of the men. His mother had not considered that it would be dignified for him to do so.

"Very well, then," he said. "But if you *do* decide to play, it must be on my side. A husband's orders."

It was the only command he had given since their wedding, even in joke.

"And you must give the prizes in the village this morning," she said. "Will you, Alistair? It is not fair that I judge the contests and award the prizes. And I am sure the winners will be far prouder of themselves if their prizes are presented by the Duke of Bridgwater himself."

Good Lord! "Very well, my dear," he said. "If you wish it."

"Oh, Alistair." She leaned across the table toward him, her face eager and animated. "There is to be dancing about the maypole. Why is dancing about a maypole so much more magical than dancing anywhere else? I used to love it of all things when I was a girl. I remember Mama being doubtful and thinking perhaps it was not quite proper for the vicar's daughter to join in, but Papa said I might. I would have *died* if it had not been allowed."

He had to resist the impulse to lean back slightly. He was dazzled. She was as excited as a girl. She was *enjoying* this. His mother had never enjoyed it. She had treated it as one more duty that must be perfectly executed.

"Alistair," Stephanie said, "give me your opinion. Will it be undignified for the Duchess of Bridgwater to dance about the maypole?"

His mother would have an apoplexy. So should he.

"Not unless it is undignified for the Duke of Bridgwater too," he said. "I intend to dance about it with you, Stephanie. I hope it does not coincide with the cricket match?"

"Oh, no." She laughed. "There have to be men to dance. It is to be afterward. Before the ox roast. And then the dance. I can scarce wait. I have never danced out of doors during the evening before."

"There is a breeze to ruffle your coiffure," he said, "and stones to cut against your slippers, and night chills to raise goose bumps on your arms."

She laughed. "And stars for candles," she said.

"Yes." There was a curious ache about his heart. "And stars for candles, my dear. We will dance beneath the stars. We will *waltz* beneath the stars. Shall we?"

"Yes." Her hand came half across the table to him, but she had drawn it back before he could cover it with his own.

"I must fly," she said, getting to her feet before he could

rise to draw her chair back for her. "I promised to be in the village early."

"Before eight o'clock?" he said.

She laughed. "Is it that early?" she said. "But I still have to change my clothes and have my hair dressed. No respectable lady can accomplish those tasks within half an hour, you know. Will you ride with me, Alistair? Perhaps I will need advice on some of the judging."

"I am the world's foremost authority on embroidery," he said.

She laughed.

"But I will come, of course," he said.

He would go anywhere in the world she cared to ask him to go—if she would but go there with him.

Chapter 17

There was a strange, happy, carefree feel to the day, even though there was so much to do every minute of it and there should have been so much anxiety that something would go wrong. There was an excitement about the day, a sense of a turning point. Everything since her marriage and her coming to Wightwick had been leading up to this day, Stephanie realized. It was as if there had been a tacit agreement between her and her husband to postpone their personal problems until after the summer fête. To postpone any decision.

Tomorrow loomed like a great empty void in her life. She could not look beyond today. And while she lived today, she did not want to look beyond. It was such a very happy day.

She moved several times during the course of the day between the village and the park and house, sometimes with her husband, sometimes alone. She wanted to be everywhere at once. She wanted to miss nothing. She judged the ladies' and the children's contests, then smiled and applauded while her husband presented the prizes. She switched roles with him during the races and complained to him that judging races was very much easier than judging who had baked the best currant cakes.

She even joined in one of the races, when there was an odd number of children wishing to participate in the three-legged race. She partnered a thin, timid little girl, and they narrowly won the race when the leaders-by-a-mile fell in a tangled heap just before the finish line and could not untangle themselves in time. Stephanie hugged her partner, laughing helplessly, and waved cheerfully to the rather large crowd that had suddenly gathered. She threw a half-laughing, half-defiant glance at her husband, and realized that just a month before she would have been horrified by her own behavior and would have been vowing never to behave thus again.

She coaxed her husband into buying her six lengths of gaudy ribbon from a peddler's stall in the village and then tied them into the newly washed, newly combed hair of the six young daughters of one of the poorer tenants. She drew him toward the tent of a gypsy, whom she suspected was no gypsy at all, insisting that they have their fortunes told. But at the last moment, after he had acquiesced, she changed her mind.

"No," she said, "not the future. This is today, and it is such an enjoyable day. Let us not find out about the future, even in fun."

"No," he agreed. "Let us enjoy today, my dear."

He too knew that tomorrow all might change.

She watched the cricket game and cheered unashamedly and partially for her husband's team. He was a talented player, as she soon discovered with interest. His steward, who came to stand beside her for a few minutes, informed her that His Grace had been on the first eleven while at Oxford University. That was one thing about himself he had not told her.

"You should have played at Richmond that day," she said accusingly when the game was over.

But he merely smiled and drew her arm through his. "When our children reach a suitable age," he said, "we will scrape together enough children from the neighborhood to make up two teams and we can captain one each."

"Mine will humiliate yours," she said.

"Yes, probably," he agreed pleasantly. "It *is* humiliating to know that one has completely annihilated another team and made them feel quite inept."

She looked sidelong at him to find that he was doing the same to her. She did not miss the assumption they had both made about the future. She wondered, as she had done several times during the past week, if she was with child. There was a definite chance, though she was always so irregular that it was impossible to know for sure. It would be foolish to hope yet—or to dread.

Usually after the cricket match, most people relaxed or strolled in the park until it was time for the feast to begin. Only the young people headed back to the village for the maypole dancing. But this year word had somehow spread that the Duke of Bridgwater and his new bride were not only planning to attend the event, but were themselves intending to dance.

No one had ever seen a Duke of Bridgwater or his duchess or any of his family dancing about the maypole. No one could quite imagine it. Everyone needed visual evidence to believe that it could possibly happen. And so late in the afternoon the main street of the village was crowded with people, and the village green was surrounded by a milling, curious, laughing throng.

Stephanie took off her bonnet and her gloves and set them aside with her parasol. There was a smattering of applause, and one brave anonymous soul whistled. Her husband took off his hat and his coat, as he had done for the cricket match, and rolled up his shirt sleeves to the elbows. He eyed the maypole and its many-colored ribbons with some misgiving, Stephanie saw.

But he knew the steps, as he proved as soon as they and the other dancers had all taken a ribbon in hand and the violins began to play. The crowd ringing the green clapped and stamped in time to the music. Only once did the ribbons become snarled and the music pause for a few moments. The crowd jeered good-naturedly. Stephanie smiled as her husband laughed, apologized abjectly, untangled the ribbons, and laughed again.

If she closed her eyes, she thought, as she performed the intricate patterns of the dance, concentrating on both her steps and the movements of her hand with its green ribbon, she could almost imagine herself back in her girlhood, in that golden time before all the harsher realities of life had intruded. She could picture her mother smiling, her father clapping to the rhythm and nodding encouragement to her. She could picture Tom whooping with enthusiasm and catching the nearest pretty girl about the waist when the dancing was finished and twirling her about.

But this was not her girlhood. She turned her head to watch her husband, who was grinning and lifting his arm higher as one of his tenant's young daughters stepped with her ribbon beneath his and around him. Stephanie was doing the same thing with the man closest to her. She smiled at the man, and he smiled back—a smile of warmth and admiration and respect.

This was not wrong, she thought. It was not undignified. She was glad she had decided to do things her way, though she would always be grateful for the training her mother-in-law had given her. She was glad she was free. She was glad she had found out in time that she need be no slave to an obligation that could never be repaid.

He might have held her in thrall for the rest of her life. She would never have known. There would have been no danger of his secret ever being disclosed. No one but Alistair had known.

What a great and wonderful wedding gift he had given her, she thought so unexpectedly that she almost lost her step and almost dipped her ribbon when she was supposed to raise it.

The dancers were treated to enthusiastic applause when the dancing was over.

"My mother," the Duke of Bridgwater said when they were walking back to the house to prepare for the evening festivities—they had not brought the carriage this time—"will suffer an apoplexy if, or when, she hears about this, Stephanie. She will believe she failed utterly with you and that I have fallen into bad company."

Oh, my dear, make him happy. He is so very dear to me, my son.

Stephanie could almost hear her mother-in-law say those words, as she had done on her wedding day. One rare glimpse behind the armor of dignity and propriety and grace the dowager duchess had worn perhaps all her life. Stephanie was not so sure her husband was right. But right or not, he sounded quite uncontrite.

"Alistair," she said, "there is nothing as exhilarating as dancing out of doors, is there? And look, the sky is still quite clear of clouds. We really will be able to dance beneath the stars tonight, will we not?"

She was even, she thought, beginning to be able to contemplate the prospect of tomorrow coming. But she would not let her thoughts dwell on it yet.

It was a day in which great happiness had warred with desperate depression.

He could not remember a day he had enjoyed so greatly. A day in which he had felt so free or so uninhibited by his rank and consequence. Or so in love.

She had changed in the month since their marriage. It was only today, looking back on the month and considering the month preceding it that he realized how different she was. All the stiffness and timidity and seriousness and submissiveness had disappeared. In their place was a warm, charming, fun-loving woman who seemed to know by some inner instinct how to deal with people.

She said and did all the things that should have lost her the respect of both her peers and her servants—according to his mother's rules. And yet the opposite seemed true. He suspected that even after just one month she was adored by everyone who knew her. And yet he had seen beyond any doubt that it was she who commanded his home, not either Mrs. Griffiths or Parker.

And he, of course, was no exception. He adored her too.

He understood the change in her. He understood that during this month he had had the privilege of becoming acquainted with the real Stephanie Munro. He understood that during the month before their marriage she had been awed into trying to change herself so that she would be a worthy duchess for him. She had thought at the time that she owed him everything.

What he had seen during the month, culminating in today's fête, was a woman who had become free and independent, a woman who had asserted her own character and personality and who liked herself. A woman he had allowed to be free because he could never have lived out his life with one who was his merely by rights of possession.

It was a realization that terrified him. And he knew something would change tomorrow or very soon. Everything until now had been focused on the fête. After tonight there would be nothing to focus upon except the fragile, uncertain state of their marriage.

He opened the outdoor ball with his wife, dancing a vigorous country dance with her. He danced with three of his neighbors' wives before leading her out again—for a waltz beneath the stars. He could not say afterward that he had enjoyed it. It was too agonizingly sweet. They scarcely spoke. They did not once look into each other's eyes. Tension and awareness rippled between them.

When it was over, he could no longer bear to smile and converse and continue to lead out the wives of his neighbors and tenants. He slipped away. It was not the thing to do, but he was beyond caring too deeply. It was late in the evening. The ball would play itself out, and people would begin to wander homeward. It was unlikely that he would even be missed.

He walked through the trees to the lake, always a favorite haunt of his when he wished to be alone. He never felt the healing power of nature as strongly as when he was at the lake. The moon was shining across it in a silver band tonight. There was hardly a ripple on the water.

He leaned his back against a tree, propped one foot against it, and folded his arms across his chest. He drew a deep breath, let it out slowly, and closed his eyes.

*   *   *

It was difficult to see everyone in the darkness, despite the moon and stars and the colored lamps strung in the trees. At first she thought he must be somewhere beyond the range of the light available. But after she had danced two sets without once seeing him, she realized that he had left the dancing area. She asked the butler at the refreshment table, but it was only by chance that the village blacksmith, who was trying to cool himself with a glass of punch, overheard and mentioned seeing His Grace walk into the trees. He pointed to the spot.

He must have gone to the lake, she thought. But why? The evening was not over. He had appeared to be enjoying himself. But she knew why. She had felt the tension between them like a physical thing as they had waltzed. She had been unable to look at him or speak to him—even though they had lived in the intimacy of marriage for a whole month. It had been the most wonderful dance of her life and the most dreadful.

He would want to be alone. Otherwise, he would not have gone off by himself without a word to anyone. She would be the last person he would want disturbing him. She must wait for him to return. Tomorrow they must talk. The time had come. But not tonight.

"Oh, will you please excuse me?" she asked, smiling warmly at their closest neighbor who had asked her to partner him in a quadrille. "There is something I must do."

After that she could not just stand there or even mingle with those who did not dance. Mr. Macy would believe she had merely offered an excuse. She turned and crossed the lawn to the trees. After a moment's hesitation she stepped along the dark path, having to feel her way from tree to tree. Very little light penetrated from the sky above. She hoped she was going the right way. She had been to the lake only once before and that had been in daylight with her husband as a guide.

And then she saw light—moonlight on the lake. She stopped for a moment when she reached the bank, her breath catching in her throat. Surely nothing on earth could be more beautiful.

"It *is* breathtaking, is it not?" he said quietly from somewhere to her right.

He was leaning back against a tree, she saw. He made no move to come toward her.

"You wished to be alone," she said. A foolish thing to say. If she knew it, why had she not stayed away and respected his privacy? His head was back against the tree. She thought his eyes were closed, though she could not see him clearly.

"I have been dreaming an old dream," he said.

"What?" she asked.

"I was a dreamer as a child," he said. "I dreamed all sorts of impossible things. Ridiculous things, all involving adventure and personal freedom. Because I knew that the pattern of my life had been marked out for me from birth, I suppose. Part of the general rebellion that characterized my childhood. I grew to recognize and to accept reality and even to rather like it. But there was one dream that clung during my late boyhood and early manhood. It took longer to die than the others."

He stopped talking, but she did not prompt him. She stood looking at him.

"I dreamed of living here," he said. "You were right that first day, you see. I do love it. It is a part of my very being. But I dreamed of living here not just as the Duke of Bridgwater with responsibilities to the land and the people on it. I dreamed of living here as a man. With a woman. And children."

She felt an ache in her chest and throat. She had never seen him so vulnerable. He had told her a great deal about himself during the past month. But she had sensed that he still kept the deepest part of himself locked away.

"I was still young enough," he said, "to believe that somewhere out there was the woman who had been meant for me before either of us was even conceived. It was a lovely dream. But naive and sad too. It finally had to be abandoned."

"Why?" she asked him. She had taken a few tentative steps toward him. "Do you no longer believe in love?"

He opened his eyes and smiled at her. But he said nothing.

"I think," she said—and she had moved close enough to touch him though she did not do so—"that you are the most loving man I have ever known." Her words took even her by surprise. But as she listened to the echo of them, she knew that they were true. And she knew that the answer to all her questions had been staring her in the face ever since the day after her wedding, ever since that dreadful revelation in the carriage.

He chuckled without humor.

"My father's favorite biblical text was the one about laying down one's life for one's friends," she said. "You know? 'Greater love hath no man than this'? You gave up everything for me the day after our wedding, Alistair."

"I merely confessed to something I should have told you a month before," he said. "And in so doing I made you miserable and myself miserable."

"No." She shook her head and spread her hands against his chest. She saw him flinch. "You gave me the gift of knowledge and freedom, Alistair. You have given the same gift continually every day since then. You have allowed me to get to know you and your home and your people. You have let me into your life. But you have put no restraints on me. You know, do you not, that tomorrow I may ask for the use of the carriage to take me and my belongings to Sindon Park, and that I may stay there indefinitely."

"Don't go," he said. His head was back against the tree again. His eyes were closed again.

"But you will not stop me if I decide to go, will you?" she asked.

She heard him swallow. He did not answer for a long time. She waited.

"No," he said at last.

"Why not?" She dipped her head and set her forehead against his chest between her hands.

"I will not hold you against your will," he said.

"Why not?" Her eyes were closed very tightly.

"Because I would rather live without a dream than with a spoiled one," he said. And more softly, "Because I love you."

She was crying then. Just when she wanted to say something, she was crying instead. She felt his hand light against the back of her head, his fingers stroking through her hair. She felt him lean his head downward to kiss the top of her head.

"Don't cry," he said. "It is all right. Everything will be all right."

"Alistair . . ." She looked up at him, all teary-eyed and wobbly-voiced. "It does not need to be a spoiled dream. I will live in it with you. You will never understand, perhaps, how wonderful it is to know that one may say no. How wonderful it is for a woman. For now I know beyond any doubt that I may say no to you, then I know too that I am free to say yes with all my heart."

Both his arms had come tightly about her. He was rubbing his cheek against the top of her head.

"Because I love you," she said.

She leaned against him in the long silence that followed and breathed in the familiar smell of him. This, she thought, utterly relaxed, utterly safe and secure, was happiness. This moment. She looked for no happily ever afters. She knew there would be none, that despite the beauty and essential reality of dreams, the real world could often be a harsh place in which to do one's living. But this now, this moment, was happiness, and this moment would take them forward into a future they would create for themselves for as long as they both lived—with love.

"Alistair," she said after a while, "I am very happy."

He chuckled unexpectedly and tightened his arms about her. "Stephanie," he said, "will you come somewhere with me?"

"Where?" She looked up at him. Even in the near darkness she could see the spark of mischief in his smile—the one she had seen very rarely in the two months of their acquaintance.

He took her hand firmly in his, but then abandoned it in order to set an arm about her waist. "You will find out," he said.

She set her head against his shoulder and her own arm about his waist, and allowed him to lead the way.

He was lying naked on his back on the hay in the barn, at the farthest side of it from the door, where there would be plenty of warning in the unlikely event that they were interrupted. Stephanie was astride him, her thighs hugging his sides. She was kneeling upright, her head thrown back, her hair hanging loose down her back. The faint light from the small window above them gleamed in a bar across half her face and one naked shoulder and breast.

She was riding to the rhythm of his deep thrusts, and he could feel her open enjoyment despite her initial shock at the posture he had chosen for their loving so that it would be his back scratched by the hay, not hers.

She was looking down at him then, and her face fell into shadow. "Alistair," she whispered. "Alistair."

"My love," he said.

He knew then why she had spoken his name and broken rhythm. Her body was tensing. With inner muscles she was clenching about him so that his thrusts met greater resistance.

"Don't fight it," he told her.

But she remained taut in every muscle as she threw back her head again and clasped his knees behind her. He held his rhythm, pushing into the tightness, coaxing her to move into the new world they could explore together for the remainder of a lifetime.

And then she cried out. The tautness remained for a few moments while he held still in her, and then she shuddered. He reached up to take her shoulders in his hands, and he drew her down so that she was crouched over him, her head on his shoulder. He held her while the tension shuddered into gradual and total relaxation, and gave himself up to the release he had been holding back for her sake.

A long time of panting silence passed. "It is ungenteel," she murmured at last.

He laughed softly. "Very definitely," he said. "Quite unduchesslike. Far worse than bowling in a cricket match or running a three-legged race or dancing about a maypole. And naked in a hay barn, Stephanie. Tut!"

"Ah, but it was so wonderful," she said.

"Very definitely," he agreed. He turned carefully with her so that she lay beside him, his coat half beneath her. He had not disengaged from her. "Shall I tell you why I brought you here?"

"Because it is very wicked?" she said. She sounded sleepy.

"Very," he said. *I lost my virginity here on a summer fête night many years ago.* He had been about to say the words aloud. He wanted her inside his soul, inside his secrets for the rest of his life. But perhaps, he thought just in time, there were some secrets best kept after all. "It is time I did something wicked. It was not enough to abandon our guests merely to take you to your bed, you see. Tonight you have earned a roll in the hay." He chuckled.

"Alistair!" She was wide awake now and bristling with indignation. "Are you suggesting . . . ?"

"Mhm," he said, his mouth against her hair. "Running three-legged races, cheering partially for one side in cricket, dancing about the maypole, looking lovelier than any duchess, or any *woman* for that matter, has any business looking—yes, you have deserved every roll you have been given or will be given tonight. I promise several more to come. Our guests may dance until they wish to go home. It is doubtful they will even miss us, and if they do, they are welcome to allow their imaginations to run riot. You have liberated me, you see, Stephanie, and now you must take the consequences."

She sighed and touched her tongue to his. "Oh," she said.

"Mm," he agreed.

She giggled suddenly, a sound he had not heard from her before. "Several more to come?" she said. *"Tonight?"* She pressed her hips closer to his. He knew she could feel him hardening inside her. "Is it possible, Alistair? I thought it could be done only once . . ."

"Let me prove how wrong you can be," he said. "My love." He drew one of her legs snugly over his hip and kissed her once more. "I am going to take you back to town soon. There is something I must buy you, and only a London designer could do it justice."

"What?" she asked. She gasped. "Oh, it *is* possible. Oh, that feels *so* good."

"A new bonnet," he said. "Pink. With three plumes. Pink, purple, and . . . what color was the other one?"

"Fuchsia," she said.

"Mm," he said. "Oh, yes, love, very good indeed. It can be done more than once in a night, you see."

"And a fuchsia cloak?" she asked.

"Mm," he said. "My bright bird of paradise. How fortunate that your gray cloak was stolen. I might not have noticed you."

"Wretch!" she said. "Was not my beauty more dazzling than a bright cloak and a plumed bonnet?" Her sigh was half moan. "Ah, I love you. Oh, yes, Alistair. Oh, yes. Oh, please."

It was his dream, he thought. And had he not been making love to her nightly for a whole month—without interruption? Ah, yes, it was his dream, right enough.

"Hush," he whispered against her ear. "Let me answer you this way. Mm, so beautiful, my love."